VOTE
VOTE
THEY
THEM
WORST-
CASE
SCENARIO

BOOKS BY RAY STOEVE

The Summer Love Strategy
Arden Grey
Between Perfect and Real

WORST-CASE SCENARIO

RAY STOEVE

AMULET BOOKS • NEW YORK

PUBLISHER'S NOTE: This is a work of fiction. Names, characters, places, and incidents are either the product of the author's imagination or used fictitiously, and any resemblance to actual persons, living or dead, business establishments, events, or locales is entirely coincidental.

Cataloging-in-Publication Data has been applied for and may be obtained from the Library of Congress.

ISBN 978-1-4197-6499-8
eISBN 978-1-64700-841-3

Book design by Deena Micah Fleming

Published in 2026 by Amulet Books, an imprint of ABRAMS.

Printed and bound in the United States
10 9 8 7 6 5 4 3 2 1

Amulet Books are available at special discounts when purchased in quantity for premiums and promotions as well as fundraising or educational use. Special editions can also be created to specification. For details, contact specialsales@abramsbooks.com or the address below.

Amulet Books® is a registered trademark of Harry N. Abrams, Inc.

ABRAMS The Art of Books
195 Broadway, New York, NY 10007
abramsbooks.com

ABRAMS is represented in the UK and Europe by
Abrams & Chronicle Books, 1 West Smithfield, London EC1A 9JU and
Média-Participations, 57 rue Gaston Tessier, 75166 Paris, France.

abramsandchronicle.co.uk and media-participations.com

info@abramsandchronicle.co.uk

IF EVERYTHING GOES ACCORDING TO PLAN TODAY, I'LL HAVE the perfect junior year.

I'm outside Mr. Harrison's classroom at the beginning of lunch, the short side hallway an oasis of quiet in the hum and bustle of the school. Beside the closed door is a bulletin board, still displaying a poster advertising last year's spring musical, an unintelligible tag graffitied next to it on the empty corkboard. On the white wall behind the bulletin board, a threefold racing stripe of the Jefferson High School colors begins, zipping down the length of the hall and around the corner, back toward the rest of the school like a highway of blue, green, and silver.

I've been imagining this moment all summer and planning everything that comes after, and now it's here.

I take one, two, three deep breaths. Three, because odd numbers are just better; they're symmetrical, with one in the middle and an equal amount on either side. And they're more memorable, in my opinion. If you gave me two reasons to do something, I'd be like *what, only two?* Two is a shrug. Three is convincing.

I do another set of three deep breaths, and one more after that. If I do sets, they have to be in threes too; that's how it works. The repetition is calming, the breaths settling my body and mind. Mostly. All the deep breathing makes me a little lightheaded, so I put my hand on the wall to steady myself, and then I step forward and open the door.

Jayden, Makayla, and Anna are already there, dragging chairs into a circle for the first Queer Alliance meeting of the school year. The classroom is a visual riot, giant posters of famous actors, movie stills, and plays on every wall, the whiteboard covered in scribbles from Mr. Harrison's theater lessons, three huge bookcases crammed to the gills along the back wall.

"Sidney!" Jayden shrieks when he sees me, face glowing with caffeinated excitement. He grew what seemed like a foot over the summer, and now we're the same height, even though he claims he's half an inch taller.

Anna puts a hand on my shoulder. "Good morning, Mx. President," she says solemnly. Her eyeshadow today is blue blended seamlessly into lavender, bright against her very pale skin and matching her sweater, patterned in swirling shades of teal. If she were an animal, she'd be a butterfly—always dressed in bright colors, usually something she knitted herself. She's trans, like me and Jayden, but unlike both of us, she's known since she was a little kid. She's been on estrogen since puberty, while Jayden just started testosterone last year. Me, I'm not sure what kind of medical transition I want, if any. Changing my pronouns was where I started, and for now, it's where I've stayed.

"Don't jinx it," I say, setting my lunch down on a chair and my poster beside it. I hope the poster is enough to convince everyone of what I know to be true: I should be the new Queer Alliance president.

Makayla smiles at me sympathetically. Her light brown skin and black curly hair are a perfect match to Jayden's, along with her wide nose, her high cheekbones, and, well, just about everything else. The only difference is Makayla's shoulder-length hair, while Jayden's is short and freshly faded. They're identical twins, but their personalities are almost opposites: Jayden is a golden retriever in human form, while Makayla is more like a shy cat. She's also our token cis person. "How are you feeling?" she asks.

"Ugh." I make a face. "I just need to get this over with."

"Don't worry about it!" Jayden says. "I don't think anyone else wants to be president."

"I can't *not* worry," I say as we sit. "I have anxiety. Worrying is my natural state." I haven't been officially diagnosed yet—I only realized it over the summer, thanks to a couple of videos Anna sent me, because she has anxiety too—but it fits. Well, mostly. But it's the only thing that can explain my thoughts. Or rather, my mental horror movies. They're anxiety daydreams that pop into my mind without warning and go from innocuous to terrifying in two seconds flat. Sometimes, the thoughts aren't movies but an internal voice, babbling about what could go wrong, telling me what I should do or say to make it stop.

Right now, they're quiet, thanks to the sets of breaths I did before I came into the room. Next to me, Jayden is already halfway through a giant sandwich, Makayla is starting hers, and Anna is munching on an apple, and the rest of the club filters in, carrying their own lunch boxes or trays from the cafeteria. There are a few seniors, a clump of sophomores, and a ton of freshmen; that happens every year, though. Most of them will drop off after a few weeks, leaving the ones who really care.

A chorus of shrieks and laughter makes us all jump, and I look up and see him.

Forrest Hirschler.

I glance at Anna and we roll our eyes at each other. Forrest travels with a gaggle of gays, but they don't all come to Queer Alliance, just the two with him today: Alexander, who's Korean and a dancer, and Stef, who's Black and obsessed with anime. I like Stef; whenever we've interacted, she's been nice to me. Alexander is intimidating, always ready with a snappy reply.

Forrest follows them in, wearing his ever-present oversized hoodie with the hood pulled up even though he's inside and it makes no sense to do that. The hoodie thing is minor, but it's one of many things about him that annoy me. He's always talking to someone in class, or shouting out commentary on the lesson, and the only ideas he ever has for Queer Alliance are distractions that won't make life better for anyone at this school.

And I've never been able to forget what happened freshman year.

It was right after I'd started attending Queer Alliance meetings. Forrest and I were in the same biology class, and we were placed in a group together for an in-class assignment. Right away, I was less than impressed; he spent the first few minutes of our group's working time face down on his arms, hidden under the hood of his sweatshirt. Anna was the other person in our group, and I'd just started getting to know her through Queer Alliance, so we were talking about it while the teacher passed out materials. A few seconds into our conversation, Forrest raised his head like a swamp monster emerging from a bog.

"You're going to Queer Alliance?" he said, voice thick with disdain.

". . . Yeah," I responded, confused, stiffening up, wary of what he was about to say.

"That stuff is so corny," he said, dropping his forehead back onto his arms.

"Um, no it's not," I said.

"Oooh, look at us, all the queer kids hanging out together," he singsonged, voice muffled by the table. "What's even the point? It doesn't actually change anything."

"That's not true—" I started, but the teacher interrupted.

"Everything OK here?" she asked, smiling down at us.

"We're fine!" Anna said quickly. The teacher moved on, and Anna suggested brightly that we get to work, and Forrest and I followed her lead. Somehow we managed to get the entire assignment done without ever saying a word to each other, Anna navigating back and forth between us as if nothing was wrong at all.

"What was that about?" Anna asked after class as we headed to our lockers. They were right next to each other in the freshman hallway, another point of bonding between us.

"Right?" I said. "Like, if you're going to hate on Queer Alliance because you think it's pointless, why not join and help us do stuff? What a sad, bitter person."

"For real," she said.

"And this thing where you keep your head down the whole time except when you have some rude comment to make? You're not funny or edgy, you're just annoying."

Someone sideswiped my shoulder with theirs, and I staggered into Anna. She grabbed my arm, steadying me, and we both saw it at the same time: the back of a very familiar hoodie as the person wearing it walked away from us.

"Oops," Anna said, covering her mouth.

"Whatever," I said, rubbing my arm. "If you don't want to be criticized, don't be a jerk."

After that, Forrest doubled down, and I did too. Whenever we made eye contact in class, I couldn't help rolling my eyes or making a face. He returned the gesture with a sneer or some creative way of flashing me the middle finger. It got to the point that our teachers sat us on opposite sides of the room. And then in sophomore year, he showed up at our first Queer Alliance meeting, studiously ignoring me the entire time, and I responded in kind. We had only one class together that year, and he'd cemented his role as class clown by then, with his own little posse of friends. This year, it doesn't seem like anything has changed.

Whatever. By the end of lunch, I'll be president, and Forrest will have to listen to me.

"What's up, motherfuckers!" he whoops, pushing off his hood and galloping across the circle to flop into a chair. His brown curls bounce as he moves, shaggy across his forehead and slightly longer in the back. From across the circle, I can see the red glow of a sunburn on his white skin. The freshmen are silent, eyes wide, like lost kittens in the wilds of Jefferson High.

"Forrest." Mr. Harrison appears in the doorway of his office, posture as straight-backed as ever, every movement deliberate, like he's aware of where he is in space at all times.

"Sorry, Mr. H!" Forrest yells—because that's how loud he is. If he has a lower volume, I've never heard it. "What's up, fools?"

It's clearly time for someone to take charge. This is a chance for me to show my leadership qualities, so I clear my throat. "Thanks for coming, everyone. Shall we get started?"

"Yes, we shall!" Forrest echoes me. I ignore him.

Mr. Harrison finds an open seat. He's the theater teacher and our club advisor, and even though I'm not in theater, he's still one of my favorite teachers. I know it's not possible, but it seems like he knows every student at Jefferson High School by name. He encouraged me to run for secretary last year, so I know he'll support me being president too.

"Welcome, all." He surveys us, eyes twinkling behind his gold-rimmed glasses. "Normally I'm fairly hands-off with this club, but today's our first meeting, and we've got to pick a set of officers for the year. You can nominate yourself or be nominated by someone else. But first, let's introduce ourselves and our pronouns. I'm Mr. Harrison, he/him." He looks to his left, at one of the seniors, who takes the cue.

One by one, we go around the circle. My leg bounces up and down as the minutes tick by. We only have the lunch period, and I want this done, both because I want the satisfaction of the presidency and because I don't want to feel anxious about this anymore.

Finally we wrap up the introductions, and Mr. Harrison gestures to the whiteboard, where he's already written the titles of the club offices: Treasurer, Secretary, Vice President, and President.

"If you want to nominate someone, step up and write their name under a position," he says. "Then we'll take an anonymous vote."

For a beat, nobody moves, and then Jayden stands and crosses to the board, just like we planned it. Under *President*, he writes my name in black erasable marker.

Sidney Walker.

"Excellent." Mr. Harrison beams at me, then looks around. "Don't everyone jump at once, now." He sounds so proper with his British accent, and one of the freshmen cracks a smile.

Anna gets up and nominates herself for treasurer, like she was last year. Riley, a senior, nominates themself for vice president again. It would have made sense if they wanted to be president after last year's president graduated, but when I asked them about it on the first day of school, they just laughed and shook their head.

"Noooo, thank you," they said, clacking their long, lime-green, bejeweled nails in my direction. "Too much responsibility. I like being the second in command." They grinned at me. "You've got my vote."

We need a new secretary, since I'm not running for it this year, and Stef nominates herself. It's quiet for a moment as we all take in the slate.

"All right!" Mr. Harrison says, clapping his hands together once. "If that's it—"

"Hold up."

We all look over. Forrest heaves himself out of the chair, where he's been slouched through the proceedings. One of his shoelaces is untied, and I watch it as he scuffs his feet toward the whiteboard, but he doesn't trip. At the board, he picks up a marker, and writes his name.

Right under mine.

I stare at him as he walks back to his seat. Why the hell is he nominating himself? He's never held any office in the club before.

When he sits down, he looks at me with a smirk and gives me a little head nod. I turn away, pressing my lips together. This is fine. I'm way more qualified, and everyone knows it. He's not a threat.

"All right," Mr. Harrison says again. "If nobody else wants to throw their hat in the ring, we can cast our votes for the president." Everyone is quiet as he gazes around the room.

"Mr. Harrison," I say. "Shouldn't we each say a few words first? Like . . . why we want the position, and why we're the right person for it?"

"Oh!" He seems a little surprised, but he recovers quickly. "Yes, of course. That's only fair, since we've got all these new faces who don't know you." He smiles at the freshmen.

"I'll go first," I say, and pull my poster out from under my chair.

"Oh, they came *prepared*," Alexander murmurs.

I stand and so does Jayden—another piece of the plan. He always has my back. I unroll the poster, handing it to him, and he holds it up, rotating slowly so everyone can see. Black letters on a lavender background announce who I am in my favorite format: a list. But they aren't just traits. They're also reasons why I should be president, bordered by a ring of silver glitter for that extra pop.

"I'm Sidney," I say, smiling at the freshmen. "I've been a member of Queer Alliance since my first year here, and last year I served as secretary. In that position, it was my job to take accurate notes that reflected the content of our meetings. This information was super useful when it came to planning, because it provided us something to refer back to."

I describe last year's Homecoming Court committee, and how I was in charge of drafting communications to the student council for our campaign to add *Monarch* as a title alongside King and Queen. "Now when someone is nominated, and when they win, they can pick the title they want. The kids who want to be kings or queens can still do that, but the kids who don't want that have an option too. That campaign was an important step in making our school a place that celebrates all its students."

Students like me. If I wanted to run for Homecoming Court, which I super don't. Queer Alliance is my life, my home. Other than that, school is just one long anxious rat maze I have to get through.

The first few weeks at Jefferson, I was a small boat lost in a sea of halls that were so much bigger than my middle school. The few friends I'd had before were at other high schools, and I didn't know anyone yet. Then, on one of my teacher's doors, I noticed a poster covered in little cartoon rainbows. "COME OUT to QUEER ALLIANCE this FRIDAY," said the bubble letters filling the flyer, with a room number and time written underneath.

So I did.

I met Jayden, Anna, and Makayla that day, along with some other freshmen who dropped off the map a few weeks later. But we stayed, and pretty soon we were hanging out at every lunch break, not just Fridays.

I can only assume Forrest joined the club sophomore year because he came out as trans over that summer. Funny how he saw the point of Queer Alliance once it was personally relevant to him. A few weeks later, I came out as nonbinary—first to my friends, then to the club. I was worried people would think I was copying him, or was just doing it to be trendy, but everyone supported me.

I take a deep breath and segue into the home stretch of my speech. "I love this community, and we've done so many important things. Before I got here, the club helped bring gender-neutral restrooms to the school. This year, as president, I want to build on our achievements and keep making Jefferson into a place where all queer and trans students can be themselves. I deserve your vote because, as my poster says, I'm dedicated, I'm organized, I'm reliable, I'm caring, and finally, I make change happen." I feel the back of my neck tingle as I hit each bullet point. Forrest doesn't have a chance. "Thank you."

I sit down, to some scattered clapping from the freshmen. Riley wiggles their fingers in silent applause, and Anna squeezes my shoulder.

"Well said." Mr. Harrison smiles at me. "Forrest?"

All eyes turn to Forrest, slouched in his chair again. He straightens up, but he doesn't stand. "Hey. So, I joined the club last year." He fidgets with the strings of his hoodie. "We've done some really cool things. When I was figuring stuff out freshman year, I used those gender-neutral restrooms a lot. I don't know about y'all, but I like having a place to pee."

The freshmen snort, and Riley cracks a smile.

"I think we could do something different this year, though. Something more fun, and less work. We've come a long way, so let's party!" Forrest grins. "Also, I need something that looks good on my extracurriculars for college." He sticks out his tongue and flashes a peace sign, and a couple people laugh.

My chest tightens, my shoulders stiffening. This is a joke to him. All the work we've done, everything there still is to do, and he wants to party? He sits back, and there's a long pause, all of us waiting for something more, but he doesn't say anything.

"All right, then!" Mr. Harrison says. I can't tell what he's thinking. He moves to the whiteboard, picking up a marker. "I'm going to have you all close your eyes, and when I call out the name of the candidate, you'll raise your hands if you'd like to vote for that person."

I close my eyes, my heart pounding. Forrest can't win. He can't. This is supposed to be my moment, where everything comes together, not where everything falls apart. *The club will lose membership*, a voice whispers. *It's going to fail. Mr. Harrison will disband it.* The voice buzzes in my brain like an itch I can't scratch, morphing into images flashing in my head, one of my mental movies trying to play.

That's not real. It's not happening, I tell myself.

That's not real. It's not happening.

That's not real. It's not happening.

I breathe out, my mind clear. The mantra worked.

"If you'd like to vote for Forrest, raise your hand!" Mr. Harrison says.

I keep my hands clasped in my lap. I hear a few rustles. His friends are probably voting for him, but no one else will. They see it too. They have to. He'll ruin everything.

"And now for Sidney!"

I raise my hand. Beside me, I hear Jayden raise his, and the tightness in my chest eases a little bit.

There's a long silence, and then Mr. Harrison clears his throat. "You may open your eyes."

I blink a little as my eyes readjust to the fluorescent lights, and my gaze goes to the board.

"Well," Mr. Harrison says. "We have eleven votes for Sidney." He pauses, and I read the number right before he says it. "And eleven votes for Forrest."

Oh my god.

We tied.

WHEN I WAS NINE YEARS OLD, A FEW YEARS BEFORE MY parents got divorced, the three of us went on a winter hike together. That was our thing, rain or shine: regular hikes, and camping trips as often as Mom and Dad could get the time off from work. It was something they'd done since they started dating, and by then it felt like the only time there was peace in our family. On hikes, they both seemed calmer. They smiled more, and held hands, and all I had to think about was avoiding puddles and getting over logs and the burn in my legs from climbing the trail, instead of watching for tension gathering between them.

The temperature was in the thirties that day, but they still got me up at eight in the morning, bundling me into a parka and snow pants, helping me fasten grips onto the bottom of my hiking boots. Once we were on the trail, it didn't take long for my face to go numb from the wind; when I moved my mouth to talk, it felt like someone had painted a mask of glue over my face, holding it in place.

That's what it feels like now, sitting in Mr. Harrison's room, staring at the whiteboard.

This can't be happening.

"Can we even have two presidents?" Jayden asks. His words sound far away.

Mr. Harrison lifts his palms up. "I don't see why not," he says. "There are no guidelines to prevent it."

"Hell yeah!" The loud voice jolts me back into my body. Forrest shoots finger guns at me. "What's up, Co-President."

I wrinkle my forehead and shake my head. "Um, no," I say, and his smile collapses into surprise. I look at Mr. Harrison. "We don't need two presidents. It'll just make things more complicated. I've been in this club way longer than Forrest has, and I've held a leadership position. It doesn't make sense for him to be president too."

Mr. Harrison's eyebrows lift slightly.

"It's just a club," Forrest says. "It's not that serious."

I glare at him. "Just because it's a club, doesn't mean it's not important."

He rolls his eyes.

"See?" I say, throwing a hand out at him. "Mr. Harrison, you can break the tie."

I hear murmurs around the classroom; someone lets out a breath nearby. I know how I probably look right now: uptight and mean, but I'm too angry to care. Who does Forrest think he is, throwing his name in the ring just because it'll look good on his college applications? This club isn't some convenient opportunity he can use to make himself look better. This club is my life.

It's everything to me.

Mr. Harrison takes a deep breath and lets it out. "Sidney, I'm not going to do that." I open my mouth to protest and he shakes his head. "I am your advisor, here to provide supervision and guidance if needed. But this club belongs to you all, and the people have clearly spoken. They want you both."

I look at Forrest, who's staring at me, his arms crossed.

"This *is* unprecedented, though," Mr. Harrison adds, "so let's do a trial run and have a reelection at the beginning of next quarter. We'll schedule the revote for the week after Trans Awareness Week." He scans the room, and people nod quietly.

The bell rings and everyone jumps up. "Teamwork makes the dream work," Mr. Harrison calls out with a smile. "I'll see you all next week."

Forrest and his friends are out the door immediately, leaving the rest of us to put the chairs back as fast as we can so we're not late to fifth period. I move numbly from chair to chair, the meeting replaying in my head over and over. This wasn't supposed to happen. This wasn't part of the plan. My year, the way I imagined it, is receding into a golden pinprick, the me I was going to be—accomplished, collected, and in control—vanishing in the distance.

As soon as we're done, Jayden and Makayla rush off in the opposite direction to their history class, Makayla throwing a worried glance at me over her shoulder.

"Well, that was unexpected," Anna says as the two of us hustle toward Algebra II. Most people are in their classes by now, a few stragglers rushing to make it in time for the last bell.

"Understatement of the century," I mutter.

"You still have the presidency," she says, picking up her pace to match mine. "Silver lining?"

"Yeah, but I didn't want to share it with someone. Especially not him." We turn a corner and beeline for the door of our classroom. The second bell rings just as we get inside, so Anna can't say anything else about it.

In my seat, I watch as Mr. Gutierrez starts a lesson on quadratics, but my mind is buzzing again, no thoughts, just an electrical hum of doom-anxiety-desperation that only I can hear. I repeat a mantra in my head three times, one on either side and one safe in the middle:

Stop, stop, stop.

Stop. Stop. Stop.

Stop. Stop. Stop.

My heart is racing, my palms sweaty.

Again.

Stop, stop, stop.

Stop. Stop. Stop.

Stop. Stop. Stop.

I feel lightheaded, nauseous.

Again.

Stop, stop, stop.

Stop. Stop. Stop.

Stop. Stop. St—

I jump up. I can't stand this anymore. Everyone looks at me as I rush to the door, and behind me, I hear Mr. Gutierrez calling out, but I don't stop. I charge into the hall, down the long corridor out toward the wing where I know Jayden and Makayla are in class with Forrest. The security guard shouts after me as I blaze past him, but I keep going, the halls blurring until I'm at the door and pushing it open into the middle of a class in full swing. The teacher looks up and so does every face in the class. Forrest stands.

"You can't be president," I tell him.

He rolls his eyes. "Fuck you," he says. "I got elected fair and square. You're just an uptight bitch."

I launch myself at him, everyone around me erupting in screams. I shake my head, and suddenly I'm sitting in math class, blinking as Mr. Gutierrez drones on at the board. My heart is racing. Did I really just storm to Forrest's class and tackle him?

No. There's a desk in front of me, the brown grain of the fake wood gently swirling across its top, interrupted by the purple cover of a spiral notebook, a pen resting beside it. I grip the desk with my hands and look around the classroom. The walls are white, the linoleum floor is blue, the lighting is horrible. All around me students are taking notes.

That's not real. It's not happening.

That's not real. It's not happening.

That's not real. It's not happening.

But the election did. I have to work with Forrest for the entire term.

How am I supposed to do that?

♥

The moment I step inside my house that afternoon, English Breakfast runs toward the door with his signature raspy meow. I take off my backpack and kneel as he flops down on the hardwood floor to expose his belly. I know better than to touch it, though. Some cats allow belly rubs, but Brekky isn't one of those cats. I keep my fingers up around his head and neck, scritching his smoky gray fur just the way he likes it.

Petting him calms me, and for a moment, his sweet face is the only thing I see, his green eyes half closed in happy relaxation.

"You're probably hungry, huh?" I murmur, and he chirps, jumping up and pushing his head against my knee.

He follows me into the kitchen and circles my feet, meowing loudly as I put some wet food into his bowl. A high-pitched squeak pulls my gaze to the floor, where our other cat, Earl Grey, has joined him. She's a dainty gray tabby, much smaller than Brekky, and where he's laid-back, she's skittish. They belong to Shar, my stepmom; she got them as kittens years ago, before she met my mom.

The cats are both equally enthusiastic about the food, though, and run to it as soon as I set it down. We feed them three times a day: Shar takes the morning, since she's up the earliest before heading to her job site, I do the afternoons when I get home, and Mom feeds them after dinner. By the way they act around food, though, you'd think we were starving them.

I grab a glass of orange juice and some chips and set up at the table with all my schoolwork. Our house is pretty small, so I don't have far to go. The main floor is where we live: the two bedrooms and the bathroom at the back, the kitchen in the middle, with its side door, and the open-plan living room and dining room at the front of the house. There's a back door in the basement, but it's unfinished down there, all concrete, cold and damp with spiders lurking in the corners. The only reason I go down there is to do laundry. Out the side door, there's a small garage where Shar does all her woodworking projects.

Gay art adorns the walls around me, thanks to Mom and Shar's love for queer artists: abstract color blocks, portraits of gay couples, a giant knitted tapestry in a rainbow ombre. The furnishings are thrifted but cozy. We don't have a ton of money, but this home is ours, and it's better than Dad's place. Or at least, the place he lived the last time I saw him, but that was almost a year ago.

It's still September and the school year has barely started, but I have plenty of homework to do already: a worksheet of problems for math, an outline for a short essay in English, and a reading for history. The essay outline isn't due until next week, so I start the math problems. That's my hardest subject, and last year, when I worked with a tutor after Mom discovered my grades had slipped to D's in most of my classes, she taught me to do the hardest thing first. Sometimes it works.

But not today.

As soon as I look at the math problem, Forrest's face flashes into my head, his ridiculous smile and cringey finger guns when we both won the election. Like he thought I'd be happy about it. Like we're friends.

It's just a club, he said.

It's not. At least, not to me. Maybe I'm more invested than other people are, but the club has made a real difference at our school, and that's not nothing. Right now, it feels like the world is closing in on us, on marginalized people, on queer people, on trans people. Yeah, Washington State is safe enough, but for how long? And how much of that safety is just in Seattle? It doesn't take that long of a drive outside the city to see something fucked-up. Sometimes there are fucked-up things inside the city itself, like last year when my friends and I found anti-trans stickers all over a telephone pole in Capitol Hill. Right in the middle of what used to be, and still is in some ways, the gay neighborhood, where we should feel safest. I worry about my friends, about my mom, about Shar every time she goes to work at the job site. She's there now, lit up golden in the afternoon sun, drilling a wall into place, and suddenly she slumps forward, blood pouring out of her hair, down her tanned temples; behind her is a coworker, his face set in a glare and hammer upraised, yelling a slur as she falls to the floor, and nobody helps her, they just laugh—

I shake my head to clear it, taking deep breaths, refocusing on the math worksheet.

That's not real. It's not happening.

That's not real. It's not happening.

That's not real. It's not happening.

Shar's face, bloody and lifeless, flashes in my mind again and I grab my phone. I need to text her, make sure she's OK. I know she is. But what if she's not?

What's for dinner tonight? I ask. I don't want her to know I was worried about her; if she knows that, then she'll ask why, and I can't tell her I was just picturing her getting attacked by one of her coworkers.

I'm making salmon and wild rice, she texts back a few seconds later. *On my way home now,* she adds, and my shoulders relax.

Brekky jumps up on the table, distracting me from my phone. I grab him and hold him close. "You're not supposed to be up here," I whisper in his ear, and he flicks it, then wiggles, trying to get out of my arms. I set him down on the floor and stare at the worksheet.

I can't share the club. I can't risk it becoming just another social hour, where people come to hang out and nothing ever gets done. I have to do something about this.

♥

I spend all evening at the table. Homework blurs into Shar's arrival and then Mom's, at the same time as Shar pulls the salmon out of the oven. They join me as I push my schoolwork aside, Mom still in her corporate professional clothes: navy slacks and a floral-patterned blouse, her long, wavy brown hair sleeker and shinier than mine will ever be. Next to her, Shar is carpenter-casual in battered Carhartt pants, her graying hair in a buzzcut, the smile lines deep around her eyes. She has 20/20 vision, unlike us. Mom's glasses are black and horn-rimmed, and my frames are round, pink-tinted clear plastic. Technically, the color was called "champagne." I picked it because it sounded grown-up, like glasses that someone who had their shit together would wear. Someone who was Queer Alliance president. But instead, I'm just the co-president.

"How was your day, kiddo?" Shar asks.

I shrug. "Fine."

"It was Queer Alliance elections today, right?" Mom asks, focusing on me. "How did it go?"

"I got it," I say, forcing a smile. "I tied with someone else, though, and Mr. Harrison is making us share the presidency."

"Honey!" She smiles warmly. "I'm so proud of you. Sharing is caring, right?"

"Oh my god." I roll my eyes.

"It'll be good for you," she says. "Keep us posted, OK? I know you're going to do some cool stuff."

"Thanks," I say, wishing I could feel excited the way I thought I would tonight.

"How's the homework going?" she asks lightly, too lightly.

"Good."

"Care to say more?"

"Math is almost done and I'm going to finish at lunch tomorrow. Essay outline assigned today and not due 'til next week; I'll start it this weekend. History reading I haven't done yet, but I'll do it on the bus ride to school."

She eyes me, and I brace for her assessment of my homework management. "I'm glad you have a plan. Just make sure you keep it up."

"Mom." I sigh. It is too soon for this.

"That's all I'm going to say." She puts up her hands, still smiling. "I want you to do well in all areas, not just what you love."

I give her a thumbs-up. Enough has gone wrong already today, and I don't want to add a fight about my grades to the list. We did plenty of that last year.

I don't know exactly when my anxiety got worse, but by last January, it was so bad I could hardly focus in class. When I went to do assignments, I didn't know how because I hadn't learned the material. So I just . . . stopped. I went to class and took home the assignments, but they sat in my folders untouched.

"What is this?" Mom said to me the night grades came in. I was curled on the couch, watching cartoons, and she grabbed the remote to pause them.

She held up her phone, and when I squinted, she came closer so I could see. My grades, right there on her parent account in the school's online learning management system. I'd forgotten she could access them too. All those D's and F's, one after another, hit me in the chest like fists.

"What happened, Sidney?" she asked.

I stared blankly at the scene frozen on the TV. I didn't know where to start: the thoughts I was having about terrible things happening to her or Shar or Dad, the ones that felt so real they left me with my heart pounding, afraid I was losing my mind? Or the drunken texts Dad had been sending me, late at night, apologizing for what a shitty father he was, raging about Mom and what a bitch she was for keeping him from me, even though he had visitation rights but just never used them? My thoughts felt too heavy, too complicated, too much to describe, much less do anything about, and I didn't want to make things worse between her and Dad by telling her how he was acting. So I didn't say anything.

"You'll have to work hard to avoid repeating the year," she'd said at the time, and I nodded my head.

The next week, I'd started with my tutor, and Mom checked in with me every night about my homework until the end of the year, when my report card came in again. B's and C's. Crisis averted.

But not the one in my head, because even though Dad's texts stopped, my thoughts didn't. Some days it feels like I'm standing at a dam in my mind, rushing from one spewing leak to another, trying to stop the images as they firehose out. I haven't drowned yet, but sometimes I'm afraid I might.

ON MONDAY MORNING, I'M READY. I'VE BEEN THINKING about this presidency thing all weekend, and I know what to do. Sometimes my brain's inability to shut up is a curse, but sometimes, it does come in handy.

I can hear Mom out in the kitchen as I get ready, and then the front door slamming as she leaves. Shar is long gone, up three hours before we are. Rummaging through my dresser, I pick out jeans, a green-and-blue-striped shirt, and my favorite hoodie. In the bathroom, I brush my teeth and wash my face, avoiding the mirror. The person I see in its reflection never looks the way I expect. Not that I really look like anything in my head; the world constantly reminds me that I'm seen as a girl, even though I'm not super feminine. I'm not masculine either, and I try as much as possible not to think about how everyone sees me. When I'm alone, I forget gender exists, and I feel like a formless blob. If I could be an animal, I'd say maybe a lizard, the kind that runs really fast, or a small bird, so I could fly. Just not who I see in the mirror: an awkward-looking kid with shoulder-length, wavy brown hair, freckled white skin, and behind my glasses, eyes gray blue like my Dad's, the only way he's ever been a constant presence in my life.

I pop on my headphones as I walk to the light rail station to catch the train, picking Olivia Rodrigo's latest album for the soundtrack to my morning. There's a slight chill in the air, big clouds drifting in front of the silvery morning sun every now and then. The air smells good: earthy and crisp, like fall, my favorite season. Late roses bloom on the bushes in our neighbors' yards, their scent fruity and light.

When I get off the train, it takes only a few blocks until the entrance of Jefferson comes into view. My heartbeat speeds up, even though there's nothing special about it; the building was constructed in the 1970s, with newer additions tacked onto it in the years before I started high school: a shiny wing for STEM classes and a giant set of sports fields, along with new linoleum floors and fresh, undented lockers put in over the summer.

My heart is pounding, not because I see the school but because of what I'm about to do. Inside the building, I wind my way through the masses of kids crowding around lockers, chattering in clumps, goofing off outside classrooms while they wait for the doors to open.

I find him at his locker, thankfully with none of his friends in sight.

"Hey Forrest," I say, and he looks up from his phone, a slightly dopey expression on his face like he just woke up.

Which he probably did. Or he's stoned. I don't smell weed, though. He's got the same hoodie on that he wore yesterday, and as he turns to me, he pushes the hood off, shutting his locker door with a bang that makes me twitch. Hopefully not enough for him to see it.

"Hey," he says. Gone is the jovial shout; his voice is subdued, and he doesn't smile as he looks at me. He points at me. "Co-President. What's up."

"Not much." I shrug. "So. About that . . . I really think it would be best for the club if there was one president, and I was wondering if we could talk and maybe—"

"If you're trying to get me to step down, it's not happening," he says.

"Um—" I start, but my brain freezes and I don't know what to say next. It seemed like a good plan last night, when I rehearsed it in my head, but Mind-Rehearsal-Forrest was way more agreeable than this Forrest.

"What's your problem with me, anyway?" he says, crossing his arms.

"I don't have—"

"You think you're better than me?" I grimace, avoiding his gaze. "That you have some kind of claim to Queer Alliance just because you got to it first?"

"No, I—" My face is hot. A few people murmur as they pass us.

"I have just as much right to be president as you, and last I checked, half the club voted me in. Fair and square. So I'll see you at lunch on Friday, Co-President." He says the last word extra loud, swivels around, and walks away into the crowd.

I stand there staring down at the ground, not wanting to see any of the eyes that might be on me right now. I really don't think I'm better than him. But I *have* been involved longer. And I *have* done more than he has. I think that gives me a little more knowledge about how to run the club.

I blink against the tears that well up suddenly. Everyone saw that. Or at least, everyone passing us in that moment saw it, and now people just see me, standing in the hallway by a locker that isn't even mine, about to cry. I hurry down the hall, in the same direction, then turn, heading for the nearest bathroom.

The gender-neutral single stall is open, and I lock myself inside, letting my backpack fall to the floor and slumping against the door. I slide down until I'm sitting on the tile and take off my glasses, pressing my hands against my eyes. I can't believe I thought that was actually going to work. I'm such an idiot. Now he really thinks I'm an uptight bitch, just like the Forrest in my anxiety movie did.

Stop, I tell myself.

Stop.

Stop.

I shake my head to get rid of the thoughts, and open my eyes, staring at the beige wall behind the toilet. My throat tightens again, and I swallow the tears down. The bell is going to ring soon, and I have to go to class, and I am not giving Forrest the satisfaction of seeing how much he's upset me.

♥

After our showdown in the hallway, I'm on guard for Forrest behind every corner. In our class together, first-period English, he totally ignores me, but every time I see him in the hall my heart rate jumps. His words ricochet around my brain, the scene replaying at totally random and completely inconvenient moments: as a teacher calls on me to answer a question; in the middle of dinner; while I'm working on homework. I do my best to get through the day, but the whole time in my mind, Forrest is glaring at me and saying I must think I'm better than him. *What if he tells his friends what I did, and they tell everyone else in the club, and everyone thinks I'm completely out of my mind, and they don't even wait for the revote, they just make me leave Queer Alliance immediately, and my friends abandon me, and—*

"Sidney?" A finger poking my shoulder makes me jump. When I look up, Anna is watching me with a concerned, wary expression on her face. It's Wednesday, and we're sitting in the hallway for lunch, and my thoughts are going haywire, like they have for the past few days.

"What's up?" I try to smile, but my lips won't make the shape; they just pull tighter, into something that feels and probably looks like a skeleton pretending to be human.

Jayden and Makayla are watching me now too, and I look down at my sandwich, swallowing against the lump rising in my throat. If I tell them what I've been thinking, I'll sound totally unhinged.

"You've been super spacey the past few days," Anna says. "What's going on?"

"Nothing," I say. "I'm just . . ." I wave my hand vaguely. "Anxious."

"Is it about Queer Alliance?" Anna eyes me. She is way too perceptive sometimes.

"Ummm . . ." I lean back, letting my head fall against the wall with a light thump. "Yeah."

"You're gonna be a great president," Makayla says.

"Co-president," I say, and I don't mean to sound bitter, but the word comes out like burnt coffee.

"Maybe Forrest will be . . . OK-ish?" Jayden says.

I raise my eyebrows at him. "What a vote of confidence."

He rubs the back of his head, grinning. "I mean, maybe he'll surprise you! He's not *that* bad."

I sit upright. "Not that bad? Are you two secret besties? Should I be worried?" I'm joking, but *what if* whispers the voice in my head. I mentally bat it away.

"No!" Jayden holds his hands up. "I'm still your right-hand man. We just got assigned to a project together in history, that's all, and he's been . . . fine. Alexander is in the group too."

"I'm very happy for you." I roll my eyes. He shrugs, smiling.

Anna squeezes my arm. "You're going to do great. No matter what Forrest does."

I wish I believed her, but I can't seem to stop replaying the confrontation with him over and over, picking out the moments where I could have said or done something, anything, different. The moments where I could have rattled off the perfect comeback speech, which of course I can think of word for word now that I'm not right in front of him. Where I could have said the right thing to disarm him, calm him down, get him to see what's best and give up the presidency. Where I could have started the whole conversation off differently, approached him with friendliness instead.

My brain is like an entity unto itself, a whole other being inside me that I have no control over. It bombards me with images and thoughts like I'm in some horrible gym class dodgeball game where no matter how I move, I get hit in the face. It's me on one side and everything inside my brain on the other, throwing itself at me.

I'm so tired.

That's not real. It's not happening.

That's not real. It's not happening.

That's not real. It's not happening.

As my friends chatter, I say it to myself three times, then again, because the thoughts are still coming. And again. I do seven sets of three, for an odd number of twenty-one. Then I do seven more sets. Then seven more, for three rounds of seven sets of three repetitions each, twenty-one times per round, sixty-three repetitions overall. All odd numbers. I'm safe inside.

♥

When my friends and I walk into Mr. Harrison's classroom on Friday, Forrest is already there, and the circle is half set up. I stop short, Jayden letting out a noise of surprise as he almost bumps into me.

"Hey." Forrest hefts a chair over his head, grinning at us. I cringe inwardly, waiting for the thunk when it lands, but he sets it down gently next to another one. Jayden crosses to him and they fist-bump. He glances back at me, and I widen my eyes at him. He shrugs, giving me a guilty-looking smile. OK, so Jayden and Forrest are cool with each other. That's fine. My friends can be friends with whoever they want.

I join the others as we push the last chairs into place. Forrest and I slide ours in at the same time, next to each other.

"How's it going, Co-President?" he asks, his voice light. Too light. And he's still calling me Co-President, like he wants to rub it in.

"Pretty good," I say back, matching his casual tone.

The others filter in, and Mr. Harrison pops his head out of his office, making eye contact with me and Forrest for a thumbs-up that we're good to go. Then he disappears again, and it's just us and the rest of the club. It's still early in the year, so the turnout from last week is holding.

"All right," I say when everyone's seated. I have the perfect idea for an event, one that will show everyone why they should stick with me when it's time to revote. "So, October is coming up. It's LGBT History Month and we usually do something for National Coming Out Day on the eleventh. I don't think we should pressure people to come out, but it would be great to do something educational around what it means to come out and how to make the school a place where people don't have to come out, they can just be who they are."

The freshmen are nodding. "Maybe, like, an assembly?" one of them says in a soft voice.

"We did an assembly last year," Forrest says.

I smile at the freshman. "That's true, we did, still a good idea though. Maybe something similar to that?"

"Like a speaker?" Riley says.

"Oh yeah!" I turn to them. "That's a great idea. We could even do a panel. Maybe from one of the local nonprofits?" Across from me, Stef scribbles in her secretary notes.

"I have an idea," Forrest says. His voice rings out even louder than normal, and when we all turn to him, he's looking right at me. "We should have a party." He grins. "A Coming Out Party."

I open my mouth but Riley beats me to it. "Like a themed party?" they ask.

"Yeah!" he says. "We could have it in the library, and have cupcakes with colored frosting for all the flags, and a super-gay playlist, and games where you have to like, I don't know, name the queer celebrity or something—"

"How is that going to make a difference at the school?" I ask, and the room goes totally silent.

Forrest raises his eyebrows. "It's . . . fun? And having fun is nice? We shouldn't have to be educating people all the time."

"Why don't we do both a panel and a party?" Riley says, chewing on their bottom lip as they look back and forth from me to Forrest.

"That sounds—" Forrest starts.

"Expensive," Anna interjects. She's on her laptop, tapping rapidly. "I have the spreadsheet for our club income and expenses here, and we can't afford both."

"Nonprofits aren't gonna charge a school to send out some panelists," Forrest says. "And someone can make cupcakes at home."

"It's not that simple," I say, keeping my voice calm, even though I want to scream. "We should have vegan and gluten-free cupcakes to be inclusive of dietary needs, and we should reimburse whoever makes them if we want to be really fair about it. And not everyone wants to eat cupcakes, so we should have some other options too. That will add up quickly."

"OK, but that's the only thing," he says. "We can print posters using school tech and put them up ourselves. We can make decorations or bring stuff from home. All of that is free."

"Have you ever set foot inside a grocery store? Do you even know how much food costs?" I ask.

"Are we seriously that broke?" he says. "I bet we can get all the food we need for less than fifty dollars."

Everyone turns to Anna, whose eyes widen, then jump down to her screen. "We have . . . ten dollars," she says.

"Huh," Forrest says. "Well. We could ask places to donate food?"

"Do you think every single business is just dying to give high schoolers free stuff?" I ask.

"Are you always this negative?" he snaps back.

"Guys—" Jayden says, but the bell rings. The freshmen stand up, murmuring among themselves as they head for the door. Riley catches my eye and grimaces in solidarity.

Or in irritation? Maybe they're mad that I got into it with Forrest today? I can't tell. My heart is pounding, anger and anxiety surging in my chest. Our first meeting, and Forrest completely derailed it. Just like I was afraid of.

"Hey, Sidney—" Forrest says, but I slide out of the desk, grabbing my bag.

"Congratulations on getting us nowhere," I say. "Co-President." I glare at him and head for the door before he can say anything else.

ON SATURDAY AFTERNOON, I GO OVER TO ANNA'S HOUSE to study. That's another thing Mom made me start doing after last year's grades fiasco: studying with my friends on weekends. She called everyone's parents, told them what happened, and set up a rotating schedule of weekend study dates for me. It was horrifyingly embarrassing. But I love being with my friends, and I do get more done when I'm with someone else.

Sometimes.

Anna's house is a small brick bungalow in a neighborhood a few light rail stops south of mine. When I knock on the door, screeching ensues from inside, and I step back.

The door swings open. "Hurry!" Anna whispers fiercely, grabbing my arm and pulling me across the threshold.

"What's going on?" I stumble after her through the living room. Footsteps thunder below us, up the stairs from the basement. She drags me down the hallway, into her room, and slams the door, locking it just as a series of thuds shakes the frame. It's like a horror movie or something.

"My brother's friends are here," she says grimly.

"We can hear you!" he shrieks outside.

"Go AWAY!" she yells, then jumps back, yelping as Silly String shoots under the door, coating her socked feet. A chorus of wild hooting echoes in the hallway, and then the sound of—three? Ten? It's impossible to tell—pairs of feet racing away.

Relative silence descends. I can hear them dimly now, downstairs again, cackling and shouting. Anna sinks onto her bed, pulling her socks off and throwing them into the corner of her room next to her laundry hamper.

"They've been here since noon," she says, "and they're spending the night. I'm losing my mind."

"I'm so sorry," I say, dropping my bag on the floor and joining her on the bed. Anna's little brother is a nine-year-old terror, full of energy that Anna's parents don't seem to know what to do with. They're older than mine; in their late forties, compared to my mom, who's about to turn forty, and Shar, who just turned forty last year. I only know that because they talk about it all the time.

"It's OK. I needed to hermit this weekend anyway." She gets up and goes to her desk, clearing the makeup off it. "I was learning how to do a sea-creature look this morning. I'm thinking maybe I'll be a mermaid for Halloween. But not a pretty one. A scary nightmare one."

"How trans of you," I say, and she laughs.

"What about you?"

"My morning?"

"No, your Halloween costume."

"Oh." I stare at her ceiling. "I haven't really thought about it. I feel kind of awkward dressing up. Like . . . too old for it."

"Never!" she says. The brushes clatter as she pushes them into her makeup case. That's something I love about Anna—she doesn't care what other people think. Well, that's not exactly true. She has anxiety too. But she does what she wants anyway, even if it's something other people think is silly, like dressing up even though we're sixteen now.

"I'll think of something," I say. "Are we coordinating this year?"

"Not sure." She goes to her closet and pulls out the extra folding chair for me, setting it at the end of her desk. "Makayla said she'd be down. Jayden has been . . . evasive."

"What does that mean?" I sit up, watching her.

She shrugs. "I asked him about it and he changed the subject. I sent him my inspo earlier and mentioned some group ideas, but he just said it looked great and didn't answer the rest."

"Weird."

"Maybe. It might just be ADHD brain."

Jayden's notorious for that—only reading part of a message, and responding to that instead of the whole thing. Or not registering what we're saying because he's distracted by something else.

"What are we doing today?" Anna asks, turning on some lo-fi beats.

I join her at the desk, pulling out my books and laptop. "I need to work on the draft of my English essay now that the outline is in," I say.

"Oh perfect, me too," she says, and sits down beside me.

It's raining outside, the clouds making the day feel darker, but the light of her lamp is golden and cozy. We each type away, the lo-fi music and the rain on her window making a chill background. Every now and then, a screech sounds from below, and we roll our eyes at each other.

"So," Anna says after a while. "Queer Alliance yesterday."

"Yes." I keep my eyes on my screen, but I'm not seeing the sentence I just wrote. My whole body is on alert for whatever she's going to say next. "That was . . . awkward."

"Forrest was super rude," she says, and I relax. I've been going over the interaction in my mind since it happened, and I'd started to wonder if maybe I'd been the asshole, if it was all me causing problems for the alliance.

"*Thank* you," I say, looking over at her. "So much attitude, and for what? It's not my fault he doesn't know how to run a club."

"Ex-*actly*." She hits a key for emphasis and stops, looking at me with Jesus Eyes. It's what we call the expression she gets when she's settling in to hear one of us rant about something; her eyes get all soft, and her mouth scrunches up, and she frowns a little as she stares into your soul. Anna is definitely the mom friend of the group.

"It's just so frustrating." I close my laptop, resting my chin in my hands. "We could be doing so much, and he wants to throw a party? This is exactly why I didn't want us to have two presidents. We can't get anywhere if one person keeps getting in the way."

"Totally," she says, nodding. "If we're gonna have two presidents, they'd need to collaborate, and he's not doing that."

"Right?" I throw up my hands.

"What are you going to do?"

I pick at the cuticle on my thumbnail. I'm out of options, and the only thing I can do now is accept that I have to share the presidency. But maybe it will work in my favor.

"I know I'm more qualified than he is," I say. "He's going to mess this up eventually; he's already on his way. I just have to wait him out, and be the best co-president the alliance has ever had, and next to him, it'll be obvious I'm the better choice. And when the reelection comes, I'll win."

♥

That night, I cocoon myself in my room. I love my room; it's small, but it's my safe space. When Mom got her fancy job, she and Shar were finally able to put together a down payment with help from a loan through a local housing organization. They told me that they might be the adults who owned the house, but it was home for the three of us, a place they called a "fixer-upper" in North Beacon Hill. So I got to do whatever I wanted to my room, right down to the color I painted the walls.

It took me a while to decide. I went to the hardware store with Shar and picked out paint chips; at home, I held them up to my walls, trying to picture what the final result would look like. Finally, I decided on green, but not just any green: sage, Shar called it. When I walk into my room, through the door on the right in our back hallway, I see four walls in a light silvery green. It feels like being inside a mossy, foggy forest, like the Hoh Rain Forest in Olympic National Park, where we go camping every summer. Directly across from the door, my bookcase sits below the north-facing window, and on the windowsill is my small collection of succulents, their light purples, pinks, blues, and greens a perfect complement to the color of my walls. To the left, my bed sits against the wall, with a cacophony of pictures pasted above it: posters of Billie Eilish, Olivia Rodrigo, and girl in red; prints of landscapes I found at the thrift store and liked; Polaroids of me and my friends taken by Jayden during his photography phase. On the hardwood floor is a soft lavender shag rug, and Brekky is curled up on it now, nose to tail, sleeping.

It's twilight outside; there's still some time before the dark cold days of winter settle in, when the sun rises at 8:00 and sets at 4:30. It's misting, that very light rain Seattleites, including me, love to complain about but secretly enjoy. My room feels cozy, but despite that, I have this sensation in my throat like I need to cry. I felt better about the QA meeting after talking to Anna, but the feeling didn't last; it never does. Now that I'm alone, the day replays, the thoughts bubbling up in my mind.

What if Anna thought I was rude too?

What if she thinks I'm fucking up the alliance, and just didn't tell me?

Maybe that's what she meant.

When she said two presidents would have to collaborate.

It's not Forrest who's the problem, it's me. I need to collaborate. Otherwise, everyone will be mad at me. At the next meeting, I'll walk in, and Anna will be there, arms crossed.

I'm in Mr. Harrison's room, and it's completely empty except for the two of us.

"Where is everyone?" I ask, glancing up at the clock.

"No one wanted to come," she says, her voice hard.

"What? Why not?"

"Because of you," she says. "You and your ego. You think you own Queer Alliance because you've been here longer, and you were a jerk to Forrest, and now nobody wants to come."

"I'm—I'm sorry!" I stammer, but she's walking toward me, fists clenched at her sides. I step back as she strides past me. "Anna, wait!"

She whirls around. "It's too late, Sidney. The club is done, and it's all your fault."

The door slams, and my knees buckle under me, down to my blanket, soft in my clenched hands. I blink back tears.

That's not real. It's not happening, I tell myself.

That's not real. It's not happening.

That's not real. It's not happening.

Brekky meows, headbutting my face. "Hi, buddy," I whisper, scratching the top of his head. He settles next to my shoulder, tucking his paws in to make a perfect loaf shape. I snap a picture and send it to Anna. If she responds, she's not mad at me.

LOAF KING, she says back, almost instantly. *I LOVE HIM.*

He loves you back, I say.

I should feel better, but I don't. The anxiety movie is still flickering in my mind, like an old film reel on a projector screen. She's going to get sick of me, just like Dad did. She'll stop texting, just like he did, and then everyone else will too, and then I'll be alone.

♥

"How was studying yesterday?" Mom asks me the moment I drag myself into the kitchen the next morning. It took me a long time to fall asleep, again, and I'm groggy, eyes crusty, stomach growling for breakfast.

"Fine," I mumble, stretching up to the top shelf of the pantry to grab a couple Pop-Tarts. I cross to the toaster and drop them in, pressing the button and staring as the innards of the appliance glow to life.

"Fine?" Mom leans against the counter, sipping her coffee. Her hair is still wet from the shower, an empty, crumb-covered plate next to the sink beside her.

"Yeah. We started our English essay drafts. I'm going to work on it more today."

"OK, wonderful." I can hear the relief in her voice, and she crosses behind me over to the table.

The Tarts pop, and I take them gingerly by the edges, setting them on a plate before sitting down on the other side of the table from her. The first bite of strawberry filling bursts in my mouth, and I feel a little less zombie, a little more human. "Where's Shar?" I ask.

"Out in the garage," Mom says, laptop open in front of her, eyes on the screen. From the floor comes Earl Grey's tiny meow, and Mom scoots her chair back slightly, making room for the cat to jump up on her lap.

"Are you working today?" I ask. Mom loves her job, but sometimes I think she loves it a little too much.

"Yeah, you know that client I mentioned the other night?"

I shake my head. I'm sure she told me, but I don't remember.

"Well, it's our biggest one yet, a start-up with some major capital behind it, and they want the full package: branding, marketing strategy, social assets, the works." I have no idea what she's talking about, but I nod like I do. "It's really important, so I'm putting in extra time to keep us on top of it."

"But it's the weekend."

She laughs. "That's why they pay me the big bucks, sweetie."

"I wish I got paid to do homework," I mumble, but she doesn't hear me; her focus is on the computer.

I savor my breakfast one bite at a time, and when I can't drag it out one moment longer, I shuffle back to my room to change out of the giant T-shirt I sleep in and into something that resembles what a functional human would wear. Brekky trots after me, nosing around my room as I put on pants and a different shirt. My phone buzzes once, twice; probably the morning meme dump in our group chat. I pick it up and see a text from Jayden to all of us, and a text from—

Dad?

I stare at his name. I feel like I'm hallucinating, like I'll shut my eyes and open them and the alert on my screen will be gone. The room fades away, the text all that's left in front of me. I can see the first few lines: *Hey kid, I know it's been a while.*

The last time Dad texted me was back in June: a picture of me, him, and Mom at the Grand Canyon when I was six. *Best trip ever*, he'd written. He sent me texts like that a lot; memories from my childhood, pictures of us camping and hiking, of him and Mom when they were happy. Which was a long time ago, so long ago I barely remember it.

Mom had me in her early twenties, right after she and Dad got married; in the photos of their wedding, she's a pregnant bride, all smiles, except for the picture right after Dad shoved cake in her face. When I was eleven, they divorced. Dad's drinking was really bad by then, and all I remember was how much they fought. Not physically. But the yelling felt like fists on the wall between their bedroom and mine. The silence was almost worse, the waiting and wondering what had happened, or what was about to happen.

I don't want to think about that.

I shake my head to clear out the memories, staring at the notification on my phone screen. I never replied to his last text; I used to try to respond every time, with a reaction at least, but in those last few months I just never knew what to say. Dad had never been a reliable texter unless he wanted something: validation, or a confidant, or whatever, and I knew he wanted me to agree with him about Mom, to say I missed him, that I wished I lived with him, but I didn't feel any of those things. So I didn't say anything.

Maybe things would be different if I had. Maybe he wouldn't have been so angry about everything. Maybe he would have stuck around.

I unlock the phone and open the text.

Hey kid, I know it's been a while. I wanted to reach out and let you know I just got out of inpatient treatment and I'd love to see you. Text me or call me when you get a chance.

Inpatient treatment. Dad's never done that before. The first time he got sober, it was cold turkey. That didn't last long. Since then, he's gone to Alcoholics Anonymous off and on, emphasis on the *off*. When he goes, he stops drinking, and then he decides he doesn't need AA, and then he decides he can moderate his drinking, THIS time, and then it turns out he can't. Rinse and repeat.

But . . . inpatient treatment. I've heard the phrase a thousand times: thrown like a dagger in one of my parents' countless fights, murmured by Mom on the phone to her Al-Anon sponsor, written in the literature she tried to get me to read when I was younger. "Al-Anon has a group for teens too," she told me, a few months after the divorce was finalized. She'd started going to meetings soon after she and Dad separated. "They support the kids of addicts just like my meetings support adult loved ones of addicts. It's a sister program to the one your dad goes to."

I could tell how much she wanted me to go, but I didn't want to sit in a room with other kids and talk about what was happening. Just the idea of it felt weird, like I was bad-mouthing Dad by even thinking about it. I didn't want to think about it at all; I just wanted to move on and live my life.

But I can't. Dad's back. And he's out of inpatient treatment and wants to see me.

I blow out a long breath, pressing a hand to the center of my chest. My heart feels fluttery. Maybe I'm about to have a heart attack, my veins constricting, arm going numb. Is that what happens when you have a heart attack? I'm not sure.

"That's not real. It's not happening," I say quietly. I don't usually say my mantras out loud, but no one's around. "That's not real. It's not happening. That's not real. It's not happening."

I have to get out of this room, out of my head, away from my thoughts. I toss my phone on the bed and stride to the back door, slipping on my sneakers and heading outside. It's raining out, the air chillier than it has been the last few weeks, and I cross the driveway to the garage with my head bowed, trying to keep the drops from speckling my glasses. When I step inside, the sharp smell of sawdust fills my nose. Shar is behind the table saw, picking something up.

"Hey," I call out, and she straightens.

"Hey you," she says with a warm smile. "Put your goggles on, OK?"

I turn to the row of hooks beside the door and grab my safety goggles. They're big enough to fit over my glasses, and I slip them on. Shar is a stickler for protective equipment anytime we're in the shop and there's even the slightest chance a power tool might be running.

"What're you doing?" I ask, putting in my earplugs next. They're bright orange, connected by a blue plastic string.

She raises her voice so I can hear her through the plugs. "Building a bookcase."

"Oh, for the . . . ?" I wave my hand at the house.

She nods. One of our cheap old bookcases fell apart a month ago, and Shar said she'd make a new one.

I sit on a stool a safe distance away from her power tool setup, and give her the thumbs-up. She gives one back and then focuses in on the saw as it roars to life.

The sound is a comforting buzz through my earplugs. Being in the garage is calming, especially when Shar is here. My friends think I'm weird for enjoying the sound of power tools, but I don't know how to explain to them that the noise helps drown out whatever catastrophes my brain might come up with. Plus, Shar is the human equivalent of an ancient redwood tree. It's grounding just being near her.

She guides the blade through the lumber she's cutting down for the bookcase. It's a natural blond hardwood, something she'll probably stain afterward, maybe walnut to match our other bookcases. She squints behind her goggles, the crow's-feet at her eyes crinkling back to her temples. She's proud of them, says they're a marker of all the good memories she's made.

Mom met Shar at an Al-Anon meeting a few years after she and Dad divorced. For a while it seemed like they were just friends, until one day Mom sat me down and told me she had realized something: She was bisexual and had started dating Shar. It didn't shock me, really; I'd come out as bi to her and Dad when I was twelve and neither of them batted an eye. It was the same when I came out as nonbinary last year.

Shar is gay, and has been since birth, the way she tells it. "Maddy in fourth grade," she told me when I asked her about her first crush. It was the night I finally met her, months into their relationship. We were all in a booth at a diner on Capitol Hill, and the waitress had just dropped off our pancakes. Shar held Mom's hand the whole time, right there on the table, and their smiles sparkled like the holiday lights on the trees outside.

I was thirteen, and I loved her right away. I felt guilty at first, like I was abandoning Dad, or betraying him. Sometimes I still feel that way. But mostly I try not to think about it. Just because I love Shar, doesn't mean I don't love Dad too.

Because I do.

And I'll text him back. I will.

Just . . . not right now.

A hand lands on my shoulder and I startle, turning from where my gaze has drifted to see Shar smiling down at me. Her goggles are pushed back onto her head, and I realize the table saw has gone quiet. Which, of course it has, because she's standing here.

I pull out my earplugs.

"Penny for your thoughts?" she asks.

I shrug. "Just spacing out."

"Wanna see what I've done so far?" She gestures at the lumber on the table and I stand up and follow her over, putting my goggles on top of my head like her. I always feel cool when I do that, kind of tough, like I could run a table saw too.

She lays out the pieces for the bookcase: the shelves, the back, and the sides, freshly cut and waiting to be put together. "I'll sand them next Sunday. I was thinking you could help me with that, and with the stain when it's time."

"I get to use the sander?" My eyes widen. Shar has been slowly teaching me how to use each of her tools, and this one has been next on the list for ages.

"Very carefully, and with my supervision, but yes," she says.

"Fuck yeah!" I pump my fist, and she laughs. Besides the noise, one of the things I love about working with tools is the consistency. All I need to do is follow a set of steps and I get the result I want. Each one has a protocol for operation and safety, and it never changes. In Shar's workshop, I always know what to expect.

I just wish everything else was that certain.

CHAPTER 5

I FEEL IT THE MOMENT FORREST WALKS INTO ENGLISH CLASS on Monday. The energy changes, the air gets thicker, and I'm aware of exactly where he is as he walks across the room, even though I'm on my phone, texting the group chat. He's like a black hole, sucking up all the energy I could be putting into my own life, ruining the one good thing I wanted for myself this year. I don't want to look at him, but it's like a magnet is pulling at my face, forcing me to glance over.

He's looking at me.

Our eyes meet, and I glance away instantly. Why was he watching me? *Was* he watching me? Was it just a coincidence? Maybe he's pissed after what went down on Friday, and he's plotting my presidential demise. I very pointedly look anywhere but at him for the rest of class. I don't want another confrontation, and I have no idea what's going through his head.

My stomach is howling by the time the bell finally rings for lunch, and the trek to my locker is like swimming upstream in rapids. I fight my way out of the current and spin my combination, then rummage through for my lunch.

"Hey," someone says, too loud, right behind me.

I straighten up, right into the top of my locker. "Ow!" I clutch my head, backing away a few steps.

"Oh shit! Are you OK?"

I know that voice. I turn, still rubbing the top of my skull, and there he is. Forrest, a few feet away, looking right at me with a concerned expression. Of course he'd be the one to startle me like this.

"I'll survive," I say flatly. I don't want to talk to him. I don't want a repeat of our last few interactions, not today, when I'm already on edge. I haven't texted Dad back yet, and his message keeps popping up in my brain, all the ways I could respond and what he might say back.

"Sorry," Forrest says.

"What do you want?" The words come out harsher than I intended, but I let them hang in the air between us.

He shifts from foot to foot. "So . . . you know what happened in the meeting last week."

". . . Yeah." All around us, people are jostling past, but we're in our own awkward little bubble, one that feels far too small.

"I know we have different ideas about what the club should do," he says. "But we have a limited amount of time every week, and I don't wanna ruin it with us arguing and never getting anything done. I was thinking maybe you and I could meet up before the meetings and talk about our ideas, just so we can, I don't know . . ." He shrugs. "Fight it out, or whatever, without fucking up club time."

I stare at him. He stares back with a wary half smile, half grimace. Of all the things I expected him to say, this was not it. And I don't exactly love the prospect of one-on-one hang time with the most annoying dude at Jefferson High every week. But . . . it's not a bad idea.

It's actually a pretty good one.

It's what Anna said: an effort to collaborate.

And I don't want this Friday to be a repeat of what happened last week. I want to actually get things done this year. Cool things. Important things. I can't do that unless I get Forrest to see that my ideas are better.

"It doesn't have to be a long meeting," he says. "Like, maybe fifteen minutes after school one day or at lunch or whatever."

"OK," I say.

"What?"

"OK," I repeat. "I'll do it."

"Cool." He grins. "Later this week? I'll just come find you?"

"Yeah. That sounds good."

He nods. "Later, Co-President." With the flash of a peace sign, he disappears into the swirling crowd.

♥

It's not like I *mean* to ghost Dad. I just . . . don't reply right away, and then it's Tuesday and I still haven't figured out whether I should call or text him back; he offered either one, but I should probably call him, and then we can just have whatever conversation we're going to have all at once instead of dragging it out, but texting would be so much easier, because then we *could* drag it out. I wouldn't have to hear his voice, and I can plan what I'm going to say instead of trying to keep up with whatever comes out of his mouth in the moment.

So I get stuck on deciding the method, and without that, I can't get to the content, and then it's Wednesday, and I'm sitting in the hallway with my friends eating lunch, going over the options in my head for the millionth time.

Jayden's elbow nudges mine. "What did that sandwich ever do to you?"

"What?" I look up from the half-eaten BLT in my hands.

"You're glaring at that thing like it's Forrest arguing with you in Queer Alliance," he says.

That makes me laugh, a little. "I was just . . ." I'm about to lie, tell him I'm spacing out like I did with Shar, but I hesitate. It's hard to admit I'm anxious, even now that I know what it is and so do my friends. Even though I know they wouldn't judge me.

At least, I'm pretty sure they wouldn't.

But they know about my family. I can tell them this.

"My dad," I say finally. "He texted me this weekend."

"Holy shit." Jayden grabs my hand, and I curl my fingers through his. Makayla and Anna stop their conversation at his exclamation and turn to us, and I repeat what I told Jayden.

"Have you replied?" Anna asks.

I shake my head.

"What did he say?" Makayla asks.

I open my phone and show them the message. "He's never gone to inpatient before. I don't know what to think. Maybe he's really taking it seriously this time, but . . ." I trail off. "Dad" and "taking it seriously" don't really belong in the same sentence. When I was a kid, he was always joking around, with sarcasm or bathroom humor or a prank—obvious ones, like switching the salt and sugar, but he loved to trick me other ways too, by pretending we were out of my favorite cereal when we weren't, or convincing me that a random noise outside was actually a serial killer, or a rabid dog, or an escaped zoo animal.

"*Psych!*" he'd yell once I believed him, and I'd groan, or get mad. Either way, he'd laugh his ass off. Sometimes his jokes were funny, but a lot of the time they were just annoying. He acted like a kid, and I wanted him to grow up.

My throat constricts, tears stinging my eyes. "Can I hug you?" Jayden asks. I nod, and his arms encircle me, squeezing tightly.

"I'm sorry your dad is a butthole," Anna says.

"*Big* butthole," Jayden mumbles in my ear.

"Cavernous," Makayla adds.

I snicker, and then we're all laughing. The tightness in my chest loosens, and gratitude floods in—for the relief of tension, for the laughter, for my friends.

I had a couple friends scattered across elementary and middle school, but I was shy and anxious and rarely saw them outside of the school day. First it was because I was afraid Dad would be drunk when they came over, and after the divorce, it was because the apartment Mom and I lived in was so run-down. When I met Jayden, Anna, and Makayla, though, it was like I'd been a piece of a puzzle waiting under some cosmic couch for a giant hand to pick me up, and then one did and placed me with them and, together, we made a picture. Literally and figuratively; the Polaroids of us on my wall at home are proof of that. They'd all come here from different schools; Anna from another state entirely. But we'd found each other. Our jokes, our interests, our personalities; everything aligns.

I hope nothing ever messes it up.

♥

When Mom gets home that evening, I'm in my usual seat at the table, working through a math assignment. She sets her backpack on the coffee table, sits down on the couch with a groan to unlace her oxfords, then groans again as she pushes herself up to standing.

"How about we order some pizza tonight?" she asks, shuffling past me toward her room.

I give her a thumbs-up. Shar goes to an Al-Anon meeting every Wednesday night, so it's just the two of us, and Mom's not much of a cook. "Can we do mushrooms and olives?"

"You got it." She vanishes into the back hallway. From the cat tower next to the window, Earl Grey watches me, slow blinking when she catches my eye. That's how I know she likes me, even if she hardly ever lets me touch her.

Mom reemerges, and gone is the tailored pantsuit of a high-level marketing executive at a company whose name I can never remember; instead, she just looks like my mom, in sweats and an old Green Day T-shirt. She sits down across from me and taps away on her phone screen for a few minutes, then smiles at me. "It'll be here in twenty minutes. Working on homework?"

"Yeah."

"That's good." She watches me. Her brow is furrowed slightly.

"What's up?" I ask.

"I . . . have some news," she says. "Your dad called me. He went to inpatient rehab this summer. Court-ordered after a DUI, but it sounds like he took it seriously. Anyway, he's been out for a few weeks, he has a job, and he wants to see you."

I stare at her, all the pieces clicking into place. Dad went to inpatient because he had to. Because he finally got a DUI, after bragging for years about how he'd never been "nailed by the po-po," as he put it. And there's that word again: *seriously*. Is he really taking it seriously, or is he just saying what he knows we want to hear? And if I believe him, will he just mess it up again?

"I know it's a lot to take in," Mom says gently.

I shake my head. "He already told me."

Her mouth closes, head pulling back slightly. "He what?" Her voice is casual still, but I know that face; it's the expression she gets when she's angry but she doesn't want you to know, when it's just simmering under the surface.

"He texted me Sunday," I say. "I'm sorry. I should have told you."

"No, no," she says. "I'm not mad at you, sweetie. What did he say?"

She says she's not mad, but she still looks that way, half smiling but it's stiff, like petrified wood. "Um. Just what he told you, except the part about the DUI and the job."

She nods slowly. "OK. And how are you feeling about that? Do you want to see him?"

I shrug. I should probably feel happy; this is my father we're talking about. Actually wanting to see me. Not drunk, for the first time in who knows how long. I should be excited, right? But I don't really feel anything at all. "Yeah, I guess."

She half smiles again, but her eyes look concerned. "You know it's your choice, right, sweetie?"

I nod, studying the math assignment in front of me. I can feel her waiting for me to say something else, I can feel her sitting on everything she wants to say—to me or to Dad, I'm not sure. He clearly didn't tell her he texted me, but for some reason I feel like *I'm* the one who did something wrong, who ratted him out.

"I'm here if you need anything," she says, and I nod again. I don't want to talk about this anymore, in case I say something else I shouldn't.

After a moment, she pushes the chair back and goes into the kitchen. The fridge door opens, followed by the sound of a can of sparkling water cracked and poured into a glass. I wait for her to say something else, but it doesn't come. She putters around in the kitchen, getting plates out of the cabinet for us, clearing a space on the counter for the pizza boxes. I stare down at the math problem in front of me. The numbers might as well be a foreign language, that's how much sense they make to me right now, but I don't want to ask her for help. If I do, it might make her worry about my progress, whether I'm really doing as well as I seem. And then it'll be Helicopter Mom all over again; check-ins every night, a tutor multiple times a week, maybe even making me quit the presidency. I can hear it now: The presidency is interrupting my focus, or taking up too much time, or distracting me from what's important. Sometimes it feels like no one takes the club as seriously as I do.

And it's not just that. If I tell her, I'm adding another worry on top of everything else she has to do: managing that important client at work, wrangling Dad and his complete inability to be a functional adult, and probably other things I don't even know about.

In the year after Mom and Dad separated, she had to work three jobs to keep our apartment after he moved out to crash on one of his drinking buddy's couches. She'd drop me off at school, and I'd come home to an empty place, where I'd sit doing homework or watching TV, eating frozen meals for dinner before going to bed. She'd come home late from her hostess gig at a local restaurant, and if I was awake, I'd hear her crying. So I always tried to fall asleep before she got home, even though it was hard to do when I was alone; I'd get all these mental movies about intruders breaking in, horror film scenarios with knives and kidnappings where my mother comes home to find only my blood on the floor, or a ransom note, or the door off its hinges. But hearing her cry was scary in a whole different way, like my whole world was unpredictable and out of my control, instead of just my thoughts.

The doorbell rings and I blow out a breath, shaking my head to get the thoughts out, but when Mom goes to the door the person on the other side isn't the delivery person but a man with a gun, eyes wild, forcing his way through the door as she screams and tries to close it—

Stop. Stop. Stop.

Stop. Stop. St—

"Thankyouhaveagoodnight!" Mom says brightly to the delivery person, grabbing the boxes and letting the door swing shut. At the counter, she sets out plates, and Brekky meows as he circles her leg, hoping for crumbs.

"Relentless," Mom murmurs, reaching down to pet him. "Two slices?" she asks me.

I nod, but it feels like I'm itching inside, like my skin is about to split open. I didn't finish the mantra. If I don't finish the mantra, my brain is going to start screaming again, and I might accidentally scream out loud, and then Mom will think I'm crazy, and then—

"I'm gonna go to the bathroom," I say, as naturally as I can, and get up, forcing myself to walk a normal pace away from the table. I can feel her eyes on me until I shut the door behind me and sit down on the closed toilet.

I close my eyes and begin my first set of three.

♥

At lunch the next day, I emerge from the crowd to find Forrest waiting at my locker. He lifts a hand as I approach, and I nod at him. The morning was stressful; a pop quiz, a complicated chemistry experiment, the history group project, and in English class, the final draft of the essay was due. I stayed up late to finish it last night, after I finally got my brain to leave me alone. Handing it to Ms. Lundahl felt like dropping a rock into a pool and watching it sink. And right on cue, here's Forrest, as if I didn't have enough to deal with.

"I thought we could talk today," he says.

"Now?" I ask. I have to step uncomfortably close to him to get to my combination lock, and I can smell something woodsy on him. It's his deodorant maybe, or cologne.

"I mean, tomorrow is Queer Alliance, so it's kind of our last chance. Unless you want to meet up after school." He shoves his hands deep into his hoodie pockets, glancing around as if he's scared his cool friends will see him talking to me.

Hanging out with Forrest after school is the last thing I want to do. "Fine. Let's talk." I grab my lunch out of my locker and turn to him. "What do you want?"

He blinks. "Do you want to like . . . sit down? We can go to the library?"

"You said it could just be a few minutes," I say. "So. Let's talk for a few minutes."

He snorts. "I should have known."

"What's that supposed to mean?"

"I'm here trying to make the club work, and it would be nice if you did the same," he says.

I raise my eyebrows. "What are you talking about? I've done nothing but try to make this work since we got elected."

He crosses his arms. "By shooting down every single idea I have?"

"Your ideas are—" *Stupid*, I'm about to say, but I catch myself just in time. "They don't make sense. For our budget."

"The Coming Out Party will *help* our budget," he says. "And then we can do more of the shit you want to do."

"How is it going to help our budget?"

He sighs. "We can have a raffle at the party. People come to the party, they have fun, they buy raffle tickets, we get money." He speaks slowly, enunciating every word, as if I can't understand him. I grit my teeth, fighting the urge to kick him.

"You didn't say anything about fundraising last week," I say.

He rolls his eyes. "Well, that's because you kept interrupting me before I could."

I take a deep breath, closing my eyes, so I won't scream. When I open them, he's still there, but now he's smirking. He can see it, how he's getting under my skin, and I hate that I let him. We're silent, facing each other in the hallway as people chatter around us. "I interrupted you because I had important information to tell you," I say icily. "Like dietary needs. Those matter."

"I know they matter, my sister has celiac disease. I've been eating gluten-free bread since I was ten years old." He spreads his hands. "Look, just give me a chance. I care about the club too."

No you don't, I want to say. *Not like I do.* His face at our table freshman year pops into my mind, lips curled back in a sneer, telling me my home, my life at this school is pointless. Until it wasn't, conveniently, when he decided he wanted to be part of it. When it benefited him.

"I thought you just wanted something that looked good on your transcript," I say.

He shrugs. "I mean, it will, not going to lie."

I glare at him. "I'm hungry. I'm going to go eat with my friends," I say. "Good talk."

"Just think about it," he calls after me, but I ignore him, speeding up until I'm around the corner.

"You OK?" Jayden asks when I arrive at our table, slightly out of breath, hand clenched around the handle of my lunch box.

I let out a huge sigh as I sit down. "I just talked to Forrest."

"You willingly talked to Forrest?" Anna puts a hand on my forehead. "Who are you and what have you done with Sidney?"

"*Semi*-willingly," I say. "He offered to meet before Queer Alliance every week. To hash things out so we don't ruin club time."

"That's . . . mature of him," Anna says, sitting back.

"Oh no, he just tried to convince me to support his idea for the party the whole time," I say. "I can't believe people actually voted for him. I can't believe I have to deal with him. He is so infuriating."

"Maybe if you give him something he wants, it'll get him off your back?" Jayden shrugs.

I groan, pressing my hands to my eyes under my glasses. I don't want to give Forrest *anything*, not one single inch. This was supposed to be my year. I had so many ideas: discussion panels with important people from local nonprofits, a library exhibit during LGBTQ History Month in October, a documentary film series with Q&As afterward, things that would connect the rest of the school with our club and educate people at the same time. It felt like this was the one thing in my life I could count on, something I knew I would be good at, somewhere I knew I'd feel safe, no matter what else was happening. If I had Queer Alliance, if I could be president, if just one thing in my life was under my control, everything else would feel a little easier.

And now everything is crumbling, no matter how hard I work to keep it together.

"TIME FOR ROUND TWO?" JAYDEN ASKS, WALKING UP BESIDE me as I head toward Mr. Harrison's classroom on Friday. He skips ahead, spinning to face me as he walks backward.

"What do you mean?"

"You and Forrest." He throws a few fake punches. "Party versus panel. Pew pew!"

"Oh. Yeah." I shift my backpack, tightening the straps. Images keep flashing in my head: Forrest and me, toe to toe in the center of the circle while everyone watches us shout at each other. Forrest pushing me, me pushing back. Mr. Harrison calling the office, security arriving, both of us at the principal's, and then Mom's face, pinched in disappointment because I let her down. Again. Jayden must hear the anxiety in my voice, because he slows his walk, coming to my side.

"Are you OK?" he asks.

I shake my head. My heart is pounding again, and I know I'm probably not having a heart attack, but what if I faint? I take a deep breath, just to make sure I can. Is that lightheadedness I'm feeling?

Jayden's hand curls around my arm, stopping me in the hallway, and he draws me over to the side, next to a bank of lockers. "I'm sorry," he says in a low voice. "I know you don't like Forrest, but I didn't realize it was this bad."

"I just . . ." My voice cracks, and I turn away from the crowd, toward him, so people can't tell how worked up I am. "I just want this year to be good."

"It will be," Jayden says, resting both hands on my shoulders. I look into his warm brown eyes, his forehead furrowed as he gazes at me. "Forrest is just one dumbass. Yeah, you have to share the presidency with him, but everyone knows how much you love this club. Don't let him ruin that for you."

I nod, even though I don't believe Jayden at all. I know he's trying to help, but he has no idea what it's like inside my head. The things I see that I have to make sure don't come to pass. Because if they do, everything else might fall apart too, and I don't know if I can handle that.

"Come on," he says, squeezing my shoulders. "We've got a meeting to get to."

I follow him down the hallway, counting my steps:

One, two, three.

One, two, three.

One two, three.

The rest of the way to Mr. Harrison's room is twenty-seven sets of three, for eighty-one steps total. All odd numbers, which is comforting, and something inside me settles a little bit, like a dragon retreating into its cave.

Forrest is there before us again, setting out chairs. We exchange nods, and I join him, pushing seats into place.

People filter in, but it doesn't take long for the trickle to stop. We definitely have fewer people this week than last week; we started the year with at least ten freshmen, and today we're down to two. None of the sophomores show, and the only senior is Riley. Stef is here, notebook already open, but even Alexander is missing.

"Hold up!" He darts in just as Anna closes the door. "Sorry I'm late."

"It's all good," Jayden says, smiling at him.

I look around the room. There are ten of us here, down from the more than twenty on the first day. Last year, we averaged fifteen people per meeting. I should know; as secretary, I was keeping track. But we're only three meetings into the year and we've lost so many people already.

Is this because of last week?

Because of me and Forrest, and our . . . disagreement?

"OK!" Forrest says, calling the room to attention. "Queerly beloved, we are gathered here today to figure out what the fuck we're doing this month." A few people giggle. He looks at me. "I've been talking with people outside of the club, and it sounds like a lot of y'all are into the party idea."

The blood freezes in my veins. He's been talking to people? Outside of club time? He came to me as if he actually wanted to work together, and this whole time he's been talking to everyone else behind my back.

"Really?" I manage through a clenched jaw. "That's the first I've heard of it."

"I like Sidney's idea," Anna says softly. She widens her eyes at me when I look at her, and I widen mine back. I know she understands what this means. Forrest is showing his true colors.

"Maybe you shouldn't speak for others," I say to Forrest.

"Well, Anna's your friend, of course she likes your idea," he fires back. "But this isn't a popularity contest. It's about what everyone wants, not just you."

I sit back in my chair. Mr. Harrison emerges from his office, looking around at all of us.

"How are we doing?" he asks. "I heard raised voices." His gaze lands on Forrest, who shrinks slightly, a sheepish smile crossing his face.

"Sorry, Mr. H," he says. "We're just, um. Passionately discussing the best direction for the club this year."

Mr. Harrison nods slowly, scanning Forrest's face, then mine. The room feels like a pressurized container, as if one wrong word will be the puncture that suffocates us all. I don't want to be responsible for that suffocation.

"Fine. Do the party." I squeeze the words out, expecting the room to relax, but instead every face swivels to me. Jayden's eyebrows raise, and he looks to Makayla, who's fidgeting with her ring, and then to Anna beside her with hands frozen in midair over her laptop.

"You sure?" Forrest asks, his voice too light, like he didn't just Julius Caesar me in front of everyone.

"I said it's fine," I say, and he shrugs.

"So . . . what do we need to make this happen?" Stef asks, eyes darting between the two of us.

Forrest stares at me a moment longer and lurches into motion, out of his seat and across to the whiteboard. *COMING OUT PARTY*, he writes in an empty space.

"Decorations," Riley calls out, and Forrest scribbles it down.

"Snacks?" one of the freshmen says.

"Posters to advertise it," Alexander adds.

One by one, people call things out, until they've got a list and start fleshing it out. Under decorations, we add streamers, balloons, signs, and a disco ball—that last one is Forrest's. Apparently he just happens to have a mechanical disco ball on hand. Under snacks, he writes *cupcakes, chips, fruit,* and *juice.* I don't know where it's all going to come from, but it's out of my hands now. Maybe that's the silver lining, if there is one; if it fails, it won't be on me.

"I'll make a collaborative playlist so we can all add to it," Alexander volunteers, and takes everyone's numbers so he can send the link in a group chat later.

When the bell rings, Forrest stays to help put chairs away instead of darting out like he has the past few meetings. I avoid eye contact with him, straightening a row of desks on the opposite side of the room. In my periphery, I can see him, his head turning toward me sometimes as if he wants me to look at him, but I don't. Maybe he's trying to get in my good graces by staying, maybe he's doing it because he really does care like he claims to. It's hard to tell, and I don't like that.

Anna comes up to me, ready to go, and I grab my stuff, following her out. A group of seniors plows down the center of the hallway toward us, Anna and I parting on either side of them, coming back together in their wake. She links her arm through mine, and the connection anchors me.

"That was . . . intense," she says as soon as we round the corner.

"Yeah."

"How are you feeling?"

I shrug.

"I know you weren't really fine with that," she says.

"No, I wasn't." I look over at her. "He basically admitted he set me up. He came to me acting like he wanted to talk it out, and meanwhile he was going around to everyone to get them on his side."

"He didn't talk to me," she says. "Or Jayden and Makayla. I'm sure they would have said something if he had."

The thought warms me. He knew my friends had my back, that they wouldn't go along with him.

"So why did you agree to it?" she asks.

Our arms unlink as we approach the stairs to the math wing, and I pull ahead of her as we climb to the next floor. My breath comes a little harder in my lungs. I still think a party is a waste of time. I still don't trust Forrest not to run the club into the ground. But he wasn't backing down.

"I didn't have a choice," I say. "If I said no, we would have been locked in conflict for another week."

"I guess," she says. When we get to the top, I wait for her, and we link our arms again. "But now . . ." She smirks, eyes sparkling with mischief. ". . . you have leverage."

Something sparks in my mind. Jayden, telling me maybe I can get what I want if I give Forrest something he wants. I didn't give in today on purpose, and I'd prefer to avoid talking to Forrest as much as possible, but maybe I can use this. I'll meet with him again like he suggested, and this time, I'll be ready. It's my turn to get my way.

♥

When Makayla's dad swings their door open Saturday morning and sees me, he grins, eyes crinkling. "Sid the Kid!"

Unlike Makayla and Jayden, he's as white as the doorframe, and he fills it completely. He's a former football player who met their mom, a tiny Black woman, in college, and he still looks like he should be out crushing yards on a field somewhere.

I give him two thumbs-ups. He's been calling me Sid the Kid ever since I started hanging out with Makayla and Jayden, but it's not just me; he has nicknames for all of us. Jayden is Jay Is the Way, because he loves the Mandalorian and all things Star Wars; Anna is, of course, Anna Banana; and Makayla is—

"Mack Attack!" he bellows into the house. "Sid's here!" He's like my dad, if my dad had an age-appropriate sense of humor and an actual presence in his kid's life.

Makayla appears at the end of the hallway. "What's up, study buddy?"

"Oh yes, my other rhyming nickname," I say dryly. She smirks.

"I'll be in the backyard ripping out the blackberry bushes," Makayla's dad says, still grinning. I'm not sure I've ever seen him *not* grinning. "Holler if you need anything, all right?"

She nods, he disappears, and she raises her eyebrows at me. "Shall we?"

"If we must." I kick off my shoes and follow her down the hallway, through the living room toward the kitchen. "Where's Jayden?"

"He said he was meeting a friend," she says, scrunching her face up in a very skeptical way.

"He has friends besides us?" I drop my backpack on their dining table with a thump.

"That's what I said!" She laughs, rummaging in the kitchen cabinets. "Do you want anything? Snacks? Tea? Chocolate?" She pulls out a bag of chips and waves it at me.

"All of the above." I follow her into the kitchen to pick out my tea as she connects her phone with the Bluetooth speaker on the counter.

All my friends like having music on when they study; Makayla's flavor is R&B, and she puts on Victoria Monèt's latest album, a mellow background that makes the room even cozier. At the table, I curl my hands around the hot mug of peppermint tea, staring down at my math homework. The assignment is due on Tuesday, with a test on Wednesday, and after asking some embarrassingly basic questions in class and ignoring the few people who whispered when I did, I understand about half of it. Which is more than I can say for the end of last year.

Sometimes, I wonder if I actually don't have anxiety. Maybe I'm just exaggerating, just another social media self-diagnosis with no real problems. Last year was bad, but also, was it? I could have tried harder. I could have pushed through. Dad was texting me, but he was just being Dad. Just dramatic and annoying. It wasn't the end of the world.

Thinking about it makes my brain go all staticky. The longer I try to pinpoint what went wrong last year, the less certain I feel. What if it wasn't real at all? The thought makes my stomach swoop.

"I have a question," Makayla says suddenly. I push the thought to a back burner in my brain, but it's still simmering. "How did you know you were nonbinary?"

I click the end of my pen into the table three times, then three more, and then another round. The sound is a satisfying anchor. "Goooooood question."

"You don't have to answer," she says. "I don't want to be invasive or anything."

I give her a look. "Dude. You're one of my best friends. It's fine."

"Sorry." She presses her hands to her face.

"Don't apologize!"

"Sorr—OK." She laughs. "You're right."

I think for a minute. It's been a while since I really analyzed my gender, though I did plenty of it when I started questioning in middle school. "I remember I started seeing a lot of videos about being trans. My feed decided that was what I wanted. It was trans content, stuff about anxiety, and gay musicians." I laugh.

"The algorithm knoooows." Makayla makes a spooky ghost noise, wiggling her fingers at me.

"For real." I click my pen again. "It wasn't just that, though. I always felt like a person, not a gender, and when people would refer to me as a girl, it startled me. Like, oh right, that's what I am. Or how people see me."

"Do you want to do any medical stuff?"

I shake my head. "Not really. I mean, maybe top surgery someday. But it's mostly the social stuff. I like my name and the way I dress, but it was the way people saw me that was uncomfortable."

"Like you're a capital *G* Girl instead of a human."

"Totally! And like, I know I could just redefine what being a girl is." I roll my eyes. I've seen that line in internet comments too many times to count. "But it's not just that. I don't really know how to explain it. It's like, how do cis people know they are the gender they are? No one asks them to pinpoint it. They just feel it. So why can't we just feel it, without having to explain it?"

"Yeah." Makayla nods. "That's so annoying."

"Yeah, it is." I look at her then. She said it like she understands what I'm talking about from the inside. "Are you . . . questioning things?"

She laughs nervously. "Maybe? I don't know. Kind of. I don't know."

"You can totally be nonbinary if you want," I say.

"I know." She doodles on her homework, focusing hard on drawing a perfect spiral.

I watch her for a minute. I've never thought of Makayla as anything but cis before, but that's the thing about people; they can surprise you. For better or worse. But this is . . . well, there's nothing wrong with being cis. But if Makayla is nonbinary, that would be really cool.

"If you want to talk about anything," I say. "I'm here."

"Thanks," she says, and when she looks at me her eyes are crinkled in a smile, just like her dad's.

♥

Shar picks me up when our study date is done, her arm out the window of her work truck. It's a battered teal Chevy, with a bazillion gay and social-justice stickers on the back. I boost myself into the cab and she smiles.

"How's your brain?"

"Um." I pause for a second, wondering how she knew about my weird thoughts earlier, and then I realize she's probably talking about studying. "Oh. It's fine. Tired." I stick out my tongue and cross my eyes and she laughs.

"You still feel up to some sanding?"

I'd totally forgotten about our plan to finish the bookcase this weekend. The vampire touch of math drained my soul out of my body, but suddenly all that energy floods back. "Fuck yeah!"

She laughs. "Perfect."

The clouds darken as we head out of the North Seattle neighborhood where Jayden and Makayla live and back toward our house. It's not evening yet, but the impending storm makes it feel that way, and the clouds open up as we cross the I-5 bridge toward downtown. I look left toward the Cascades instinctively; sometimes Mount Rainier is visible there too, but today they're all hidden. Shar turns her wipers up to the highest setting, the blades whacking back and forth to keep the rain at bay.

When we pull into the driveway, we jump out of the truck and beeline for the garage, both of us shrieking as the downpour hits us. Shar fumbles with the lock for a second and then we're safe inside, the bite of sawdust hitting my nostrils as she turns on the space heater. I stand in front of it, letting my slightly damp sweatshirt dry while she drags the lumber she cut last week for the new bookcase out of the corner where it's been waiting. I put my safety gear on and join her at the sander.

"All right," she says, setting a power tool on the table in front of us. It's black and teal, the brand's letters in red across the side. "This is a random orbital sander." The tool is a lot smaller than I expected, a cylindrical part on top where you hold it attached to a short cone-shaped base with a dust filter. The bottom is the widest part, and it's where the sandpaper attaches. She shows me how to grip the top, where to turn it on, and how much pressure to apply as the base spins. "There are different kinds of sanders, but for most projects like this, a random orbital will do you just fine. I'm going to have you watch me for a bit now, and then you can do it yourself, OK?"

I nod and stand back as she sets the wood up on her work table. There are small holes drilled into the table's length, and she positions the wood along them, pushing small pegs into the holes on either side of the wood to hold it in place. “These are bench dogs,” she says, and I giggle at the unexpectedly cute term.

She turns the sander on and presses it to the wood. The grain goes smooth under the tool, and a few minutes later she turns it off and steps back. “Feel that.”

I put my fingers on the lumber where she was working. “Whoa, it’s so soft.” The wood grain is more muted now, as if it’s being blended like eye shadow in the makeup tutorials Anna loves to watch.

“Your turn.” She hands me the sander. “Always pay attention to what your other hand is doing while you sand; you don’t want your fingers anywhere near that base. In fact, why don’t you hold it this way.” She positions both my hands on the sander.

I take a deep breath and press the red button to turn it on. The roar of the tool is dampened by my earplugs, but the vibration is unmistakable, tingling in my hands and up through my wrists as I hold the sander in place. I move it across the wood, slowly and smoothly the way Shar did, leaving perfectly sanded lumber in my wake. I don’t know how much time passes between the press of the button and the moment I reach the other end of the board, but my hands are warm and still tingly when I turn it off.

Straightening up, I look around, and Shar grins at me from her perch on a stool nearby. “Nice work. How’s your arms?”

I lift them up and watch my forearms tremble slightly. “Noodles.”

She laughs. "Why don't you take a break? I'll work on the next piece. It can take a minute to get used to the feeling."

We switch places, and I watch her work. It's so cool, the way we can take lumber and shape it into something completely new. After a while, my arms are feeling less noodley, and I have another go. Pretty soon all the lumber is sanded, and she gives me a high five.

"I don't know about you, but I'm getting hungry," she says. "Wanna work on this together with me next weekend?"

"Do I get to learn more tools?"

She nods. "Absolutely."

♥

In my room a little later, I sit on the edge of the bed and open the text thread with Dad. It's been almost a week since he texted me, and I'm done procrastinating. If I can use a random orbital sander without crushing my fingers, I can text my dad.

Hey, sorry for the late reply, I type. *School was a lot this week. Do you want to hang out next weekend?* For a moment, I hover over the blue button beside the text box, then hit it, sending the text.

I toss the phone aside and sigh, flopping back onto my bed. My stomach is swooping, legs tingling, but I did it. I feel a little bad about blaming my ghosting on school, but it's not a complete lie. School *was* a lot this week.

The phone buzzes and my stomach isn't just swooping now, it's full-on flapping, like a crowd of angry crows chasing an eagle. I grab my phone.

Hey kid, good to hear from ya. Next weekend is great. How about Sunday? We could go hiking for old times' sake.

I stare at the text for a minute, then switch over to my calendar app. The only thing I have next weekend is studying with Jayden on Saturday. Part of me wishes I had a lot more plans, just so I could put it off longer. But I shouldn't feel that way. I should want to see him. I should want to spend several hours walking through a forest with nothing to do but talk to him. It'll be great. Absolutely fantastic.

Sounds good! I say before I can chicken out.

Pick you up about 11:30? he asks.

See you then. I add a smiley face emoji, delete it, then add it again. It feels fake, but it also feels weird not to include something that shows I'm happy and excited about this. Even though I'm not. But I don't want Dad to know that, so I send the text, smiley face included. It grins up at me from the screen, a little digital lie.

I COME INTO SCHOOL MONDAY MORNING WITH A MISSION: Find Forrest at lunch and make him agree to do whatever I want with the club next. First, though, I want to make him sweat a little. However he justified it, he went behind my back, and he deserves to feel like shit for it. So in first-period English, I ignore him completely. I'm aware of exactly where he is at all times, of course, because my brain can't seem to turn off its Forrest scanner, but I don't make eye contact with him even once.

At the end of fourth period, I have all my stuff ready to go, and I book it to the junior hallway lockers so fast I almost knock a freshman down the stairs. At my locker, I grab my stuff and then dawdle, pretending to text someone while I wait for him to walk up.

When he does, Alexander's with him, the two of them laughing about something. Alexander leans against the wall beside him while Forrest digs something out of his locker. I stuff my phone into my hoodie pocket and march up to them.

"Hi," I say. They both turn to me, and I cross my arms. "Forrest, can I talk to you?"

"Oooop," Alexander says, raising his perfectly manicured eyebrows. "I'll see you there." He points at Forrest and slides away, to wherever "there" is.

Forrest shuts his locker. "What's up, Co-President?"

"You can just call me Sidney, you know," I say, rolling my eyes. I wanted to play it cool, but I can't help it; now that we're up close and personal, I'm seething again, the memory of Friday's meeting bubbling up unbidden.

"I like Co-President," he says. "It fits you. Very official. Businesslike."

I have no idea what that's supposed to mean, so I ignore it. "I thought we could talk about Queer Alliance today. Get it out of the way for the week."

"Oh. Um. OK." He looks around. "Do you want to go somewhere and sit down, or just talk in the hallway again?"

"Hallway is fine," I say. "Here's the deal: You got your party, but only because you went behind my back and won the rest of the club over, so I had no choice but to say yes."

"I didn't go *behind* your—"

"Yes, you did," I say, voice rising.

"OK!" he says, holding up his hands. "You're right. Technically, yes, what I did could be seen that way." I open my mouth and he speeds through, talking louder. "But I swear I didn't mean it like that. I didn't even think about it. I just thought it would make things easier."

"Easier how? Easier for you?"

"Fuck," he breathes out, rubbing the back of his head. "Yeah, OK, fine. After we talked, and you were clearly not down, I thought it would help to get a read on how the rest of the club was feeling. And yeah, I hoped they'd see it my way, and they did."

I nod slowly. So he did talk to me first, at least. Maybe it wasn't all planned out. But still. "Well, you got what you wanted. And now, I should get something I want."

He raises his eyebrows. "And fuck the rest of the club, I guess?"

"I—that's not what I meant."

"What did you mean?"

"Just that . . . I don't know, you got your party. But I have ideas too, and I want to bring one to the meeting this week," I say. "So, when I do, don't block it."

He snorts. "You make it sound like we're in Congress negotiating over a bill."

"I'm just saying. I meant what I said in my speech. I want to get some real things done this year."

"All right, fine, I'll stay out of your way," he says, holding up his hands, and then smirks. "*This* week."

I stare at him silently.

"Kidding," he says. "Oh my god, you need to get a sense of humor."

"And you need to get a sense of reading the room," I snap back.

"I'm going now," he singsongs. "See you Friday." He side-steps around me, heading down the hallway, and I stomp in the other direction. I won, but I'm so irritated I can't even be happy about it.

♥

A couple people are out sick on Friday, so the Queer Alliance meeting is even smaller than last week. I push down the anxiety movies about that, trying to stay focused as we discuss the remaining pieces for the National Coming Out Day party next week. Forrest pulls together a list of folks who are available to set up in the library that morning, and I volunteer; I'm usually at school early anyway, so why not? And if I'm there, I can head off any potential Forrest-induced disasters.

"And there will be cupcakes," he says, grinning. "Stef?"

She looks up from the black polish she's been slowly chipping off her nails. "My aunt runs a bakery. She does all kinds of dietary restrictions, gluten-free, vegan, whatever we need, and she's donating two dozen, plus a gift card we can raffle off."

"That's amazing," I say.

Forrest shrugs. "Told you we could do it."

I almost roll my eyes, but I catch myself. Instead, I do my best impression of a smile, but I don't say anything back. We agreed to keep our issues out of Queer Alliance, not to become besties.

"Do we wanna do anything else this month?" Riley asks. "It's LGBTQ History Month, might be cool to do something on that theme."

Thank you, Riley, for the perfect cue.

"Actually, I was thinking we could do an exhibit about that exact subject," I say. "I know the month is half over, and it'll take some time to put together, but we could run it through Trans Awareness Week in November."

Everyone's eyes are on me. I look at Forrest, who's slouched back in his chair, arms crossed; I remember our conversation on Monday, and I'm hoping he does too.

"We could put it up somewhere in the school," I add. "Maybe they'd let us use the display cases in the front hallway, or we could do the library again. Mx. Prager loves us." Our librarian is nonbinary and has hosted more than their fair share of Queer Alliance events.

"Oh my gosh, yes," Makayla says, clapping her hands.

"I just watched this movie about Stonewall," one of the freshmen says, baby face obscured by heavy eyeliner and black lipstick. "We could do a whole section about that? It was this night where all the gay people in New York City rioted, they even threw bricks at cops—"

I open my mouth to tell them of course we're going to talk about Stonewall, it's only one of the most important events in queer history, but Forrest beats me to it.

"Hell yeah, we can have a Stonewall section," he says, smiling at the freshman, and they smile back, a bright blush spreading across their face.

"Sounds like we're all down for this?" Riley asks, looking from me to Forrest.

Across the circle, Forrest meets my gaze and nods. "I'm down."

Something lifts off me then, like some huge bird has been perched on my back, digging its claws into my neck, whispering to me about all the ways this would go wrong,

Forrest would hate the idea, everyone would agree, the club would fall apart again—but it hasn't, and everyone thinks it's a great idea. Or an OK one, at least. Finally, I'm getting a chance to show what I'd bring to the presidency. Every meeting so far has felt like a tug-of-war that Forrest is winning, but now I'm pulling the club back to my side. I just have to keep this up until the revote.

"Maybe we talk about this more next time?" Riley says, glancing at the clock. Lunch is almost over. Everyone agrees, and we get up to put the desks back. I know Forrest is nearby, I can hear him talking to Stef about some video game they're playing, but I don't look in his direction. I can't quite believe that was so easy, but I'm not questioning it.

♥

Dad is late to pick me up for our hike Sunday morning, because of course he is. I sit on the living room couch, checking and rechecking my phone, waiting for a text from him. Maybe he slept in, or maybe he just forgot. Maybe this was a terrible idea. Am I really prepared to spend multiple hours with him? Is it too late to back out? I pick up my phone to check our text thread again, but there's nothing. This is it, he's not showing up. Fear surges in my chest, hot and tingly.

My phone rings, an unknown number, and I answer it.

"Sidney? I'm calling from Swedish Hospital on First Hill," says the voice on the other end. "Your father listed you as next of kin, and—"

STOP! I scream in my head, shaking it back and forth. *Stop. Stop.*

That's not real. It's not happening.

That's not real. It's not happening.

That's not real. It's not happening.

Brekky bumps my hand and I lift it to pet him, focusing on the velvety fur behind his ears. He arches his neck, purring loudly.

"Do you have everything you need for today?" Mom asks, coming up behind the couch.

I twist to face her, patting the backpack on my lap. "It's all in here."

"Snacks? An extra layer? Lots of water?"

"Mom, I've got it." I don't mean to snap at her, but I can tell she's anxious, and it's making my own anxiety worse.

"OK, honey," she says, raising her hands in front of her. "Just remember, you can ask to come home whenever you want."

"I'll be fine."

From the door to the hallway, Shar gives me a thumbs-up and disappears again, into the room she shares with Mom. She keeps a low profile when Dad is around; the first few times they met, in moments like this, when Dad was picking me up, Dad would say things to her. Nothing homophobic, just . . . unfriendly in a way I couldn't quite pin down, something to needle her or Mom, so they'd respond, and then he'd get defensive and weird. It never ended well, so now she avoids him. I don't blame her.

A knock sounds on the door, and I suck in a breath.

"You ready?" Mom says, crossing to it, hand on the doorknob.

I take a deep breath and blow it out. I'm not at all ready. I don't want to do this. I'd rather rot in my bed, watching videos until my brain leaks out my ears. "Yeah."

I get up, Brekky complaining at the loss of attention, and head to the door as Mom opens it. And there he is. My dad, standing on the walkway to our house.

"Sidney!" He spreads his arms wide. He's bulked up since the last time I saw him, shaggy blond hair glowing in the bright morning sun, cheeks red, but not from the cold. They're always red like that; when I was younger, Mom told me it's something that happens when you drink a lot, and eventually it doesn't go away, even if you stop.

I smile as wide as I can and step into his arms. Even though I've been anxious all week, even though I'm waiting for this day to go south, something about the way he squeezes me makes my shoulders relax. In these moments, he feels like my dad, the dad he can be when he's sober and hasn't said anything stupid yet. He smells like Old Spice and cigarettes, like he always has.

"Hi, Kyle," Mom says behind me.

"Nicole. What's up." His voice vibrates against my ear where my face is pressed to his chest, arms still around me.

"When should I expect you back?"

He glances down at me. "What do you think, kiddo? I know we talked about running away to Mexico."

I half smile, and look at Mom. The line between her eyes deepens as she frowns. Silence reigns, broken only by a car passing by, and someone's dog barking a few houses down.

"Aaaaall righty then," Dad says when neither of us responds. "Three or four hours max; the trailhead isn't too far of a drive. I'll bring them back in one piece and I'll text you if we're running behind."

"Great." She looks at me. "See you soon, honey."

I follow Dad out to his car, the same Corvette he's been driving since I was a kid, just worse for the wear now. He used to take really good care of it before the divorce, but now the paint is scratched, rust stains spreading on the roof. Inside, it smells like cigarette smoke, and I do my best to breathe through my mouth. As we settle in, Dad blows into something attached to the dashboard; after a minute, he turns the key, and the car starts.

"What's that?" I ask, gesturing at the device.

"Breathalyzer," he says, eyes on the road. "Gotta blow into it to start the car now. I know I didn't mention it in my text, but I wanted to tell you in person." He glances over at me. "I got a DUI. That's why I was in treatment."

I nod, and something about my expression must give it away, because he shakes his head. "Your mom already told you, huh?"

"Yeah." I watch the side of his face as his jaw clenches. "She just told me it happened. She didn't say anything bad."

"Of course, of course," he says. "It's just not something you should have to hear about from someone else, why I'm in . . . rehab." He falters on the last word, punching the brakes a little too hard for the red light ahead of us.

I bite back the responses that spring to mind: *Because being in the dark and thinking you were dead is any better? Because*

I'm so shocked you finally ended up in treatment? What else was she supposed to do? Instead, I roll the window down and stick my arm out, letting the wind buffet my hand up and down.

"How about you?" Dad asks.

"I'm good," I say automatically. "I'm president of the Queer Alliance. Co-president, I mean. I'm sharing it with this guy Forrest."

"Good for you," Dad says. "I always knew you would be good at the leadership thing."

"Thanks."

"Any crushes? Boyfriends, girlfriends . . . whoever-friends?"

I grimace a little, but he doesn't see. "Not really. I'm trying to stay focused on school."

"That's my kiddo," he says, turning at the bottom of the hill toward the freeway entrance. One hand dials up the volume on the stereo, and I recognize Kurt Cobain's voice immediately; other than Eminem and '90s hip-hop, grunge is Dad's favorite.

"You recognize this, right?" he asks.

"'Heart-Shaped Box,' by Nirvana," I say. It's an old game we used to play when I was younger, where he'd choose a song and have me identify the title and artist.

"I taught you well, young Padawan," he says. "Wish I would have been around to see them live. But I got to see Pearl Jam, so there's that. Have I told you that story?"

I nod. I've heard it before, but that doesn't stop Dad.

"I was eighteen. Just a couple years older than you," he says, accelerating up the freeway ramp. "Me and your mom had just started seeing each other, it was maybe our second or third date. High school sweethearts." He flashes me a grin. "I got tickets from a buddy of mine who was sick and couldn't go to see them play the Showbox. It was a benefit concert for voter registration."

The song changes, and I recognize it within a few notes: "Rooster," by Alice in Chains. Dad speeds up to merge in front of an oncoming car, muttering curse words as he tries to make it in time. In my lap, I weave my fingers together, clenching them tightly until we're safely in the flow of traffic heading east through the tunnel, toward the bridge.

"Where was I?" He settles back in his seat. "Oh yeah, Pearl Jam. Anyway, your mom and I got pizza beforehand and then we hit the show. It was electric, the place was packed, and we somehow got right up against the barricades at the front. Your mom was wearing a cute little dress over some jeans, that was the style at the time. And a few years later I proposed." He snorts. "And now we're divorced. Should have seen it coming."

I want to ask why he says that, why he thinks he should have known, but I also don't. The conversation is veering sideways now, like a semitruck hitting the rumble strip of a highway, the loud grinding a reminder: Get back on track, before you crash. Get back on track, before you die.

Dad curses, and I jerk my head up in time to see him brake, but he does it wrong, too hard, or too slow, and the car drifts, screeching sideways toward the edge of the bridge as we leave the tunnel, and—

"Earth to Sidney." A hand waves in front of my face, and I look over. We never hit the brakes, never hit the railing. It was an anxiety movie. It was all in my head.

"Sorry," I say. "I spaced out."

"It's all good," he says. Loud guitar rips through the car and he bops his head side to side, gaze staying on the road as he does the gentlest headbang I've ever seen. We're halfway across Lake Washington now, and I look to the right out of habit, across the water.

"The mountain is out!" Dad whoops, and I can't help but smile. Mount Rainier is fully visible today, snow just starting to speckle her sides, the distance rendering her in hazy blues and white, massive ridges sloping down from the sky into the valley below. "Maybe we can go pay her a visit next," he adds.

I nod. "Yeah. That could be cool." My stomach tightens. I knew somewhere in my mind that a text to Dad meant I was signing up for a whole lot more than one hike, but now it's real. He's back in my life, and I have no idea how it's going to go.

We drive for almost an hour in silence, the suburbs slowly dwindling and trees taking their place, green ridges rising up around us as we climb toward Snoqualmie Pass. The wind rushes past the open windows, the white noise a comforting curtain shielding me from having to make conversation. There aren't that many cars on the road, just some semis dragging loads over the mountains to who knows where. Finally, Dad changes lanes and we exit, turning onto a road that crosses above the freeway.

It's later in the morning now, the light golden on the trees. I lean my head closer to the window, breathing in the air; it's fresher already, all pine and earth and a slight hint of smoke from somebody's chimney somewhere.

"Do you remember where we are?" Dad asks. A sign ahead of us lists trailheads to our left and right. I scan it.

"Denny Creek?" I look at him. "Didn't we go here all the time?"

"That's right." He grins. "I thought you might enjoy it. You loved it when you were younger."

The images rush in: glittering water rushing down shallow grooves on a wide expanse of smooth-rock creek bed; an eagle soaring high up in a hot blue sky; Dad's face, less red, more smiley, the sun behind him. I don't know why, but there's a lump in my throat, tears stinging my eyes. I stick my head out the window before he can see, letting the wind blast my face.

He slows down as we turn onto the Forest Service road, winding through the trees, taking another turn, until finally we pass a giant parking lot.

"That's new," he says. "Used to be a big rock field."

"I played on it," I say suddenly. The memory is so clear. I haven't thought about it in ages. "There were all these big boulders, and we'd jump from one to another."

"Your mom got so pissed at me," he says, laughing.

He parks and gets a day pass for the dashboard from the pay station, and after a stop at the bathrooms we're heading up the gated road across from the parking lot, toward the trailhead. I feel different, lighter, like the air out here is going straight to my head, clearing out all the bad thoughts. I stride ahead of Dad.

"Hey, listen." The tone of his voice makes me turn around and look at him, walking backward as he follows me. He swallows, then takes a deep breath and blows it out.

"I know I haven't really been . . . present the past year. Or at all, really." He barks out a laugh. "But this time . . . I don't know. It feels different. Rehab taught me a lot. I'm going to be around more, and I'm going to make it up to you. All the times I was . . . yeah." He clears his throat. I slow down, falling into step beside him. "I'm back at AA, I've got a sponsor, and I'm working the steps. When it's time, I want to make amends to you. How does that sound, kiddo?"

"Sounds good," I reply softly, because I don't know what else to say.

"All righty." He grips the straps of his backpack in his hands, staring straight ahead. We pass the sign at the trailhead, and I drop behind him to walk single file on the narrow path. Above us, the trees spread their limbs, the sun filtering through.

I've never heard Dad apologize before. Not that this is an apology. For that, I think someone has to actually say the words "I'm sorry." But it's something. I scan my body, looking for what I should be feeling: happy, or grateful, or *something* good. Because this is good. I love my dad, and he's finally getting sober, for real. He's finally going to be *here* again, the way he was when I was little. At least for a while.

He looks over his shoulder, smiling at me, and I smile back automatically.

"I'm glad we could do this," he says.

"Yeah," I say, focusing on my feet as I navigate the rocky path. "Me too."

"HEY, CO-PRESIDENT."

I look up from my locker Tuesday morning to see Forrest leaning against the wall a few feet away. The hall is crowded, students chattering in clumps before the last bell rings for first period.

"Wow, you didn't scare the shit out of me this time," I say, rolling my eyes.

"Yeah, I'm trying not to give people concussions lately? It's a new thing." He grins.

"Personal growth! Impressive." I snort, then stop myself. No friendly banter with the enemy. I grab the last book out of my locker and shut it. "What do you want?"

"I was thinking we could talk about club stuff today?" He shifts from one foot to the other. "Maybe we could actually sit down and have a conversation like normal people this time."

I give him the side-eye. "What are you, like, allergic to standing?"

"I just think it's more professional if we sit," he says. "We are the presidents, after all, and this is serious business, according to you."

"OK," I say. "Fine. I will meet you in the library at lunch."

"Excellent." He puts his hands together like an evil scientist, just as the bell rings. We look at each other, and I can tell when we both realize we're going to the same class. I take a step forward, then another, and he follows.

Forrest and I are walking to class together.

"Soooooo . . ." he says. "How are . . . you . . . ?"

I think of Dad, dropping me off at home on Sunday, how he hugged me for way too long before I climbed out of the car. How I stood at the window, waving as he drove away, and it felt like I was a kid again, watching him go to work, looking forward to when he'd come home and we'd watch cartoons.

"I'm fine," I say. "And . . . you?"

"Pretty good," he says.

The classroom appears ahead of us, a shining beacon of hope in this horrifyingly awkward moment. I speed up, heading inside, and Forrest peels away to talk to his friends on the couch at the back of the room.

The second bell rings, and everyone scrambles to their seats. Ms. Lundahl brings out a stack of packets and starts passing them out. One lands on my desk with a thump that hits me like a stone.

"I'm working on reading your short essay assignments right now," she says. "As I mentioned at the start of the year, these were a warm-up for the main event of our first two quarters: your long essay and presentation."

Groans echo around the classroom. "Love the enthusiasm," she says cheerily, heading back to the front and grabbing the remote. With the projector on, she walks us through the assignment step by step. With every section, the cloak of dread that settled over my shoulders the moment she said the words "long essay and presentation" gets heavier. This time, instead of writing about one of the three excerpts we read at the start of the year, we have to compare, contrast, and analyze all of them. There's a deadline for an outline, and for a first draft, and for the final draft. Our presentations will happen in January, and we'll have to give our argument to the class.

"No visual assistance," Ms. Lundahl says. "It'll just be you up here, and I'll be grading on public speaking elements alone. I know that was a core component of tenth-grade curriculum for you all, and this will be a level up."

"Fuuuuuck," Stef mutters behind me. Beside me, Alexander murmurs in agreement. I chance a look over, and he widens his eyes at me. I grimace in response, and the impulse startles me. I don't dislike Forrest's friends, exactly; I've just never really associated with them. But that felt . . . friendly, almost. I didn't even second-guess the reaction before I had it.

As Ms. Lundahl keeps talking, I pull my phone out, opening the group chat under my desk.

I can't join for lunch today, I'm meeting with Forrest to talk about club stuff, I tell them.

We'll miss you! Anna says.

Text if you need us to rescue you, Makayla says.

Don't tempt me, I say. I put my phone back in my pocket and try to focus on the board. I can do this. The assignment, and the meeting with Forrest. It will be fine.

♥

When I walk into the library later that day, I spot Forrest right away: in the back, eyes on his phone as he shovels pasta into his mouth.

"What are you looking at?" I ask when I get close, and he jumps, noodles falling off his fork into his lap.

"Fuck!" He sets the phone down, laughing. "You scared the shit out of me."

I shrug. "I guess now we're even."

He rolls his eyes, picking food out of his lap. "And it's queer stuff, dance trends and politics."

"What?"

"What I'm looking at. My feed."

"That's . . . cool," I admit, sitting down across from him. And it's unexpected too. I don't know what kind of stuff I assumed he'd watch—dumb prank videos?—and I'm surprised by his answer. Though I guess it makes sense; queer stuff, for obvious reasons, and the dance trends, since he's friends with Alexander. "You follow politics?"

"Kind of?" he says. "I follow some creators who talk about what's going on with anti-trans legislation, and anti-racism stuff. There's this one account that does queer history videos. I love it."

"You do?" It slips out before I can filter my surprise.

He laughs. "Wow."

"I'm sorry," I say, shaking my head. "I didn't mean it like that. It just . . . I didn't . . ." I trail off, because I don't know what to say, or what I actually meant. *You're an asshole*, a voice whispers in my mind. *You're an asshole. You're a fucking asshole. He thinks so and so does everyone else.*

Stop, I tell myself.

Stop.

Stop.

"It's cool," he says. "You wanna talk about the exhibit?"

"Yeah! OK." I pull out my notebook, pushing down the frantic murmuring in my head. "So, here's what I've been thinking. The library has a display case out front, and it still has the summer reading stuff from the end of last year in it, so this would be a perfect place to put part of the exhibit. I want it to be eye-catching, something that directs people inside the library, where we can have the rest of the exhibit, which I'm thinking could be freestanding around the room. Maybe we could make it like a scavenger hunt, where people go to every installation, write down a fact they learned, and turn it in for a prize?"

"You wanna give people homework?" He tucks in his chin, staring at me from under his eyebrows.

"It would be *optional*." I glare at him. "And it's just an idea. Way to shoot me down."

"Yeah, doesn't feel good, does it?" he says.

I stare at him silently. His lips are pursed, eyes flat and peering right back into mine. I want to come back with a snappy reply, but I'm also just . . . tired. I don't want to do this today.

"OK," I say. "I know you said we could use this time to fight things out, but I don't really want to spend my lunch break arguing with you. I . . ." I blow a breath out. Time to be the bigger person. For the millionth time in my life. "I'm sorry I shot you down. When the club got started. But we're stuck with each other until the reelection, so I want to make this work, at least until then."

He glares at me a minute longer, then sighs, looking away. "Yeah, all right. And you're right. I want to make this work too."

For the second time today, I'm surprised. I look down at my food, pretending to be very interested in deciding whether I want to eat my apple or my sandwich first. Across from me, Forrest is quiet too.

"It's not a terrible idea. The scavenger hunt," he says after a while.

"I don't know." I grimace. "I want it to be interesting, but maybe that's not it."

"We'll figure it out," he says. "What do you want in the exhibit?"

"Well, Stonewall, of course, and other big events in queer history. And important historical figures, like Marsha P. Johnson and Leslie Feinberg, along with people who are well-known right now."

"Lady Gaga, Lil Nas X, Elliot Page, Laverne Cox, Janelle Monáe . . ." He lists them off on his fingers.

"Yes!" I scribble the names down.

"We should definitely talk about when the DSM stopped classifying queerness as a mental illness," Forrest says. "And some of the gay marriage milestones."

"And the current anti-trans legislation."

He nods, his mouth a grim line. "Yeah."

We toss ideas back and forth and my paper starts to fill, enough for more than one exhibit. Forrest knows way more about queer history than I expected; as much as me, and maybe more. "We should include Lou Sullivan in historical figures," he says. I tilt my head, the name unfamiliar. "People think he's probably the first trans man to openly identify as gay. He founded the first organization for trans guys in the United States and had to fight for the right to medically transition because the criteria for gender identity disorder used to require trans people to identify as straight. But he helped change that, and a bunch of other stuff too."

"Wow." I stare at him, wide-eyed. "That's so cool."

"I know." He grins.

I look down at my lists. The one for pop culture is particularly long. "So many celebrities are out now," I say. "We can't include everyone."

"What if we have the alliance vote for the top five, and include the rest on a list in the exhibit? That way, people can still read it and see all the names."

"That's . . . a really good idea."

He snorts. "You keep acting surprised."

My face heats up, and I stare down at my paper. "Well, you didn't exactly show you were capable of having them when you ran for president."

"Well, you didn't exactly show that you were capable of having a genuine conversation with me, but here we are."

"Hey!" I glare at him, and he smirks back, spreading his hands wide in a sign of surrender. "God, you're so fucking annoying."

"Back at you," he says, still grinning. The bell rings, and he jumps into motion like a tornado, pulling his hoodie and backpack on at lightning speed. "See you later, Co-President."

♥

"It's so early," Anna mumbles, her eyes still half closed as we head through the halls to the library Friday morning. Here and there, posters for our party are tacked up on the display boards; Jayden and Makayla put them up on Monday. "Remind me why I decided to help set up for the party again?"

"Hey, you live two blocks from here," I say. "I had to catch the earlier train while you were still asleep."

"Let's not compare suffering," she says dryly, and I burst out laughing. The sound echoes through the still-empty halls; the school buses haven't arrived yet, teachers just starting to get to their classrooms. Ms. Lundahl waves to us as she unlocks her door, and we wave back.

"I'm so behind on my outline," I say after we're around the corner. "It's due Monday, right?"

"Yeah. We can work on it this weekend. I still need to finish mine."

"Perfect."

In the library, we find Riley, Forrest, and the goth freshman who mentioned Stonewall gathered around one of the tables, sorting through decorations. People brought things from home throughout the week, stuffing them into Forrest's locker, and now they're all spread out on the table: streamers, sparkly lights, bead curtains, balloons, and a whole pile of Pride flags, including the bi, lesbian, ace-spectrum, nonbinary, and trans flags.

Riley waves to us behind the balloon they're puffing into. It swells in front of their face, translucent and full of glitter.

"That's so cool," I say.

"Nyx brought them," they say as they tie it off. The goth freshman waves shyly, and I smile back at them.

Mx. Prager joins us at the table. They're a full head shorter than all of us, their round form swathed in bright yellow overalls, a flamingo-print shirt underneath, with a long rainbow sweater completing the look. Sometimes they're in a wheelchair, but today they're using their cane, the length of it wrapped in gold.

"Anything I can help with?" they ask.

"Do you have tacks?" Forrest asks. They nod, and he follows them up to the front.

I join Riley in untangling the strands of lights, and when Forrest returns with a tub of tacks, we grab chairs to stand on and start hanging the lights up around the perimeter of the library. Nyx and Riley get to work on the balloons, and Forrest starts putting up the Pride flags. Pretty soon the library looks like a gay hurricane hit it, lights glowing on every wall, a bead curtain hanging in the doorway, streamers adorning every aisle.

A few of the chess club kids come inside and stop short, gaping at the decorations, and Forrest invites them to come back at lunch for the party. Chatter from the halls seeps into the library, breaking the quiet of the morning, and Mx. Prager busies themself with students coming in to print papers, turn in books, or hang out.

We finish just in time for first bell. We gather back at the table, collecting empty plastic from the opened packets of balloons, shouldering our backpacks.

"I have to say, this really came together," Riley says, glancing at me, and I nod along. As much as I hate to admit it, Forrest did a good job spearheading this. The library looks inviting. Now we'll see if anyone comes.

♥

By the time lunch rolls around, I'm on edge. I want to feel excited, but what if no one shows up except Queer Alliance members? Should I have fought harder for something more meaningful as our first event? I grab my lunch box from my locker and link up with Jayden outside the cafeteria.

"I saw Stef with the cupcakes this morning," he says, taking a huge bite out of his corndog as we head for the library. "Dayloosohgoog."

"What?"

He chews frantically and swallows the corndog. "They look so good!"

"Oh. Great! Cool."

"What's up with you?" he asks.

"Nothing." I try to smile.

"Sidney." He eyes me as we turn into the library hallway. "Has anyone ever told you you're a bad liar?"

"You do, all the time." I stick my tongue out at him.

"OK, well. I say that because it's true. So what's up? Was Forrest a dumbass during setup this morning?"

"No! No. He was fine. I'm just . . ."

"Anxious?"

"Yeah. As usual." I laugh, but it's half-hearted.

"Hey." He curls a hand around my upper arm and squeezes gently, stopping me just outside the library. "I know you think you're responsible for the success or failure of Queer Alliance, but you're not." I blink, looking down. I don't know how he does it, but Jayden always seems to know what's going on with me. "Plus, if this fails, you can just blame it on Forrest," he adds. "And then you'll be a shoo-in when it's time to revote."

I laugh, meeting his eyes again. "You're right." As much as I want to win the presidency, though, I don't actually want this event to fail. Even if it means getting an edge on Forrest. The club's well-being is more important than that.

"You know it!" He points at me. "OK, let's get in there."

I take a deep breath and follow him through the open double doors, the bead curtain tickling my face. Inside, people are crowded around the tables—way more than we usually have at Queer Alliance meetings. Music is blasting through a portable speaker on one of the tables, and at the front desk, Mx. Prager bobs their head as they study their computer screen.

I follow Jayden to the first table, where we find Makayla and Anna stuffing their faces with cupcakes. The whole table is covered in rows of them, each one labeled with the appropriate dietary restriction: vegan, gluten-free, nut-free, ones that are all three, and ones that are none of those things. I pick one of the latter, a chocolate cupcake with tiny sour gummy worms resting in its pink frosting. The first bite makes my eyes widen. It's moist and rich, the icing flavored like actual strawberries, not just generic sweetness. The gummy worms add a perfect tartness.

Stef appears beside me, her long beaded braids swinging forward as she leans over the table to grab a vegan one from the other end. "Hey Sidney," she says, smiling at me.

"These are *incredible*!" I say, taking another bite. "Your aunt is a genius."

She laughs. "Thanks."

"How long has she been doing this? Where's her bakery? Do you get to just eat these whenever you want?" The questions spill out of my mouth, Stef's eyes twinkling as my words trip over each other in excitement.

"She opened it a few years ago down in Rainier Beach. It's become a real community spot. It's called Sweet Tooth, if you ever wanna go."

"That's really cool that she donated."

Stef shrugs. "She's always been super supportive of me. She's gay too, she lives with her wife."

"Was the rest of your family not supportive?" I watch her face, the small glitter hearts pasted at the corners of her eyes moving with her expressions. I don't think I've ever had this long of a conversation with Stef before. Not that I don't like her. But she's just always been Forrest's friend, and I guess I kind of wrote her off by proxy.

"Eh, my parents were fine, so were my sisters; some of my extended family was weird, and my grandma . . ." She grimaces. "I'm not out to her yet. She's old and super Christian, like she's still convinced I'm gonna marry my dad's best friend's son."

"Oh my god." I face-palm and she laughs. "Why are boomers like that?"

"I don't know, but I'm ***not*** into it," she says.

"What's up, nerds?!" a familiar voice bellows. Forrest pushes between us, snagging a cupcake. "This party is pretty great, huh?" He grins at me, face inches from mine as he licks the frosting off. "I told you."

I roll my eyes and step back. "Yeah, OK, I'll give it you." I glance around at people chattering to each other over the music as they dig into the chips, fruit, and drinks we brought. "This . . . was a pretty good idea."

"Wow." Forrest shakes his head. "*You* approve of something *I'm* doing. I never thought I'd see the day. Now I can die happy."

"You are so annoying," I say, but I can't help smiling.

"So I hear." He smirks. "OK, I gotta get back to Skittles pong."

"Skittles pong?"

"Beer pong, but with Skittles!" He's already walking away.

"Did Mx. Prager OK that?!"

"It's fine! We'll pick up anything that spills!"

I follow him and it's exactly as he said: Each end of the table has three rows of cups, in bowling pin formation, filled with Skittles. Nyx is waiting for him at one end.

"Finally," they say when he walks up. They seem a little more relaxed today, not so much like a cat I could scare off with a sudden movement.

"I was just getting them in on the game," he says, jerking a thumb at me.

"I'm not playing," I say quickly, and look over at the other team. Jayden smiles at me sheepishly from his place beside Alexander. "Jayden!"

"It's not messy like beer pong is!" he says quickly.

"You don't even drink," I say, but I can't help it; I'm grinning.

Alexander flutters his fingers at me. "We do need a referee."

I side-eye him for a second, and then I nod, and they all cheer. A glow swells in my chest, and I take up my position beside the table, at the center.

♥

We're mid-game, Jayden and Alexander winning, when the bell rings to signal the end of lunch. It jolts me out of the warm, happy glow of the party and back to reality, where we have a ton of stuff to clean up and only five minutes to do it in before fifth period.

"We're good," Forrest says, his eyes catching mine just as I'm about to panic. "I asked Mx. Prager to write us all passes."

"Oh." My shoulders settle. "You really did think of everything."

"Not so bad having a co-president after all, huh?" He smirks at me as he sweeps Skittles from the table into a cup.

I smirk back. "It's not the worst."

He snorts and I join him in tidying. Jayden and Alexander are at the next table, putting the remaining snacks into a big reusable bag, while the rest of the Queer Alliance bustles around the library taking down decorations.

"Forrest!" We both look up at the voice to see someone I don't recognize, tall with long blue hair, golden-brown skin, and dramatic cat-eye makeup.

"Mercury!" Forrest steps forward and the two of them hug. He turns to me. "Sidney, this is Mercury. She's a sophomore, and is in theater with me. I've been trying to get her to come to Queer Alliance forever."

"Hi!" I smile up at her. "Thank you for coming."

"This was so fun," she says. "I didn't know Queer Alliance did stuff like this."

"Well, we do now," Forrest says.

"I gotta get to class, but . . . the meeting is on Friday next week, right?"

"That's right," he says.

She flashes us two thumbs-ups and slides past, toward the double doors. Forrest turns to me. "She just came out," he says in a low voice. "We started talking last year while we were both on set crew and she was questioning things."

"I didn't know you did set crew." I glance back at Mercury, her giraffe-like frame disappearing into the hallway. Forrest has a whole life outside his posse, is friends with people I didn't know he knew. And he told them about Queer Alliance. Got them to come to this party, this thing I thought was a terrible idea, a waste of time, and . . .

It wasn't.

He winks. "There's a lot of things you don't know about me."

I huff. "Oh yeah, you're so mysterious."

He wiggles his fingers at me like he's casting a spell, then turns to take the cup of Skittles to the trash. I scan the library; almost all the decorations are put away, and Riley is pulling down the last of the flags. The only one left is Mx. Prager's Pride flag on the wall behind their desk, which has every single color including the trans Pride chevron with the black and brown stripes, and the yellow triangle with the purple circle that signifies intersex people. It hangs there year-round, a comforting reminder that there are people working at this school who have our back no matter what the outside world is like.

This party was a reminder of that too, that there's a bigger community of queer people and allies at this school than just the people who come to Queer Alliance. I've been focused on making sure my ideas get heard so I can win the reelection, but Forrest's ideas are good for the club too. And it might not have happened if I'd kept trying to shut him down.

"So, I was thinking," Forrest says as he rejoins me at the table. "It might be easier to plan our meet-ups if we exchange numbers."

I scan the floor, looking for any escaped Skittles. The thought of texting Forrest, of all people, makes my brain short-circuit a little. It's just so . . . weird. His request makes sense, though; it would be easier to just text him than look for him at school. And I want to keep up our collaboration. Yeah, I want to win the reelection, but more than that, I want the club to succeed.

"I promise I won't spam you," he continues. "Scheduling purposes only."

I scoop up an orange Skittle from where it lodged under a nearby bookcase. "OK."

"Really?"

I turn and he's looking at me, head cocked to the side, eyebrows raised. "I can change my mind and say no, if you prefer," I say dryly.

"No, no! Here, just a second," he says, searching his pockets for his phone. I tell him my number, and a moment later my own pocket buzzes. I pull my phone out, and there it is: an unknown number, and a single text:

Hey it's Forrest.

I hope I don't regret this.

CHAPTER 9

ANNA'S HOUSE THAT SATURDAY IS A HALLOWEEN FEVER dream. Huge fake spiders adorn the windows, porch, and trees on her front walkway, synthetic webs stretching everywhere, light-up plastic jack-o'-lanterns hanging from branches, and the crowning touch, an animatronic witch sitting on the porch swing who cackles when you get close to her. You'd think after all these years, I'd be used to it, but she still startles me when I step up to the front door.

It swings open before I can knock. "Welcome to our haunted mansion," Anna intones, and gives me a horror-movie grin.

I come inside and kick my shoes off in the hallway. "Your dad really went all out this year."

"He did. He's already got his costume locked down too."

"Which Hollywood monster is it this time?"

"Freddy Krueger." She leads me into the kitchen, a large room with honey-colored wooden cabinets and a freestanding island, and opens the fridge. "The original *Nightmare on Elm Street* version, of course."

"Of course." I set my backpack down on the island and slide into one of the chairs. Jayden and Makayla are joining us for a movie night after my study session with Anna, and I'm looking forward to it. Between homework and extracurriculars—Makayla has guitar lessons, Jayden's playing volleyball—and the lead-up to the Coming Out Day party, we haven't all hung out as a group outside of school since the year started.

"It's weirdly quiet here," I say, swiveling back and forth in the chair.

"My brother is spending the night at a friend's house," she says, setting an open bottle of ginger ale in front of me, and popping the top off hers. We drink in silence for a moment, then head into the dining room, where we spread out across their huge table.

"What did you think of the party?" she asks, setting up her laptop on its pink stand.

"Um." I pull up Ms. Lundahl's assignment from the online portal. "It was . . . really fun, actually."

"Right? Those cupcakes, oh my god." Her eyes roll back in appreciation. "And there was a great turnout. How are things with you and Forrest?"

I shrug. "I mean, not to jinx anything, but . . . I think we might not be mortal enemies anymore?"

Her eyes widen. "So, just regular enemies?"

I laugh. "Maybe not even that. I don't know. He's not terrible."

"The bar is on the floor," she says dryly.

"It's not like we're friends or anything," I say. "But we're collaborating, and it's working."

"Well, good," she says.

I look at her over the top of my laptop. Her eyes are on her screen, fingers tapping as she scans whatever is in front of her. "Are you working on the Lundahl assignment?"

"Yeeeeeeeah." She grimaces. "She did *not* fuck around."

We brainstorm arguments together, coming up with a list of ideas for analysis. Anna latches on to one right away, so I delete that one from my list, and work on formulating my own thesis. It's hard to focus, though. Anna is typing away, clearly having no problem writing her outline. The sound blends with the rain pouring down outside, and my phone vibrates, pulling my attention. For a moment I wonder if it's Forrest, but it's not.

Was scrolling through old Facebook photos and found this, Dad says.

It's the three of us at Mom's family Christmas, six months before they told me they were getting divorced. In the photo, we're all wearing matching reindeer sweaters, a gift from Grandma that year; I'm smiling, and so is Mom, but with her lips closed. Dad is in the middle with his arms around us, one hand making bunny ears over Mom's head.

I remember the day as soon as I see our faces. It's not obvious in the photo, except for his red nose and cheeks, but Dad was drunk, and had been since we'd woken up that morning. The day started with presents at our place while he sipped spiked coffee; he'd spent too much money on everything, and I could tell Mom was angry even though she tried to hide it. When it was time to go, I waited in the car for fifteen minutes while they fought over whether Dad was sober enough to drive. Eventually, he threw the keys at Mom's feet and got into the passenger seat, slamming the door hard enough to rattle the whole car.

Miss Christmases with you, he says. *We gotta take a new photo without your mom. I'm not good enough with Photoshop to take her out.*

And a goofy-face emoji. Like he's joking. Let's erase Mom from the photo! Won't that be funny!

I text him back, before I can think: *Why would you Photoshop her out? You're the one who broke up our family.*

My heart is pounding; I can't believe I just said that.

The response is swift. *Are you fucking kidding me? It's just a joke. I should never have had you. You're the reason I started drinking in the first place.*

"Sidney?"

I look up at Anna, then down at my phone. There's nothing there, just Dad's initial text, and the photo. I didn't reply. It was an anxiety movie. None of it actually happened.

It felt so real, though. My hands are shaking, chest fluttering, pressure rising behind my eyes. I shift my gaze back to Anna.

"You OK?" She frowns. "You seem . . . upset."

"I'm . . . I'm fine." I set my phone face down on the table and scrub my hands against my face. "It's just . . . Dad stuff. Anxiety."

She clicks her tongue. "Oh yeah. I feel that. Did you talk to your mom about a diagnosis yet?"

I wrinkle my nose. "No. I just . . . last year sucked, and I don't want to give her another reason to do her Helicopter Mom thing."

Anna watches me, her mouth screwed up in a skeptical grimace.

"I'm fine! Really. It's not that bad."

"OK," she says, but I can't tell if she's convinced.

The doorbell rings then and her face lights up. "They're here!"

I look at my laptop screen as she heads to the front door to let in Jayden and Makayla. I have a thesis formed, sort of. It needs to be fleshed out. But it's fine. It's good enough for now. I can finish my outline later this weekend.

"Sidneeeeeeeeeeey!" Jayden gallops into the room, wrapping his arms around me, still in my chair.

"Hello to you too," I say into his elbow. He pulls back and I straighten my glasses, grinning up at him.

"What are we watching tonight?" Makayla asks. "Can we play Betrayal first?"

"Abso*lute*ly," Anna and I say at the same time, and high-five each other. Betrayal at House on the Hill, or Betrayal for short, is one of our favorite board games, a horror-themed one where you play as different characters trying to navigate a haunted mansion. One player turns rogue eventually, and then you have to fight the monster in your midst to get out alive. It's just the right amount of rules and chance, with a touch of role-playing.

“’Tis the season,” Jayden says, wiggling his eyebrows at us, and zooms ahead down the stairs into the basement.

“A wild teenager appears!” I hear Anna’s dad say, and when the rest of us reach the basement, he widens his eyes. “*Several* wild teenagers!”

“You’re sooooo corny,” Anna says.

“I’m corny but I’m free,” he says cheerfully, and vacates the couch with an elaborate bow. “Enjoy your coven meeting.”

“We will!” Makayla says as he leaves, then turns to us. “We should totally form a coven, though.”

“That could be our group Halloween costume.” I plop down on the couch and glance at Jayden, who’s trying to do the worm on the carpet. “What do you think, Jayden?”

“About what?” he says, breathing hard as he rocks back and forth on his stomach.

“Halloween. Group costume. Coven of witches.”

“Oh!” He rolls over onto his back. “That could work. Witches are kind of . . . basic though.”

“We could be creative witches,” Anna says, rummaging through the game cabinet. “Like a sea witch. I call that one. And a fire witch.”

“The witches of the four elements!” Makayla says.

“I don’t really want to be a witch,” Jayden says, pulling a face. “I’m sorry.”

“It’s OK!” Anna says quickly. “We could do something else.”

“I . . .” Jayden closes his eyes. “Idon’tthinkIwannadoagroupcostumethisyear,” he says really fast, then opens his eyes, looking at all of us, mouth stretched into a grimace.

Silence reigns, expanding like a too-big balloon in the space left by his words. I make eye contact with Anna, and she holds my gaze. A phrase flashes into my mind, a fragment of conversation from one of our study dates: *Jayden has been . . . evasive.*

We've coordinated our costumes the past two years. I know logically it's not that long a time, but it feels like longer. I got used to it. And now it's not happening, I guess.

"Why not?" Anna asks. Her voice is mom-friend calm.

Jayden shrugs. "I just want to do my own thing this year."

"OK," she says. Her face is pleasantly neutral; she's good at that face. It's hard to tell what she's really thinking sometimes. I don't even really know how I feel either.

"Are you all mad at me?" Jayden asks.

"No!" Anna says, at the same time Makayla says, "Kind of?" They look at each other, and Anna gestures for Makayla to talk.

"I'm not *mad* mad," Makayla says. "It's just like . . . two weeks out from Halloween, and we've done it the past few years, and you could have told us earlier."

"I'm sorry," Jayden says.

"It's OK."

Makayla looks at me and Anna. "The three of us can do something still."

I nod, even though it feels weird to do it without Jayden. "We can text about it."

"Perfect," Anna says, and she sounds relieved. "Betrayal?"

"Fuck yeah!" Jayden claps his hands and sits upright, and we all gather around the coffee table to set up the game. As

Anna passes me one of the character figurines, she catches my eye, and this time, I can read what she's asking without a word. I smile back, reassuring her that we're good, all of us, our whole little group. I know she doesn't like conflict. She wants everything to be all right, and it sounds like Makayla's basically fine.

So I am too.

♥

I sleep late on Sunday, and wake up to my phone buzzing with texts. There's a new group chat—me, Makayla, and Anna, and from the look of it, they've been sending costume ideas back and forth for at least an hour. The thread is full of pictures and categories: big cats, book and anime characters, houseplants, fruits, and, of course, witches.

If we do houseplants I get to be a cactus, I text them.

Of course, Makayla says.

Houseplants feel like a lot of work, Anna says.

Makayla laugh reacts. *That was YOUR idea.*

I don't know what I was thinking, Anna says.

I like fruits, I say. *Plus we're all gay, so it works.*

And it's easy, Makayla adds. *Just get a bunch of same-color clothes and maybe draw the fruit on our faces or something?*

Yes. Perfect. Love it, Anna says. *I'll be an orange, I already have those tights.*

I call lemons! Makayla says.

I'll be a strawberry, I say.

Good job, team, Anna says.

I roll out of bed and pull on sweats and a fresh T-shirt, then head downstairs. Mom is gone, out with her friends for brunch, and on the table is a fresh loaf of banana bread, clearly Shar's handiwork. I grab a slice and head out to the shop.

Shar is there, setting up. "Top of the morning to ya!" she says.

"This is really good." I hold up the bread.

"Glad you like it. You still want to help with the bookcase today?"

I nod and scarf down the rest of the bread before putting on my protection gear. When I join her at the worktable, she's laid out the lumber we sanded last week, along with a can of walnut-colored wood stain, tape, and a pack of small white microfiber squares.

"So, I lied last week," she says. "I forgot we have to stain this puppy before we finish it. So no power tools."

"That's OK."

"Great." She measures the lumber and tapes off the places where the wood will be glued together later. Then she opens the can and dips one of the microfiber squares into the stain. I watch as she applies it to the wood in even strokes, then I do the same.

We work quietly for a while, the music playing in the background. The wood soaks up the stain nicely, the color slowly turning from light blond to a dark, ashy brown.

Shar clears her throat. "You seemed a little subdued when I picked you up last night."

I'm quiet, focused on the wood. She's right; even though I had a good time with my friends, the conversation with Jayden cast a shadow that never really faded. The pauses in our conversation felt heavier, my friends' smiles and laughs a little too bright, like we were all trying to just move on. Because we should move on. It shouldn't be a big deal.

"We usually do costumes together every year," I say. "Well, since I met them freshman year. So we thought—well, Makayla and Anna and I thought—we'd do it again. But Jayden didn't want to."

Shar hums in acknowledgment, filling in the last of her wood with its first coat of stain.

"It's stupid, like I shouldn't even be upset," I say, finishing mine and grabbing another. "But he waited until the last minute to tell us he wants to do his own thing. Whatever that means." I move quicker and quicker over the lumber.

"Ouch," Shar says.

"It's fine. But like. He could have told us earlier. And I don't get it. Why does he want to do his own thing? What's so bad about doing a costume with all of us? Like, does he secretly not want to be friends with us anymore and just doesn't know how to tell us?" My voice cracks, and my eyes fill with tears. I stop staining, staring down at the table.

"I doubt that," Shar says gently, coming over to me and taking the pad from my hand. I look up at her; not by much, because she's only slightly taller than me. Her dark brown eyes crinkle gently. "This is the age where people want to do their own thing sometimes. You're all figuring out who you are, with each other and without."

"Well, he doesn't *need* to figure it out without us," I mumble.

She laughs. "I know that feeling."

"I just . . ." My voice cracks again, and she opens her arms. I step into them, her hug enfolding me like the world's best weighted blanket. "I just don't want things to change."

"I know." She squeezes me. "Change is hard. But it's going to be OK."

I want to believe her. I want her hug to make me feel better. I want it to be enough. But it isn't. She lets me go, and we keep working, and this feeling stays with me, the same feeling that's followed me for years, right on the heels of my horrible thoughts like some medieval plague. Like my insides are crawling, buzzing, and I need to do something to make it go away.

So I remember the scene, the moment Jayden told us, and I scan it over and over. Every facial expression, every note and cadence of our words, looking for the hints, for the evidence, for the cracks.

Then I scan it again.

And then one more time.

Is he going to leave us?

Or will everything be fine?

♥

That evening, I curl up on my bed, staring at my text thread with Dad. His message is still sitting there, our faces smiling at me from the photo. I should reply. I don't want to leave him hanging like I did a few weeks ago.

Sorry for the late text! Those sweaters, omg.

I stare down at my text, waiting for a reply. The ellipses pop up, way faster than he usually responds.

Took you long enough.

My hands shake as I type, and delete, and retype: *I got distracted with school stuff, I'm really sorry.*

I get it. You've got more important things to do.

Tears fill my eyes. He's in his trailer right now, probably reaching for a beer can, and it's all my fault. What if he's doing worse than before? What if he wants to ki—

Brekky jumps on my bed, headbutting the hand holding my phone and I drop it onto the comforter. I snatch it up again, but in my thread with Dad, there's only my text about the sweaters, waiting for his reply.

I toss my phone away from me on the bed, but it vibrates again and I snatch it up. The message is from a new number, though, one I haven't saved. *Meet up at lunch Monday?* the preview asks.

From my pillow, Brekky watches me, eyes half closed. I open the conversation, and when I see the text before it, I know who it is: Forrest. I save his number in my phone and text back. *Sounds good.*

How's your outline going?

Oh my god. The outline. I've been so in my head about Jayden that I completely forgot about it, and it's due tomorrow. I'm not telling Forrest that, though. *Fine*, I say back, and jump up, rushing to my backpack where it sits languishing next to my closet, clothes strewn on the floor around it. I rummage through, pulling out the readings and my notes and my laptop. It's going to be a late night.

My phone buzzes. *Lundahl's nice but she goes way too hard with the essays sometimes*, Forrest says.

I crouch on the floor, staring at the phone. I don't really know what to say back. It's not a question, so there's nothing for me to answer. *For real*, I say finally.

You're in third period history, right? How's the group project going?

OK, I guess we're having a conversation. School is a safe subject, and—*How do you know what class I'm in? Stalker*, I say.

LMFAO noooooo! Stef mentioned you're in it with her.

Oh, right. That was a stupid thing for me to say. Why did I call him a stalker? I didn't actually think that, it just . . . came out. Like when I'm joking with my friends, and we call each other names, but it's all in fun.

Which class are YOU in? I ask.

Fourth period. With Jayden.

I knew that, of course, because Jayden's in the group project with him, but I'm not about to let Forrest know that I know anything about him.

On my bed, I arrange everything I need for the outline in a perfect half circle in front of me. If I study at the table, Mom will notice, and then she'll ask questions, and I can't tell her I'm this behind on an assignment.

I grab my phone again, staring at Forrest's last text. I could ask how his outline is going, whether he's come up with a thesis yet, what his arguments are. Do I really want to open that door, though? We just barely came to a truce, and the peace between us feels delicate, like a glass too close to the edge of a table waiting to be knocked off. Better to give it space, let it stay where it is.

I put the phone back down and open my laptop instead.

AT LUNCH ON MONDAY, FORREST ISN'T ON HIS PHONE WHEN I get to the library; instead, he's watching the door, and he grins when he sees me come in. I'm dragging today, eyes squinty from lack of sleep, a dull headache forming behind my eyes.

"I couldn't let you scare me again," he says when I get close. I crack a smile, but it's half-hearted, and his expression shifts to a questioning frown. "What's up with you?"

"Nothing." I sit across from him, opening my lunch. "I was just up late finishing the outline." Actually, I was up all night, writing the entire outline from scratch, but I already feel like enough of a failure for falling behind in the first place; I don't need Forrest to know about it too. If I want to keep the presidency, I can't show the cracks.

"Same here," he says.

"Really?"

"Yeah. I actually, uh . . . didn't start it until Sunday morning." He rubs the back of his neck.

I burst out laughing, and he purses his lips, tilting his head. I wave my hand. "I'm not laughing *at* you! I started it Saturday morning and then forgot about it until you texted me."

He nods slowly, lips curling upward again. "Niiiiice."

"School is just a lot sometimes," I say, biting into my apple.

"Agreed." He leans backward in his chair until the front legs lift off the ground, then lands with a thump.

"So. About the exhibit," I say. "I've been thinking about it. How about on Friday, we bring it to the meeting and get everyone's input, vote on what we want to include, and figure out when we can have a work party to put it together. Maybe this weekend? My house is too small for a big group, though."

"I can host," Forrest says, then pulls a face. "Actually . . . no, yeah. It'll be fine. I'll host."

I tilt my head. "What do you mean?"

He waves a hand. "Nothing."

"Are you sure?" I say. "I don't want to inconvenience anyone."

"It's all good. It's just my parents." He rolls his eyes.

"Oh, are they strict?" I ask.

"Not really, not with friends," he says, then lets out a long sigh. "They're getting divorced. And they fight. A lot."

"Oh." I didn't expect Forrest to tell me something like this, and my brain scrambles, trying to think of the right thing to say.

"Yeah."

"We can go somewhere else if it's awkward," I say.

"No, it's really fine." He scrubs his face with his hands. "I think my dad is out of town on business this weekend anyway."

I watch him, with his face still buried in his hands. I want to tell him something comforting, and the impulse surprises me. He exhales and sits back, hands coming down, face blotchy from where he rubbed it.

"Sorry," he says. "I know we're not friends or anything. You don't need to hear about my family drama."

We're quiet. I look down at my notebook, at a small flower I doodled on the cover. When Mom and Dad divorced, I didn't have anyone to talk to about it, because I didn't feel close enough to the few friends I had to say anything. I thought if I did, I would just bring them down, or even worse, maybe they wouldn't care at all. Now I have Jayden and Anna and Makayla, and I can tell them anything. And most of the time, I do.

But their parents are happily married, and they don't know what it was like to live in a house with two adults on the brink of breaking down, where every moment felt like a held breath. Forrest and I may not be friends, but I know what he's going through, in my own way. A few weeks ago, I couldn't have imagined even listening to, let alone caring about, whatever was going on with him. And now . . . well. It's not that I care, exactly. But I don't *not* care. If my parents were still together and fighting the way they used to, I'd feel hesitant to have friends over too.

"I'm really sorry," I say. "My parents divorced when I was eleven. It sucked."

"Thanks," he says quietly. "Yeah. They were fighting more, but I didn't really think they'd actually do it."

"Mine fought, like, all the time."

"That's rough."

"Yeah. I didn't think they would get divorced either, though. That was something that happened to other kids, you know?"

He nods slowly and heavily, staring at the table, tracing the grain with his finger. The bell rings, signaling the end of lunch, and the stampede to fifth period, but we both just sit there for a minute. I don't know how to move out of this space, this weird and quiet pocket we've fallen into.

And I don't know if I want to. It was surprisingly easy to talk with him this way. Nice, even.

He scoots his chair back, grin coming on like a light bulb. "Thanks for the therapy," he says, and stands up.

I snort. "You're welcome."

We pack up, and I follow him out, both of us still quiet. He disappears ahead of me into the halls, and something twinges in my chest; I don't know why, but I was expecting him to say goodbye. But that's something friends do, and we're not. Even if we both have divorced parents.

♥

On the train home, I get a text from Anna. She'd looked at me quizzically when I walked into fifth period after lunch, and I'd just shrugged at her. *Forrest*, I'd mouthed, and she'd nodded slowly. We didn't get a chance to talk.

So . . . how was lunch? Her message reads. And I don't know why, but I'm a little annoyed. She knows I've been meeting with him for a while now; why is she asking?

Uneventful, I say back. *We talked about what's next for the exhibit.*

We missed you, she says, and my chest warms. She's just checking on me, and here I am being a jerk.

I missed you all too, I say. *How was it?*

It was fine, she says, and I know that's Anna-speak for not-fine.

Annaaaaaaaa, I say.

It was fine! she replies. *Really. It was just me and Makayla.*

I stare down at the text. That's weird. Volleyball is an after-school thing, which means Jayden must have been doing something else. But what?

That's . . . different, I say.

Yeah :/, she says. *Makayla didn't know where he was either.*

Even weirder. What if Jayden is getting into something . . . bad? That wouldn't make sense. But that's how it starts sometimes, right? He could have tried something, maybe from one of the guys on the volleyball team. At a party, surrounded by them, and someone presses it into his hand. I don't know what a drug looks like, but probably a pill. Small and white, easy to pop in your mouth, and now he's pulling away from us. No Halloween. No lunchtimes. No Queer Alliance. He'll fade like a ghost, dark circles under his eyes, avoiding us in the halls. *Signs your friend is on drugs*, I type into Google, and wait as the results populate. I'm being ridiculous, but I need to know. Just in case. If I know, then I can look for the signs. If I know, then I can stop Jayden before something really bad happens.

I look through article after article—"Warning Signs of Drug Abuse," "7 Signs Your Friend Has a Drug Problem," "Signs of Drug Use in Teens"—and catalog the answers in my head: physical appearance changes, cravings, poor judgment, risky behavior, strained relationships. That doesn't sound like Jayden.

But what if it's just starting, and the signs are more subtle, things I'm missing, things that wouldn't be on any of these lists?

Someone settles into the seat next to me on the train, jarring me out of my thoughts. I stare at my face in the window, the darkness of the tunnel behind it as we rattle down the track. I feel afraid, afraid that everything is about to collapse, that I'll lose Jayden forever, and what happens after that?

That's not real. It's not happening.

That's not real. It's not happening.

That's not real. It's not happening.

My phone vibrates again, but it's a message from someone else. From Forrest.

My mom says I can host, he says. *I was right, Dad's gonna be on a business trip. Saturday?*

That's my study date with Jayden, but . . . this is important too. And maybe Jayden will come, and so will Anna and Makayla, and everything will be normal. Because nothing is really wrong. My brain is just freaking out for no reason, like it always does. I can miss one study date. And if Jayden is using drugs, then I can watch him, and see if he gives any of the signs, and I can check with Makayla and Anna after to see if they notice anything too.

Sounds good, I say to Forrest.

Hope you like big dogs, he says.

You have dogs?

Just one—Simba. He's a pit bull mix. A picture pops up, of a golden dog, his muzzle gone white with age, mid-lick with his tongue over his nose.

OMG he's SO CUTE, I say. *We have two cats at home, English Breakfast and Earl Grey.*

LMFAO that's amazing, he says. *You must really love tea.*

They're my stepmom's cats, I say. *She had them before they started dating.*

Ohhhhhhh that's cool! he says. *So your mom is dating a woman now?*

Yeah, she's bi.

That's super cool. So was she chill when you came out?

I smile down at my phone, remembering. *Yeah. Both times.*

Oh you're out to her as nonbinary too?

Yeah, my whole family knows. They've been fine with it. My extended family isn't the best at pronouns, but they try. What about yours?

They were fine with it too. I kinda wasn't expecting it . . . my parents voted conservative when I was little, he says. *But things really changed the last few elections for them and . . . idk. They've been really good about it. My mom took me to the doctor to get on testosterone like a week after I told her.*

That's awesome.

I know. I feel lucky. Even if they're being assholes to each other, at least they're not assholes to me. Most of the time, lol.

The train stops and I look up. We're at my station, and I stand, murmuring an *excuse me* to the person next to me. The doors almost close on me, but I dart through and head to the elevator, composing a text back to Forrest. I don't want to ask him more about his parents, in case it's a touchy subject, so I ask him about Simba instead, and then suddenly we're talking about how long they've had him, what his personality is like, and he asks me if I have any siblings, and I learn that he has an older brother in college and a little sister in elementary school, and then he sends me a song he's really into, and I listen to it, and then I'm home, walking in the back door, English Breakfast running toward me.

I slide my headphones off and kneel to pet him. "Hi Brekky," I whisper with a smile. The bad thoughts are a distant echo in my mind, muted by the conversation with Forrest. I never would have thought someone who annoyed me as much as he has could be this fun to talk to. It's a little weird, how much I'm enjoying it. Maybe I was wrong about him. Or maybe he's grown since freshman year. Either way, I don't really care anymore. I'm tired of spending all my energy on hating him.

♥

Forrest and I text back and forth throughout the evening, and the next morning, I have a video waiting for me when I wake up, a silly one of a cat. I laugh as I watch it, shaking my head, and send one back.

When I get to school, I look for him as I pass his locker, but I don't see him. I round the corner and someone fills my vision, a split second before we collide.

"Ah, fuck!" a familiar voice says as I stumble back, something warm and wet soaking the front of my sweatshirt. It's Jayden, mug clasped in his hand, the contents splashed down his clothes too.

"Sid, I'm so sorry," he says, holding his arms out as they drip. "It's just tea, don't worry, it won't stain."

"I don't care about that," I say, looking him over. He's got dark circles under his eyes, but he always does in the morning. He's making a sheepish face at me, no hint of guardedness in his eyes. "Are you OK?"

He frowns. "Yeah, I'm fine, it's just liquid. Are *you* OK?"

"Yes! Yeah." I look down at myself. "I needed to wash this hoodie anyway." It's my black one from the last time Billie Eilish played here.

"OK. Hey, you stay here. I'm just gonna grab some paper towels and I'll be right back."

I nod, and he beelines into the boys' bathroom next to us, a small puddle on the floor where he was standing. I set my backpack on the ground and take off my hoodie. It's not that wet, just damp on the front, and I'm wearing a long-sleeve shirt, so I won't be cold while it dries.

Jayden reappears and kneels down to soak up the spilled tea with a handful of paper towels. He does it with his usual energy; no hint of lethargy, or a hangover of some kind. It doesn't seem like he's on drugs. And now that I see him, I realize how silly that idea is. It's *Jayden*. Like the rest of us, he's never even smoked weed, let alone done anything else.

"I heard we both ditched lunch yesterday," he says as he stands up.

"Forrest and I had another meeting," I say. "We were talking about the exhibit."

"That makes sense." He wads the paper towels together and chucks them into the nearest trash bin. "Whoosh! Nothing but net."

I snort. "You're such a jock."

"Someone's gotta balance the rest of you nerds out," he says cheerfully. "You going to first period?" I nod. "Sweet, I'll walk with you."

We fall into step, the halls thinning out; the first bell must have rung. I was so caught up in our collision, I didn't even notice. It feels good to be walking beside Jayden, beside one of my best friends.

"So what about you, what's your excuse for missing lunch yesterday?" I ask as we arrive outside Ms. Lundahl's room.

"Oh! Um. I was . . . breakdancing."

"Breakdancing?" I can't help it; the word comes out incredulous.

He flushes. "Yeah. The club meets at lunch on Mondays."

"Cool!" I say quickly. I don't want to make him feel bad with my surprise. But he's never once shown an interest in any kind of dancing, let alone breakdancing.

"Thanks!" He scratches the back of his head. "So . . . see you at lunch? Like usual?"

"Yeah!"

He shoots me finger guns and darts away, leaving me watching his retreating back. I'm no stranger to Jayden's sudden hyperfixations; I guess this is the latest one. I take a deep breath and let it out slowly. He's not leaving us. He's fine. We're fine. The Halloween thing was just a weird blip.

♥

That night, I lie on my bed after dinner, scrolling on my phone and feeling accomplished. I did my math homework and worked on my portion of the history group project. It's due next week, and I'm not going to let myself fall behind again like I did with the English assignment. Now that my outline is in, the rough draft is next.

My phone buzzes, a text dropping in from the top of the screen. It's Dad. I thumb open the message, my heart rate only speeding up a little bit at its appearance.

So, about that visit to Mount Rainier, he says. *You game? Sunday, maybe?*

It's been a long time since I visited the national park, even though the mountain is a constant presence watching over the city. The last time I was there was with Mom and Dad, and it's a barely there memory, a few snapshot images in my mind: bright green grass, wildflowers, a deer peering at me from within the trees. It would be nice to go back.

Yeah, I say. *I'm game.*

ON SATURDAY MORNING, I STAND IN FRONT OF MY CLOSET, trying to pick out what to wear. Mom and Shar are both at an Al-Anon meeting, which means I don't have to do the awkward work of explaining why I want to take public transit all the way to Jayden and Makayla's house instead of getting a ride from one of them. Because I'm not going there. I'm going to the Queer Alliance work party at Forrest's house.

I know I should tell them. But if I do, then Mom will ask me what my plan is for rescheduling my study session, and how I'm doing on my assignments, and if she finds out I already fell behind in English, I won't get to go. And I need this. Queer Alliance makes me happy, and I need to feel happy.

I finally settle on a long-sleeve shirt with thin gold, orange, and pink stripes, faded flared jeans, my now-dry Billie hoodie, and my chunky sneakers. Since coming out as nonbinary, picking my clothes has been easier in some ways and harder in others. I used to cycle through feminine phases followed by masculine ones, never comfortable in either, like something was wrong and I didn't know what it was. Like *I* was wrong, and I didn't know why. I didn't feel what other girls seemed to feel; a sense that they were what everyone perceived them to be. But I didn't feel like a boy either. In Queer Alliance, I got to know other nonbinary and trans people, and for the first time, I felt what cis people seemed to have: an anchor, grounding me without weighing me down. I realized that clothes could mean whatever I wanted them to, no matter how people saw me in them, and a lot of other realizations followed: I don't like it when shirts cling to my chest, or when my silhouette is all box and no softness. I don't think I want to try hormones, but I might want top surgery someday. I don't want to be seen as a girl, or as a boy, just as a person, and I wish society would see that too. Right now, a lot of days are a balancing act between what I want and how other people might see me, and some days are easier than others.

Today is an easier day. I feel good about the way I look. And I'm going to hang out with people who see *me*, not a gender. Yesterday's QA meeting was the best one yet. I felt at home again, at ease, the way I used to feel before the presidency, and this time, Forrest was part of that feeling. Leading the meeting with him was effortless. I'm not even worried about seeing him today, which is nice. The longer this peace between us goes on, the more I get used to it.

The bus ride to Forrest's is short. I make it to the stop just in time, and we rattle up from Rainier Avenue into the

Central District, where I get off across from a park and walk into the neighborhood. The houses get a little nicer as I go east, in the direction of Lake Washington. A few blocks in, I check my maps and take a right, then a left, and then I'm standing outside.

Forrest's house is bigger than I imagined it, but not a mansion. The house is painted dark green, camouflaging it behind the hedge and the garden that line the walkway to the front door. I step onto the low, wide wooden porch and hear laughter from inside. It sounds like people are already here, which is fine. I kind of wanted to arrive first, but it's OK.

I ring the doorbell and a chime sounds inside, followed by a bellowing bark. A moment later the door swings open, Forrest grinning at me as he restrains a whining, jumping golden pit bull.

"Come in, come in!" He backs away, dog in tow, and I edge inside. "I'm going to let him go, just turn around if he jumps on you and don't give him any attention until he stops doing it!"

Before I can say anything, he releases Simba and the dog barrels toward me, whole body wiggling. I brace myself, but the jump never comes; instead, Simba knocks me back a few steps, against the wall, and buries his face in my hands as I bend to pet him.

"You are such a good boy," I murmur, petting his short, soft fur as he settles, the wiggles subsiding, his weight leaning against my legs.

"Whoa," Forrest says, and I look up to see him watching me thoughtfully. "I've never seen him calm down so fast. Did you grow up with dogs?"

"Nope," I say. "We never had pets when I was a kid."

"He must just like you," he says. "You've got the Simba stamp of approval."

My cheeks warm, and I smile. Forrest's eyes glimmer, and we stand there quietly for a moment in the hallway. I don't know why, but my chest is fluttery all of a sudden, and I'm nervous and excited at the same time.

"We've got snacks in the living room," he says, taking a few steps away toward the rest of the house. I follow him, Simba trotting at my heels, my heart still racing.

The hallway opens up into a large, light-filled living room lined with soft-looking blue couches on a gray carpet. The walls are cream, and a fireplace, its bricks painted white, faces the couches. Riley is cross-legged on the carpet at the huge wooden coffee table, eating a cracker from the giant plate of snacks. Stef and Alexander lounge on one couch, and Anna sits at another, Nyx perched beside her.

"Sidney!" Anna jumps up and we hug.

A knock sounds and Simba zooms off toward the door, barking his head off. Everyone laughs as Forrest follows him, shaking his head. From the door, we hear voices, and Jayden and Makayla walk in to a flurry of hellos. They both spot me and Anna at the same time and beeline for our couch, Jayden settling on the floor in front of the table and Makayla sitting on Nyx's other side. It feels like we're warring families, my friends and Forrest's friends facing off across the coffee table, but no one is fighting. Forrest smiles at me from where he's standing behind his friends, and I smile back.

"So, what's the vision?" Alexander says, pulling everyone's attention. He missed the meeting yesterday, so we fill him in on the exhibit as he nods along. Forrest runs to a closet somewhere and comes back with a huge box of art supplies, Stef pulls some paints out of her backpack, and Jayden and Makayla dump out a bag filled with several packages of construction paper in all different colors. We spread out across the floor, divvying up the exhibit into small groups.

I end up beside Stef and Forrest, cutting posterboard into squares. Construction paper gets pasted onto each poster, so the white board makes a neat border behind the bright color. Each one will display a picture and biography of a famous queer person from our list. In another corner, Makayla, Anna, and Nyx are researching each person, finding the photos and writing up the bios for us to print out. Riley, Jayden, and Alexander are working on the timeline of historical events, two of them researching while the other cuts construction paper into triangles. We'll string them all together to make a banner of historical events people can follow from the entrance to the library all the way to the start of the exhibit, marked by a display of our library's queer books. Beyond it, we'll mount each profile on the end of a bookcase, making a perimeter around the tables in the center of the library.

A chorus of giggles bursts the silence, and I look up to see Jayden smacking Alexander's arm. I guess the history group project must be going well if they're this comfortable around each other.

"We need *music*," Forrest announces to the room and scrambles to his feet, almost stepping on my fingers as he dashes to a Bluetooth player on the fireplace mantel. He turns it on and stands there connecting his phone, and a moment later "Hot to Go!" by Chappell Roan blasts out at top volume. Anna shrieks and covers her ears, Riley flinches, and Forrest frantically presses the buttons on his phone until the sound is a normal level.

"Thanks, I'm awake now," I mutter as he sits back down beside me.

"You're welcome!" he says with a toothy smile. I roll my eyes and he smirks back. It feels like we're friends, bantering back and forth, the bitter edge that used to color our interactions now gone.

The music is a playlist of pop hits from the last few years, and I hum along as I glue construction paper to posterboard. Stef harmonizes with me, and I smile at her.

"You have a nice voice," I say.

"Thanks!" she says. "I'm in choir with this fool." She jerks a thumb at Forrest, who presses a hand to his chest, feigning hurt.

"You're in choir?" I ask him.

"Yeah, I love singing, and I thought it would help me not lose my singing voice when I started testosterone." He presses purple construction paper to a posterboard square.

"And theater? Does that mean you get to waive gym class?" I say.

"Hell yeah I do," he says, grinning. "I avoid sports at all costs."

"Closest he gets is coming to my breakdancing competitions," Alexander calls out from where he sits tapping away on his laptop.

"Always support the homies," Forrest says, shooting finger guns back.

"How long have you been breakdancing?" I ask.

"Since I was like . . . twelve?" Alexander says, running a hand over his close-cropped black hair. "I was really into hip-hop and some of my friends were taking classes, so I got my parents to let me go."

"And now he's winning everything," Forrest says with a grin.

Alexander blushes. "Not *everything.*" His expression turns mischievous. "Just *most* things."

"When's your next one?" I ask.

"November," he says. "Y'all should come."

"We'll be there," Jayden says, and I glance at him, but he's looking at Alexander. It does sound cool; I've never seen breakdancing in person before, just on my feed for whatever obscure reason the algorithm has decided to show it to me. I've been noticing more videos popping up for me lately, but I don't mind. It's impressive to watch.

Something pings in my brain. Jayden said he'd gone to the breakdancing club that Monday we both missed lunch with Anna and Makayla. Is he hanging out with Alexander? I mean, he must be, if he's gone to the club. But maybe he's been seeing the same videos as me and just thought it was cool.

Or he's ditching us. Maybe he's not on drugs, maybe he just found people better than us. Why would he want to be friends with us, anyway? He's probably pulling away, right now. On Monday, he'll be gone again, having a great time with Alexander and not even thinking about us. My chest aches, the beginning of tears stinging inside my nose. The grief is strong, surging inside me, and it feels like I'm going to drown.

That's not real. It's not happening.

That's not real. It's not happening.

That's not real. It's not happening.

Everyone else chatters around me, but they recede like shapes in a heavy fog as I repeat my mantra. A laugh cuts through my second set of three, and I look around. Everyone is smiling and talking. No one knows what I'm thinking, which is good, because if they did, they'd think I'm crazy, and then they'd pull away for sure.

♥

By the time parents start arriving, we've finished everything we wanted to do. We decide to set up the exhibit at one of the lunch periods this week, and one by one, as people leave, we clean up. My thoughts have faded to whispers, but I'm still in an anxious haze, not really paying attention to the others as I gather up the materials around me.

I take an armful of paper scraps to the recycling bin in the kitchen, poking around for a minute before I find it at the end of one of the butcher block counters, by the back door. The kitchen is nice, as big as our living room at home, with an island, a porcelain sink, and three times the counter space. Simba follows me, snuffling at the ground while I throw the paper away. I crouch to pet him, and he licks my face. It makes me smile, and when I stand up, I feel a little more present.

Back in the living room, Forrest is the only one there, dropping the last few markers into his bin of art supplies.

"Did everyone leave already?" I ask.

"Jayden's in the bathroom," he says.

"And I'm in the hallway," Makayla calls out, poking her head around the corner into the room. She frowns at me quizzically. "Sid, how are you getting home?"

"Uhhh . . . can I get a ride?" If Mom and Shar are already home and see me get dropped off by Jayden and Makayla, they'll never suspect I wasn't studying.

"Totally!" She smiles.

I follow her into the hallway and slip my shoes back on. We turn to Forrest, who waves at us awkwardly.

"See you in class," he says, and we echo it, standing there in a moment of silence. Jayden appears, zipping up his jacket, and then we're hustling out the door while Forrest holds Simba back. The twins' mom is waiting for us in their sedan.

I look back before I reach the car, just in time to see the golden glow of the hallway and the side of Forrest's face before the door shuts. His mom never came out to say hi, and I never heard a sound from his little sister. Where were they? Is he home alone? It must be weird, being all by yourself in a giant house.

In the back seat of the car, I pull up our text thread. I want to say something, but everything I think of sounds too earnest, so I find a funny video in my likes and send that instead.

Thanks again for hosting, I add.

A moment later, a reply pops up. *No problem. Simba's helping me clean up the food.* And a photo of Simba with very guilty eyes, a slice of cheese hanging out of his mouth. I laugh.

"What's up?" Jayden asks from the front seat as Makayla looks over beside me.

"Oh, uh, just a meme," I say. I don't know why, but I don't want to tell them I'm texting Forrest. They'll probably think it's weird that I'm suddenly so friendly with someone I hated not that long ago. And I don't want anything to make this weird.

THE NEXT DAY, DAD IS ON TIME TO PICK ME UP FOR OUR hike. When I slide into the passenger seat, he pulls me into a tight hug with one arm, and I hug him back.

"Perfect day for it, huh?" he says as I buckle my seat belt. It's almost Halloween, but the weather hasn't quite turned to unending rain just yet; instead, it's cool and sunny today, just a hint of crispness in the air, the leaves on the maples around our house starting to turn.

I nod, and he smiles before turning to the Breathalyzer. A moment later, he puts the key in the ignition and the car starts. "Had just enough whiskey not to tip it off," he says with a wink.

I can tell he's joking—*I got a DUI and didn't talk to my kid all summer, ha ha ha!*—but it's not that funny. I know Dad, though, and it's better if I react like it is, so I summon a smile, and that seems to satisfy him.

"You wanna pick the music today?" he asks, slapping the dashboard as we pull away. I settle my backpack on the floor between my feet and dig my phone out of my jacket pocket, plugging it into the car stereo. I skip past all the pop girlies and finally land on Paramore, something both of us can enjoy listening to.

"Man, I haven't heard this one in a minute," he says as the first song comes on. "What a classic. Your mom used to listen to this album all the time. It came out a few years after you were born."

I can see the year in my music app, but I just nod. I remember being in the back seat of the car as Mom drove me to and from elementary school, how she'd smile at me in the rearview mirror as she sang along. This album tastes like chocolate milk, feels like a seat belt strapped across my body. Even though it's a rock album, to me it's a moment of calm before the chaos of going to school and coming home. I hope it's a good omen for today, something to keep us anchored.

♥

The trail Dad picked starts out near one of the visitor centers. The place is busy, but as we climb, the groups of tourists and other hikers fade away. Concrete under my boots turns to dirt, rocks, and twigs as we snake up a ridge. Dad takes the lead and sets a slow pace, which is fine with me, because I'm not the speediest hiker either.

The trail is quiet except for birdcalls and the occasional piercing whistle of a marmot. I scan the rocks around us, hoping to see one, and am rewarded by the sight of a small, furry, beaver-like creature standing upright to stare at me from a nearby outcropping. He screams and disappears, and Dad and I both burst out laughing.

As the path gets steeper, my breathing gets heavier. Physical exertion isn't really my thing. My thighs are already burning and I'm sweating despite the chillier temperature at this elevation, so I stop to take off my jacket and stuff it in my pack. A few minutes later, the trail slacks off, and we emerge from the tree line into a meadow.

"Would you look at that," Dad murmurs as we stop, staring across the meadow in front of us. It rolls away like a soft green carpet, and across from us is Mount Rainier, no longer a distant vision on the horizon. Even far away, she's got the gravitational pull of a planet, but now we're close enough to see the surface, and the view is breathtaking. She's cloaked in snow across the broad, rolling curve of the peak, and swathes of white blanket her sides, broken by spines and valleys of dark gray rock that slope downward from the sky to the earth. I can see a waterfall pouring over one of them, tiny in the distance, continuing its path down a glacier toward the basin.

Dad hands me a granola bar, and we stand there together eating our snacks, gazing at the mountain. I gulp some water from my water bottle without taking my eyes off her; I want to memorize this moment, this image, this feeling. Dad motions me forward, phone in hand, and takes a few photos of me smiling with the mountain behind me. Then he comes forward so we can take selfies, and I lean into him, both of our faces beaming on his screen.

I pull out my phone and snap a few of my own pictures, wishing I could send them to my friends, and to Forrest too. There's no reception up here, so I don't know if he's texted me this morning. Maybe I'll have messages waiting for me when we get back to civilization.

After a few more minutes, we turn away, cutting through the meadow. The mountain looms in my peripheral vision, pulling my gaze back to it again and again. I wish I could live in this meadow. Up here, my thoughts are clear the way they are in the garage with Shar. It feels, for a moment, like my brain is my friend instead of my enemy.

"How's the Queer Alliance thing coming along?" Dad asks.

I blink. He remembered. "Um, it's OK?"

"You mentioned you were sharing the presidency with someone. Started with an *F*?"

"Forrest," I say. "Yeah, at first I was . . . not sure how that was going to go. But it's working out. I don't know. We're kind of . . . talking?"

"Oooh!" Dad says, turning back to waggle his eyebrows at me. "Talking?"

"Oh my god, not like that." I roll my eyes. "Just, like, friendly, which is weird."

"Weird how?"

"We didn't have the best history," I say. "He is—was pretty annoying. And I was worried . . ." I trail off. I've never really talked like this with Dad. When I was a kid, it was Mom who cuddled me when I cried, Mom who talked to the principal when a kid was bullying me in elementary school, Mom who was always watching over me. So it was Mom I turned to when I needed something. After the divorce, Dad was so in and out of my life that confiding in him never even crossed my mind; instead, I was busy wondering where he was, whether he was OK, and if he'd even be coherent the next time we talked.

I swallow hard, blinking back tears.

"You were worried . . ." Dad prompts me, a few steps ahead, his back to me as we approach another stand of trees. The trail is looping, heading back to the start, and there's an incline ahead.

"Worried he'd mess it up, I guess," I say, digging my toes into the sudden steepness of the trail. For a moment, we're both silent, concentrating on pushing up the hill, and then we're over the top and hiking down into the trees again.

"But he hasn't," Dad says.

"Nope," I say. "Kind of the opposite."

"Well, sometimes people can surprise us," Dad says. "Do you like talking to him?"

I nod, then remember he can't see me. "Yeah, I do actually."

"Then don't overthink it," Dad says. "Just do what feels right."

I catch myself before I laugh. Dad has no idea what goes on inside my head; overthinking is an understatement. But up here, it almost feels that easy. Just do what feels right.

Which I guess means that Forrest and I might be . . . friends?

♥

On Friday, I wake up early to put together my Halloween costume. Strawberries are my favorite fruit, but I don't have a whole lot of clothes in the right color palette. I'm more of an earth tones person, my coat hangers full of dark green, navy blue, burnt orange, gold, and black.

I pick out a shirt that's more of a red-orange, and in the back of my closet I find a red velvet blazer I got at the thrift store last year. I put on dark green corduroys—my legs can be the strawberry vines—and my olive green beanie, for the little leaves on top. In the bathroom, I draw a strawberry on my cheek in bright red marker.

When I come out to grab breakfast, Mom is standing at the counter capping her coffee thermos. She sees me and her whole face lights up.

"Look at you!" she says. "Are you a . . ." She squints at me, taking in the whole outfit from my hat to my shoes.

"A strawberry," I say after a few moments of silence.

"Yes, of course," she says. "So cute. I love it."

"Aren't you usually gone by now?" I ask.

"I know," she says, rushing to the door and stuffing her feet into her loafers. "I'm late! I stayed up working on a new brand direction for the client—they did *not* like what we came up with originally, and I'm the lead, so." She grimaces. "It's my responsibility! OK, your lunch is in the fridge, HappyHalloweenIloveyoubye!'

And she's gone, the door slamming shut behind her. I wait for the click of the lock, but she must really be in a hurry, because it doesn't come. A moment later, her car starts up and peels away outside.

"Thanks, I love you too," I mumble, as if she's still here, and pull open the fridge, snatching my lunch box. She didn't have any idea what my costume was. I want to run back into my room and rip off all my clothes, scrub the stupid strawberry off my cheek. If I'd been thinking about it, I would have gone thrifting or borrowed clothes from one of my friends, but it's too late now.

I'm a strawberry. And it's time to go.

♥

When I get to school, I see only a few people in costumes. Most people are dressed normally, and next to them I'm a pimple on unblemished skin, bright red and way too obvious. On the way to my locker, I definitely hear giggles. They're probably not about me, but I keep my eyes ahead. Either way, I don't want to know.

I text my friends to find out where they are, and weave my way from my locker to Anna's, where I find her and Makayla. It's not hard, because Anna is dressed in head-to-toe bright orange. Her earrings are huge orange slices made of acrylic, her dress is practically fluorescent, and her tights have a pattern that matches her earrings. Her eye makeup looks like a sunrise.

"Wow," I say, stopping in front of them. Makayla is wearing a yellow shirt and mustard-colored pants, and gold eyeshadow that pops against her brown skin. She's drawn a small lemon at either temple, just under the outer corners of her eyes. I should have done something cute and subtle like that. The giant strawberry on my right cheek feels like a bad tattoo.

"All the fruits are here!" Anna says, throwing her arms out.

"We look like the first half of a Pride flag," Makayla says. "Plus the green." She gestures to my pants.

"I forgot until, like, last night," I say, grimacing.

"It's all good!" she says. "You look cute."

"I don't, but thank you," I say, and she's about to respond, but the bell cuts us off. I head to class, feeling eyes on me. I wish I'd brought a change of clothes. I wish I'd thought about this ahead of time. Maybe Jayden had the right idea about doing his own costume. This is probably why he didn't want to coordinate with us. We're dumb, and dorky, especially me. At least Anna and Makayla made their costumes look cute. It's just me who ruined it.

Maybe I'm the reason he's pulling away. If he is pulling away, that is. I want to ask him, the urge crawling under my skin like a monster about to burst out. I'd seem weird and possessive, though, and he would definitely stop being friends with me after that. It's probably fine.

But what if it's not?

♥

I'm the first one in Mr. Harrison's classroom at lunch. He waves from his office, and I grab a chair to start setting up for Queer Alliance.

"HO HO HO! MEEEERRY CHRISTMAS!" a familiar voice bellows behind me. I turn around and there's Forrest in full Santa mode, from the hat, wig, and fake beard, to the stomach that's probably a pillow buttoned under red velvet, to his shiny black boots. His hazel eyes glint behind gold-rimmed costume glasses.

"Santa? In October?" I snort, scanning him up and down.

"It's a commentary on how capitalism starts marketing us Christmas stuff way too early," he says.

"How intellectual."

"I try," he says, eyeing me up and down. "And you are . . . one of my elves?"

I look down at my clothes. It didn't occur to me this morning, but now I see it: the red and green color scheme.

"An elf who really likes strawberries?" He's looking at my cheek now, and I cover it with one hand. "That's very non-binary of you."

"I'm supposed to be a strawberry," I say. "Just a strawberry. No elf. Me and Makayla and Anna—"

"Ohhhh!" he says. "I saw them earlier. Now it all makes sense. All of you together make a gay little smoothie."

"Strawberry, orange, and . . . lemon?" I make a face. "That's so random."

"The tartness would be good!" he says.

"OK, weirdo," I say.

"Takes one to know one." He drops his bag as I groan.

"Do you ever *not* have a comeback?" I say, joining him as we drag more chairs into place.

"Nope. I'm always prepared. Like a Boy Scout." He dashes around me, pushing a chair ahead of him. I wince as its legs screech across the floor. "It would have been cool if you were an elf, though. You'd look cute in a little elf hat."

I stop, staring at him, but he's oblivious, racing to get more chairs into place as the other club members trickle in. Forrest thinks I would look cute in an elf hat? Forrest thinks of me as someone who is, or would be, cute?

Forrest thinks of *me* that way?

What alternate reality is this?

"Sid!" A hand claps my shoulder and I twitch, snapping back to earth. Jayden's beside me. "The exhibit is a big hit. Mx. Prager said people are really getting into following the little history trail thing."

"Oh, sweet!" I scan him up and down. I may not be an elf, but he's decked out in a costume that looks a lot like—"Link?" I ask. Jayden is a huge fan of the *Legend of Zelda* games.

He grins. "You got it."

"You look *so* good!" I say, touching the fake pointed tips attached to the tops of his ears. "What are these made of?"

"EVA foam!" he says. "Alexander showed me how to make them. He's really into cosplay."

"Oh!" I tilt my head. "I didn't know you two were becoming, like, *friends* friends."

"Yeah, I don't know!" He rubs the back of his neck, looking around the room. "We've hung out a few times outside of school to work on group project stuff and it was chill."

"That's cool." I stare at the ear tips. They look almost real, painted a color that very nearly matches Jayden's skin. "Those are seriously good."

"I know, right?" He touches them lightly. "Hey, we gotta start planning for Trans Awareness Week soon. It's only a few weeks from now."

"Yes. You're right. Totally." I look around. The seats are filling up, and there's even a few people standing. I don't recognize some of these faces. I see Forrest's friend from theater, though—Mercury—standing outside the circle. She catches my eye and smiles, waving at me.

"We need more chairs," I say.

"On it." Jayden steps away, directing people to scoot outward and widen the circle to let more people join it.

I look around the room, watching everyone take their place. By this time of year, we usually have a set group of people, smaller than the beginning, but a solid core that will carry us to June. We've never gotten an influx of new members like this before. Is this from the party? Or the exhibit?

Or both?

Is this whole co-presidency thing actually . . . working?

AT MAKAYLA AND JAYDEN'S THAT WEEKEND, THEIR PARents are having friends over to watch a football game, so Makayla and I hole up in her room instead. I lie on the floor, working on my rough draft of the long essay for English, and Makayla sits on the bed, working on hers. I can hear Jayden dimly every so often through the wall, cursing and whooping in turn at his video game. When he whoops at the same time as a loud cheer from the living room, we both flinch.

"Love a nice screech with my studying playlist," Makayla says dryly.

"Really elevates the production." I roll over onto my back, away from the laptop, and stare at the ceiling. "I'm so glad no one in my family watches football." Which is technically true; none of the family members I live with watch it. Now that I think about it, though, I don't know if my dad watches football. He did a few times, when I was younger, but after the divorce, I didn't see him often enough to know.

I guess I can ask him when I see him next.

What if he's dead right now? a voice whispers out of nowhere. *He got in a car accident and I just don't know it.* I squeeze my eyes shut. Why is my brain like this?

That's not real. It's not happening.

That's not real. It's not happening.

That's not real. It's not happening.

I grab my phone. I don't have to wait until I see Dad; now that we're talking again, I can just text him and ask. And when he answers, I'll know he's OK, and not dead. It's like a special two for one deal, sponsored by anxiety.

Do you like football? I ask him. A minute goes by, and then he texts back.

I don't follow it closely, but I watch a game here and there when I'm bored. Why? You getting into it?

God no, I text back, and he laugh reacts. I smile. *What are you doing right now?*

I'm about to meet up with my AA sponsor, he says. *What about you kiddo?*

Studying. We have this huge assignment for English class and I'm trying to keep on top of it.

Good, good. Let me know if you need a proofreader.

I heart react to the message. This might be the most normal text interaction we've ever had: no snarky comments about Mom, no drunken ranting, no nostalgic reminiscing about my childhood. It's the kind of conversation I imagine my friends get to have with their dads all the time.

If he's willingly seeing his sponsor today, then he really must be taking this sobriety thing seriously.

"Hey, so . . ." Makayla says. She waits, like she wants me to fill in the blank.

I turn away from my phone. "What's up?"

"I was thinking . . ." She doodles something on the corner of her notebook page. "I might want to start using they/them pronouns. And still use she/her."

"Makayla!" I sit up. "I love this for you. She/theys are so cool."

She blushes. "Thanks."

"How long have you been thinking about this? I know we talked about it a while ago, but . . ." I haven't thought about our conversation since it happened, but now it comes flooding back. I should have remembered and checked in with her. Or maybe not. Maybe that would have made her feel self-conscious.

"I don't know, since the end of summer? Just watching Jayden's transition, and knowing you and Anna . . . it got me thinking." She twirls one dark curl around her—their finger. "I feel like a girl some days, and some days I just feel like . . . something else. Undefined. My own thing. I don't have words for it yet."

"That's totally chill. You don't have to have words." I get to my feet and sit on the end of the bed, facing them. "Do you want to change anything else, like try out a different name?"

She shakes her head. "No, I like my name."

"Oh my god." I smack my forehead. "You were never our token cis person."

They half laugh. "Yeah, that was part of it. I knew y'all were joking when you said stuff like that, but after a while it didn't feel right. But I didn't know how to correct you because I wasn't sure why it didn't feel right. I wasn't sure if I was allowed to be . . ." She trails off and shrugs.

"Oh." I clasp my hands together in my lap. "Makayla. I'm so sorry."

She nods, looking down at the page in her lap. "Thanks."

We sit in silence for a few minutes, my thoughts swirling over the muted beat of the music in the background. It's like my brain is a canvas and there's a monkey hurling paint at it. Or maybe my brain is the monkey hurling paint at *me*. Either way, the words are coming fast, one over another like a cacophony: *You're a bad friend you don't deserve Makayla they don't want to be friends with you anymore they're going to ditch you they hate you—*

"Have you told anyone else yet?" I ask. The words from my mouth sound far away, the ones in my head clamoring above them, images joining them now in flashes: *Makayla's face angry, Makayla turning away, I'm in the hallway at school screaming after her and everyone's watching her leave me because I'm selfish and I never noticed—*

"Yeah, I told Jayden a few days ago, and I'm gonna FaceTime Anna later," they say. "I'll tell my parents at some point. I don't think I'm going to do a big coming out. The people who get it get it, you know?"

"Totally." I nod vigorously. "Hey, I'm going to the bathroom. I'll be right back."

She gives me a thumbs-up and I exit the room, forcing myself to walk at a normal pace down the hall, past Jayden's closed door, and into their bathroom. I close the door and sit on the white tile floor, pulling my legs up and resting my forehead on my knees, staring into the space between my thighs and my chest. *All your friends are going to leave you they hate you you're a bad friend that's not REAL! IT'S NOT HAPPENING.*

THAT'S NOT REAL. IT'S NOT HAPPENING.

THAT'S NOT REAL. IT'S NOT HAPPENING.

How can I even think this way when Makayla just fucking came *out* to me? They came out to me and all I can think about is my own reaction, my own fear.

I'm so fucking selfish.

♥

I'm relieved when our study session ends and Shar picks me up. The longer I was with Makayla, the harder it was to act like I was fine. When I came back from the bathroom, they didn't seem to notice anything was wrong, but my thoughts didn't stop. I'd stare at my laptop, and a thought would pop up, and I'd whack it down, and another would take its place. I closed my laptop with exactly two more sentences written, bringing my draft total to one of the six pages I need.

But as we drive away, the anxiety stays with me. I rest my head against the car seat, closing my eyes. I'm exhausted, but the voices are a dull roar, a buzzing itch in my skull, in my whole body. I need to ask Makayla if everything's OK, I *need* to, before this feeling spins out of control, but I don't want to make their coming out about me. In my pocket, I grip my phone, fighting the urge.

Shar pulls up outside the house twenty minutes later and I follow her up the walk without a word, heading for my bedroom. I close the door behind me and lean against it, sliding all the way down to the floor.

My phone is in my hand and I'm typing. I have to stop, I can't send this text, but I'm still typing and then my thumb is over the button and I send it, I sent it, it's there on the screen, Makayla's profile picture smiling at me and the three dots appear, she's responding, she saw what I wrote and it's over, it's all over, all my friends will know what a pathetic, needy freak I am, and—

Yeah of course we're OK! she says.

I clutch the phone to my chest and sob silently into my knees. She doesn't hate me. She doesn't hate me. She doesn't hate me.

Or is she just saying that?

Stop. I tell myself.

Stop.

Stop.

Stop. Stop. Stop.

Stop. Stop. Stop.

I repeat the mantra for what feels like forever, until my brain finally goes quiet.

♥

I wake up in the morning feeling drained. Thoughts pulse in my mind, nothing clear, just shapes circling below the surface, waiting to strike. My group turns in our history project, but I just watch them as they high-five. At lunch, I eat my food quietly, listening to my friends talk, and when I come home, I sit at the table and stare at my homework like it's written in another language. I copy the answers out of the back of the book for math, not bothering to even try to show my work. My rough draft for English sits untouched on my laptop. I'm afraid. Afraid to move too fast, afraid to try too hard, afraid whatever I do will wake the thoughts up again and this time I won't be able to stop them.

Dad texts me that night. *How's it going?*

OK, I say.

Just OK?

I'm just feeling kind of anxious, I type, then stare at the words for a second. Confiding my feelings in Dad is not something I've ever done, but I did talk to him about Forrest on our hike, and that turned out all right. Helpful, even. I send the message, and wait for his response.

About anything in particular? he asks.

I don't even know where to start with an answer to that one, or if there is an answer at all, one that would make sense to my dad, anyway. *It's more of a general feeling*, I say.

That's a tough one, he says.

Yeah, I say, and all of a sudden I wish he was here, hugging me. *Do you want to go hiking again soon?*

I sure do! he says. *I know we talked about doing Olympic National Park next. How about Sunday?*

I say yes without a second thought. Being surrounded by trees, as far away from my life and my thoughts as possible, sounds like exactly what I need this weekend.

♥

On Thursday, I'm at my locker between second and third period when someone pokes my arm. I turn and Forrest is standing there, hoodie cinched tight around his face for some reason. We've been texting back and forth all week, sending memes, songs, pictures of our pets, and the odd snarky comment about school. His messages are little anchors in my day, something I've started to anticipate every time I pick up my phone.

"What's up?" he says.

"Not a lot," I say. My voice sounds flat, and I hope he doesn't notice.

"I just realized we didn't meet this week," he says, doing a little dance move in place. It's so random, and so silly, and it makes me smile. He's right, and not only that, but the idea of meeting didn't even cross my mind.

"Do you think we still need to?" I ask. "I feel like things with Queer Alliance are going really well. And you don't annoy the shit out of me anymore." I smile again, to show I'm joking.

"What a compliment," he says, placing a hand over his heart. "Yeah, maybe we don't need to?"

"OK," I say, and we both stand there. I should feel glad, I think, but I kind of wish I hadn't said anything at all. The little energy left inside me deflates. *He's glad to be rid of you NO STOP.*

STOP.

STOP.

I look at my locker, then at him, and he scratches the back of his head.

"How's your essay going?" he says.

"Ugh." I close my eyes and bang my forehead lightly against my locker door. "Don't ask."

"That bad, huh?"

I side-eye him. "Sounds like yours is going fine."

"I mean . . ." He grins. "It's coming along."

"Can you . . ." I can't believe I'm about to ask this, but the words come out of my mouth before I can think twice. "Help me?"

His eyes widen. "Wait. What? You want *my* help? You. Want *my*. Help."

"I don't know! Never mind."

"No, it's all good," he says, laughing. "I'm sorry. I just . . . I don't think I've ever heard you ask for help before. Let alone from me."

"I ask for help sometimes!" I say. "Like, um . . ." I search my memory.

"See?" he says, then puts his hands up when I glare at him. " OK, OK. Meet at lunch today?"

"I guess," I say. "If you really want to."

"Hey, you asked me," he says, backing away as the bell rings. "Remember that! You asked me!"

I wave my hand at him like I'm swatting a mosquito, and he turns, booking it down the hall to wherever his next class is.

"Jerk," I mutter, but I'm smiling.

♥

When I walk into the library at lunch, Forrest waves from our usual table. I sit across from him and pull out my laptop, trying to ignore the anxious fluttering in my chest that's been there since yesterday.

"So, are you really doing all right with this essay?" I ask. My laptop comes out of sleep mode, the document still open on the screen. Seeing it there makes my stomach swoop. I'm so behind. If Mom finds out—she's working so hard right now and this will just add to her burden, I'll add to her burden, I'm such a burden, the laptop goes fuzzy and she's there, in my head, or I'm there, in the living room, and she's glaring at me. "I never should have let you do Queer Alliance this year," she says, voice raised. "It's just a distraction, a waste of time. You'll need to drop it and let Forrest take over. God, I'm so tired of your bullshit, I—"

"Hey," a voice says. "You OK?"

I look up, blinking. Forrest is watching me. I nod. "Sorry. Spaced out."

"Yeah, seemed like it."

"Oh god." I cover my face.

"Hey, it's all good," he says. "What do you have so far?"

"Exactly one page," I say, clutching my face tighter.

"Wow," he says. "You really are behind. You know it's due at the end of next week, right?"

"Hey!" I drop my hands, glaring at him. I know he's joking, but it stings. *I never should have let you do Queer Alliance this y—NO.* "Are you offering me help or brutal honesty?"

"Both?" He grins.

I snort. "Fine." I show him the lists Anna and I brainstormed, and we start picking out elements that support what my thesis is trying to argue. As we do that, the thesis sharpens in my mind, and I revise it, deleting one phrase and typing another, finessing the words until we both exclaim and high-five.

Once I have the thesis and the supporting arguments, we match each one to the right section of the essay format Lundahl wants us to use. Forrest is patient, asking me questions about where things fit without rushing me for the answer, and when I get frustrated, he's ready with a joke.

"You are weirdly good at this," I say, sitting back in my chair.

He shrugs. "I've had a *lot* of tutoring. I'm just doing what they did with me."

"Did it work for you?"

"Kind of? Sometimes? Not always. Once I got diagnosed with ADHD, my mom found a tutor who specializes in it, and that's been great. She's super cool, never judges me or anything, and she has it too."

"When did you get diagnosed?" I ask without thinking, and grimace. "Sorry, that's rude."

"You're good. I don't mind talking about it." He waves a hand. "Freshman year. I wanted to go on meds, but my parents weren't into the idea at first. They thought I'd have to go on a stimulant and they were concerned about it affecting my brain. But there are more options now and my tutor talked to them about it. She takes a non-stimulant, so I think that helped them get over it."

"Nice."

"What about you?" he asks.

"Oh, um, I'm not diagnosed with anything."

"But you've got something, right?"

I flush. "What makes you say that?"

He raises his eyebrows at me. "Come on. You brought a posterboard of reasons why you should be Queer Alliance president to the election meeting. And you made a speech."

"That's called being prepared."

"Like how you're so prepared for this essay?"

I gasp. "You are so shady!"

"The real Slim Shady, that's me." He pats his chest, smirking.

"An Eminem reference? Really?"

He turns up his palms. "Hey, you understood it."

"Only because my dad's a superfan."

He laughs. "Oh my god, so's mine. He still has a concert T-shirt he wears around the house."

"Wooooowwwwwww."

"I know."

The bell buzzes and we both startle, then snicker. I gather my notebooks, and he dumps his lunch wrappers in the trash can nearby.

"What's your next class?" he asks as we walk out.

"Math," I say.

"Oh, sweet. I'm heading that way too." He smiles at me, and I smile back.

"Are you doing anything after school?" I ask. If he's got rich parents, he's probably in a million extracurriculars.

"Nothing today," he answers. "Usually it's either tutoring or golf."

"You play golf?"

"That's right." He makes a motion like he's swinging a club. "I suck at it, but my parents made me pick a sport and that one has the least amount of running. You will *not* catch me chasing a ball up and down a field."

I laugh. "Relatable."

"What about you?"

I shrug. "This essay, I guess."

"If you need more help, I could come over," he says.

I look down at my feet, threading through the crowd ahead of him. Forrest, in my house. The thought freaks me out a little bit, but it also feels . . . well, fine. I'd rather be with him than alone with my thoughts, trying to focus instead of spiraling for three hours until Shar and Mom get home. If Mom is even home at the usual time; she's been staying at work later and later.

Talking to Forrest today made me feel better, made the thoughts fade to a faint fog hanging in the back of my mind. So maybe, if I keep spending time with him, they'll stay that way. That itching buzz, that sick black-hole pull that puppets me into someone I don't want to be, will leave me alone.

"Are you sure?" I ask as we come to a stop in front of my classroom.

He grins. "I don't have anything better to do."

I cross my arms. "Oh, because hanging out with me is such a chore?"

He sighs dramatically. "It is, but someone has to do it, I guess." I shove his shoulder and he darts away, cackling. "Have fun in class!"

I HALF THINK FORREST WILL DITCH ME AFTER SCHOOL, BUT when I get to my locker, he's there, winding one string of his hoodie tight around a finger.

"You're losing circulation," I point out as I open my locker.

He grins. The tip of his finger has gone bright red. "I know."

I snort. "OK then." I get what I need, then shut the door and turn to him. "You ready?"

"Take me to your lair," he says.

"You are so corny," I say, heading for the doors.

He falls into step beside me. "You like it."

"Do I?" I raise my eyebrows at him as we step into the cold gray afternoon. It's not raining, but it feels like it should be.

"You're hanging out with me, aren't you?" he says, elbowing me. It's light, just a little bump, but I feel it like an electric shock. I don't think Forrest and I have ever touched before. I grab the straps of my backpack, holding them tight.

Don't overthink it, Dad said. I guess I really am friends with Forrest.

As we walk to the train, he asks me if I've seen the newest episode of an animated show he's into, and when I say no, he spends the next ten minutes explaining the entire backstory and the characters until he can tell me about the episode with the proper context.

"You are deeply invested in this," I say when he's done.

"It's one of my hyperfixations," he says. "Was it too much?"

"Not at all." We scan our transit cards at the train entrance and ride the long escalator down to the platform. It's like descending into a bunker, all concrete and metal and fluorescent lights. "You make it fun. I feel like I've seen the whole show and I didn't even know about it until you told me. I could hold a whole conversation with someone about it now."

He laughs. "Do you have anything like that? A hyperfixation-type thing?"

"I mean, I'm not neurodivergent that I know of," I say. "So it's not really the same, but I guess queer stuff. Queer history, and queer musicians, and Queer Alliance . . . if it's gay, I'm into it."

A rumble starts deep in the tunnel, signaling the train's arrival, and a moment later it whooshes in front of us, slowing until it stops and the doors open. We step aside to let people out first and then get on, finding an open two-seater by a window. The seats are small, and our legs touch, my light blue denim against his black sweats, our bags perched on our laps.

"What made you get into all that?" he asks, right as I'm about to start overanalyzing whether or not I should pull my leg away. "Besides the fact that anything queer is just objectively superior."

"Right?" I say. "We moved around a lot when I was little, my dad had a hard time keeping a job, so I always felt like anything could change at any time. But when I figured out I was queer and joined the alliance, it made me feel at home, like I was part of something solid. Like, history exists. Queer people exist. None of that can be changed, even if people try to."

"Damn." He nods, raising his eyebrows. "That's deep."

I blush, shrugging. "I don't know."

"No, it is. That makes a lot of things make sense." He jiggles his leg, fingers tapping on his knee as he gazes past me, out the window, even though there's nothing on the other side but the dark tunnel before the next station.

"What do you mean?" I ask.

"Don't take this the wrong way, but when the year started, I thought you were kind of . . ."

"Uptight?" I say quietly, my heart sinking.

"No, no!" He waves his hands. "Well, you obviously wanted things your way and it was annoying, but mostly you just seemed so *serious*."

"I mean, that's how things get done," I say, hugging my bag tighter.

"No, I get that. And I'm not that good at getting things done, so—"

"Do you really think I think I'm better than you?" I blurt out.

"What?"

"That day . . . when I asked you to give up the presidency."

He frowns, deep in thought for a minute, and then his eyes widen. "I totally forgot about that. Oh my god." He claps a hand to his face. "No. That was just . . . I was texting with my dad right before you walked up, and he was just really pissing me off, so I was already in a bad mood. I . . ." He grimaces. "I'm sorry. Have you been thinking about that all this time?"

I shrug, staring out the window as we pull into one of the downtown stations. "Not really. I just remembered it now. Because of what you were saying."

"Sidney."

I turn my head slightly so I can look at him, just barely. His eyes are fixed on me as he pulls off his hoodie and turns his body toward me. His knee presses into my thigh.

"You are serious, but it's not a bad thing," he says. "You're also super funny, and really smart, and you have really good ideas."

"What?" I crinkle my nose.

"It's true." He smiles. "Look, I'd almost always rather have a party, because I think you can't really get work done unless you have fun too. Look at Pride parades. They started as a protest, *and* they were also a way for the community to get together, support each other, and celebrate who we are. Now they're giant parties, and yeah, the capitalism of it all is irritating, but they're also fun, and beautiful, and we need that. We need that to keep going." He pauses. "Sorry. I'll get off my soapbox, but the point is, we need fun because it keeps us going through the serious shit. The work. Changing things, and raising awareness, and building power. Like your exhibit idea. Yeah, some of our newbies at QA came because of the party, but half the new people who were there came because of the exhibit. Because it taught them something new, or made them curious, or whatever." He clasps his hands. "It all works together."

"*That* is deep," I say.

He blushes, something I've never seen before; his cheeks and forehead redden, even the bridge of his nose under his freckles. "Thanks."

"I had no idea you were into social justice like that," I say.

He tilts his head. "You thought I was just an annoying class clown?"

"No, no—" I protest, even though that's exactly what I think. Or used to think. The longer we're co-presidents, the less I remember exactly why I found him so annoying before.

He laughs. "I'm just teasing you. But yeah, that's one of my other things. My hyperfixations, or whatever you wanna call it."

"That's cool."

He shrugs, smiling. It's hard to believe the revote is happening in two weeks. I haven't been thinking about it as much lately, and the idea of not sharing the presidency with Forrest anymore feels a little odd, almost wrong somehow. Add that to the list of feelings I never thought I'd have. It seems like there's more and more of those lately.

I look out the window as we pull into another station, and—

"This is us!" I jump out of my seat, and he follows me off the train with a crowd of commuters headed home.

We're both quiet on the elevator ride up to street level, checking our phones, and I text Mom and Shar to let them know I have a friend coming over. It doesn't even feel weird to call Forrest a friend.

Should it feel weird that it *doesn't* feel weird?

When we get to my front walk, the nerves kick in. Did I leave anything embarrassing lying out in my bedroom? Maybe my journal is open on my bed, or there's a box of tampons on the bathroom counter, or—but this is Forrest. He's trans. He knows what a tampon is. *Don't overthink it.*

Inside, the house is quiet, except for Brekky's demanding meows as he trots toward us, tail high. He goes straight for Forrest, bypassing my outstretched hand altogether.

"Betrayal!" I gasp, and Forrest chuckles, kneeling to scratch Brekky behind the ears. The cat arches his neck and purrs, leaning his head into Forrest's hand.

"Guess I'm not the only animal whisperer," I say. "Earl Grey will be the real test, though."

As if on cue, a tiny mew comes from the direction of the kitchen. Earl Grey peeks around the corner and, as I watch, slinks along the wall until she stops a few feet away from Forrest. She sits upright, gazing at him with her round green eyes.

"Wow," I say, and she flinches, dashing behind the armchair. We both laugh.

Forrest sets his stuff down and follows me to the kitchen, boosting himself up to sit on the counter while I scoop the cats' food into their bowls. Once they're eating, I rejoin him.

"Do you want anything?" I ask, opening the fridge. "We have some soda, and sparkling water, and juice . . ."

"What kind of soda?"

"Ginger ale."

"I'll have that."

I hand him the bottle, open one for myself, and we each take a sip. Now that we're here, in my house, I realize that I did *not* think this through when I blurted out my invite. What are we supposed to do now? I could show him my room, but the thought sends a ripple through my stomach.

"Can I have a tour?" he asks, as if he knows my thoughts.

"Sure!" I say, a little too enthusiastically. Probably. I don't know. I'm second-guessing everything. I take a deep breath and turn with my arms out. "So this is our kitchen."

"Oh, I was *wondering* what this room was called," he says, smirking.

I roll my eyes. "And of course, our living room and dining area." I gesture toward the front room, and take a few steps out of the kitchen. He jumps off the counter and follows me into the hallway, where I show him the bathroom with its yellow walls and sunflower-pattern shower curtain.

"It's nice on rainy days," I say. "It makes me feel more awake and less depressed."

He snorts. "I feel you."

"The door at that end is my mom and her partner's room." I point, then turn. My room is a few steps in the other direction. "And this is me."

I push open the door, quickly scanning inside, but there's nothing to see. All my laundry is put away and I even remembered to make my bed this morning. Good job, past Sidney.

Forrest follows me in. I watch him look around, taking in my posters, the rug by the bed, the bookcase. Crossing to the windowsill, he bends down to look at my cactus lineup. He puts out a finger, as if to slide it between the spines of one, and—

"*Ow*!" He pulls his hand back.

"You OK?" I ask.

"So *that's* why you don't touch cactuses," he says, examining his pointer finger.

"Cacti," I say. "And also, *obviously* you don't touch them!"

"I just wanted to see if I could do it without getting stabbed," he says, grinning at me.

I shake my head, laughing. "Come on, we have tweezers in the bathroom."

He follows me out, and a moment later we're both squeezed into the bathroom as I rummage around the cabinet. "Sit on the toilet," I say, and he does. I find the tweezers in our medicine box and perch on the edge of the bathtub, grabbing his hand and pulling it toward me.

We're touching again.

His skin is soft. I don't know what I expected, but it wasn't that Forrest Hirschler is well-moisturized. Remnants of chipped black nail polish adorn his fingernails, and I turn his palm up, tilting it until the light catches a tiny cactus needle embedded in his fingertip. The tweezers close on it, I pull ever so slightly, and—

"There you go," I say, looking up.

He's inches away from me, leaned forward so his elbows rest on his knees, his hand still in mine. This close, I can see the green and brown swirling together in his eyes, and the freckles scattered across his nose. He blinks once. His eyelashes are long, and dark brown, like his hair.

"You smell like a Christmas tree," I say.

"It's my lotion," he says. So he really *is* well-moisturized.

"It's nice." I'm still holding his hand. He hasn't moved it.

"Thank you," he says. His eyes look soft, and he holds my gaze. A movement draws my eyes down to his mouth. He's biting his lower lip.

"So, yeah!" I say, releasing his hand, and he straightens, and I slide away down the edge of the tub until I can stand without knocking into his knees. "You should be good now, I got the needle."

"Thanks," he says as I put the tweezers back. My heart is pounding. Am I sweating? Oh my god. I don't know what just happened, but I feel weird. Shaky, like I'm vibrating insidc, the warmth of his hand still imprinted on my palm.

"Do you want to study? We can sit in the dining room. And we have snacks. I can get us some snacks." I'm at the doorway now, smiling brightly to cover up how unbalanced I feel.

"Hell yeah." He gets to his feet, grinning at me. His eyes look normal now, the gentleness gone, replaced by his usual prankster gleam.

"Great! Cool. Sweet." I lead the way and grab chips, crackers, and dried fruit out of the cupboard while he gets comfortable at the table, pulling his homework out of his backpack.

I take my time arranging the snacks onto a plate, willing my body to calm down. The last time I felt this way, it was freshman year, when I had a crush on—

I freeze, hands full of dried mangos. That's what this is, this static electricity circling just under my skin, the lurching in my stomach, the sudden awareness of exactly where Forrest is and what he's doing. The way I can hear every little sound as he shifts in his chair and rifles through his notes.

I have a crush on Forrest.

How the fuck did this happen?!

"SIDNEY!" MAKAYLA'S VOICE SHAKES ME OUT OF MY HEAD the next morning. I've been staring into my locker, lost in swirling thoughts for who knows how long, and when I look over I'm surrounded by my friends: Jayden on one side, Anna on the other, and—

"Check it out," Makayla says as I turn around. She fluffs her hair with a grin as my mouth drops open. "Got it done after school yesterday."

"Oh my god! It looks so good!"

When I saw them yesterday at school, their hair was long, past their collarbone, but today, their curls have been sculpted into a short mullet, halo-like around the crown of their head, longer strands tapering below their ears, with fresh blond highlights woven into their natural dark brunette, almost black color.

"Makayla, you look . . ." I search for words, not sure what will feel right to them.

"Like a nonbinary baddie?" They strike a pose, one hand under their chin, eyes tilted to the ceiling like a glamorous diva.

"Exactly." I smile back. "Do you love it?"

"I've been wanting to do this for so long, you don't even know," she says. "I can't wait to show it off at Queer Alliance. Everyone's going to freak."

"Now we're all trans!" Anna said. "The agenda is working!"

My friends chatter on, but Makayla's words echo in my head. Queer Alliance is today. I'm going to see Forrest, which makes me happy, but also, I'm going to see Forrest, and that's terrifying.

He stayed yesterday for a few hours, typing away on his laptop while I stared at my own, willing the words to come for my essay. But all I could think about was him, sitting across from me; him, in my house; him, sitting in my bathroom, face inches away from mine, and the way he bit his bottom lip. His lips, and wanting to feel them on mine. And then I'd glance at him over the top of my screen, and he'd look up and stick his tongue out, or crack a joke, or just smile, and I could feel myself blush.

Has he guessed? After he went home, did he spend the whole night thinking about me the way I was thinking about him until I finally fell asleep? Will he see it on my face the moment I walk in?

Does he have a crush on me too?

♥

When the lunch bell rings, my heart jumps like it's been electric-shocked. I haven't seen Forrest all day. Maybe he's absent? I rush to my locker, grab my lunch, and head for Mr. Harrison's classroom, scanning the hallways around me. No sign of him.

As I near the door, my steps slow. I can hear voices inside, the squeak of chairs pushed across the floor, and Forrest's laugh cuts through the noise, ringing out to where I'm standing now. Just a few more steps, and I'll be inside. Just a few more steps, and I'll see him.

I take one step forward, then another, until I'm standing in the doorway.

Then I see him, at last. Forrest is setting up for the meeting with a couple other people. No one has noticed me yet, and a wild thought spikes in my brain: *RUN AWAY.*

I don't want to. Queer Alliance is my space, my home.

RUN AWAY.

I force myself to lift my foot and set it down in front of me, *RUN AWAY,* and again, *RUN AWAY,* until I'm inside the classroom.

The second he glimpses me, Forrest's whole face lights up and it's like I see every moment of it in slow motion: his mouth unfurling into a broad smile, all his teeth showing, his cheeks scrunching up, eyes filling with sparkle, the corners of his eyes crinkling back to his temples. Oh my god, I noticed his eye crinkles.

"Hey," I say, and it sounds like I'm underwater. My heart is thumping like it's going to burst out of my chest. *I'm going to have a heart attack and die.* No, you're not. *I AM I AM. My chest hurts it's happening now I'm going to collapse and—*

No, I tell myself. I cross to a desk and plop my lunch down on it, my bag in the seat, and pull it into the circle. Forrest is beside me, dragging another chair.

"You weren't in first period," I say, as casually as possible.

"Dentist appointment," he says, and bares his teeth.

"Very nice. Very white." I look away. I probably shouldn't stare at his mouth.

"I was thinking that today, we could keep chatting about Trans Awareness Week, figure out what we want to do, maybe break out into groups depending on who wants to run what thing?" he says. His eyes are still sparkling. They're so pretty.

Oh my god, no. Stop.

"Yes. Yeah. That sounds great!" I force a smile, hoping it masks how absolutely weird I must look right now. My thoughts are so loud, I'm surprised everyone can't hear them. *Maybe they CAN—*

No.

"Cool," he says, and turns away suddenly, and it feels like dropping off a cliff, the absence of his attention. Alexander is there, gesturing about something.

"It's tomorrow, are you coming?" he asks Forrest.

"Fuck yeah!" Forrest says.

Alexander's eyes land on me. "You should come too, Sid! Jayden's going to be there, and he said he was going to invite you all."

"To what?" I say, forcing the babble of words and images in my head into the background.

"My breaking competition," Alexander says. "It's hosted by the studio I dance with and there's like thirteen crews coming from around the area, local ones, Portland, even Los Angeles. Mine is the best though." He pretends to flip invisible long hair.

"That's so cool," I say.

"What's up?" Jayden joins us, followed by Makayla and Anna. Alexander tells them about his competition, and they all clap and say yes of course, and then everyone exclaims over Makayla's hair, and I stand there like a gargoyle, frozen in stone, seeing it all unfold:

Tomorrow.

The competition.

A whole day with Forrest, laughing at his jokes, breathing in the pine forest smell of him, feeling the warmth of his body radiating next to mine, the way I can feel him now, even though we're not touching, the way I could feel him last night on the other side of the table. He jumped up when Shar got home and shook her hand as if he was forty years old instead of sixteen, and then made small talk with her for ten minutes before running out to his mom's car, and then he rolled down the window and flashed me a peace sign that turned into an enthusiastic wave until the car rounded the corner out of sight. I'd gone back inside, straight to my room, and sat there for thirty minutes straight, staring at the wall, replaying the entire afternoon, how good it had felt, how easy, how right. Even though the knowledge of my crush was like a swarm of bees swirling under my skin.

The second bell rings and we all take our seats, Forrest right next to me.

"So, we were working on locking down stuff for Trans Awareness Week last meeting," he says, clapping his hands together. "How's that looking?"

"I heard back from that nonprofit I mentioned," Nyx says, raising a hand. "They're down to send someone to speak next week, and they're going to do it for free. I guess one of their employees was a student here back in the day?"

"Mx. Prager said we could host the speaker in the library as a pull-out event," Riley adds. "So anyone who wants to attend needs to get signed out for fifth period. Trans Awareness Week doesn't start 'til Thursday, but the library is booked by other classes the last half of the week, so we'll need to do it Tuesday."

"More Trans Awareness Week?" Mercury interjects, smiling. "Sign me up. Everyone should be aware of me." She twirls one long blue strand of hair around her finger.

"More like *be*-ware," Riley says, clicking their nails at Mercury.

"That too," she says, letting out a villainous laugh.

"Hell yeah," Forrest says, and turns to me. "Sidney, are you still good to co-moderate the panel with me? I thought we could take turns asking questions."

I make a noise of assent, nodding. Forrest's leg is inches away from mine, and all I want is to put my hand on his thigh.

I have a crush on Forrest. In all these weeks of meeting with him, it turned out he wasn't annoying, or awful, or out to ruin the club. He's the opposite: funny, and caring, and thoughtful. When I'm around him, my anxiety movies turn off, and I feel like I'm actually living in the present instead of fighting off a million possible catastrophic futures.

I want to tell him how I feel, but at the same time, I'm scared. What if it changes everything, and for the worse?

I can't. Not just yet.

I can hide my feelings at Queer Alliance, but can I manage a whole day? I don't know, but I want to go to Alexander's competition. I want to be with my friends. I want to be with Forrest.

Oh my god.

I want to be with Forrest.

♥

"I heard you're going hiking again this weekend," Mom says when she gets home that evening. I look up from my laptop, midway through page two of my essay. "Your dad told me," she adds, setting her bag near the door and sitting on the couch with a groan.

"You need anything, love?" Shar asks, coming in from the back room where she's been napping since she got home.

"A glass of wine and a shoulder massage?" Mom asks. "We presented the new strategy to the client today and they loved it."

"Of course they did!" Shar says, popping a cork on one of the bottles in the rack on the kitchen counter. A moment later, she brings a glass out and hands it to Mom, then settles in behind her on the couch. Mom sighs, sipping the wine as Shar presses her fingers into the muscles at the base of her neck.

"What's that about hiking?" Shar says, smiling at me. "You and your dad have been doing that a lot lately."

"Only like three times, counting this one," I say.

"He seems like he's making a good effort," Mom says, watching me.

"Yeah, he is," I say, half surprised at my own words. Part of me is still waiting for him to stumble, to show up drunk or go radio silent, but this time really does seem different. He even said he wanted to make amends, and he's never even taken the first of the twelve steps of AA seriously, let alone any beyond that.

And I'm looking forward to Sunday. Dad doesn't see me every day, doesn't have a big stressful job, doesn't monitor my study habits; he won't ask me questions I don't feel like answering. That thought is freeing. Maybe I could talk to him about Forrest, how I decided to just do what feels right, like he said to, and now we're friends, and I've realized I have this crush.

"You're studying with Jayden on Saturday, right?" Mom says.

I nod, pretending to be focused on my computer screen so I don't have to look her in the eye while I lie. I'm going to be with Jayden, but we won't be studying; once again, Mom and Shar's Al-Anon meeting will cover my ass when the twins pick me up for the breaking competition. "The three of us are all going to hang out afterward," I say. "Jayden said his mom can give me a ride home."

That's at least partly true. I am getting a ride home from him, and the three of us *are* all hanging out. Just not in the way Mom and Shar assume we're going to.

"Maybe you and I can have a little post-meeting date," Shar says, looking down at Mom, who twists her head back so they can kiss.

"I would love that," Mom says. "I've got some time this weekend before things kick up again on Monday."

I stare at the half-written second page of my essay. I have to work on it, but I have to go to Alexander's competition too. I'm scared Forrest will see right through me, see my crush, but I want to be near him. And if I'm being honest, I kind of want him to see through me. I have plenty of time to finish the assignment before next Friday. Skipping one study session won't kill my grades.

You skipped one already, a voice says. *Mom's going to find out, and she's going to be so angry, she'll hate you, she'll send you away—*

That's not real, I tell the voice. *It's not happening.*

That's not real. It's not happening.

That's not real. It's not happening.

Images form, bursting like fireworks in my mind: Mom locking me in my room, Mom so angry she leaves the house, Mom in the car, headed somewhere, and another car spins out of control, smashes her across three lanes into a building and her car goes up in flames, and the last thing that ever happened between us was a fight, and I'll have to live with it the rest of my life—

I push away from the chair and head to the bathroom, locking the door behind me, sliding to the floor, pressing my face into my knees, and scream at myself in my head.

THAT'S NOT REAL. IT'S NOT HAPPENING.

THAT'S NOT REAL. IT'S NOT HAPPENING.

THAT'S NOT REAL. IT'S NOT HAPPENING.

Over and over, until I lose track of how many sets I've done and have to start again.

THAT'S NOT REAL. IT'S NOT HAPPENING.

THAT'S NOT REAL. IT'S NOT HAPPENING.

THAT'S NOT REAL. IT'S NOT HAPPENING.

JUST BEFORE NOON ON SATURDAY, JAYDEN AND MAKAYLA'S mom steers her van into the community center parking lot to drop us off for Alexander's competition. The building sits across from a small park that hugs the shore of Lake Washington, and the lot is already packed, a line of cars circling around to drop people off before heading out in search of parking elsewhere. When it's our turn, the van doors slide open and we pile out.

Inside, we follow Jayden, who seems to know exactly where to go, into the center's huge gymnasium, where a wide stage is set up at one end, the floor filled with people milling around in groups and practicing dance moves in the open spaces.

"There he is!" Jayden exclaims a moment later and changes direction, veering through the crowd to the opposite wall, where Alexander stands tapping away on his phone next to a group of people stretching and talking.

He looks up and breaks into a smile, throwing his arms open as we approach. "You came!"

"Of course," Jayden says, stopping in front of him. "How are you feeling?"

"Oh my god, *terrified*," Alexander says, pulling a face. "I'm definitely the youngest person here."

"And just as deserving," says a girl from the group next to him. She's Asian, wearing big jeans and a baggy shirt.

"Oh my goddddd!" Alexander turns to her, hands pressed to his face. "Thank youuu." He twirls back to us, gesturing toward the group. "This is my crew."

A jumble of hellos echoes back and forth, all of the crew members shifting to smile and wave back at us. Alexander squeals and darts around the three of us, and we turn to see him tackle Stef in a hug, Forrest following behind her. His eyes find mine, and the corner of his mouth lifts. I smile without even thinking about it, then feel myself blush, and look away quickly, at the stage. He's here, and I'm here, and we're both here together. For the whole day. Ohmygodohmygodohmy-god. This is terrible, and wonderful, and I don't know what to do about it.

"What's up?"

I look back, and there Forrest is, right in front of me. He's traded the hoodie for a dark green parka over a flannel over a T-shirt, and the color of the jacket makes his eyes look like moss, soft and inviting.

"Hey!" I say.

"You excited?" he says, just as the speakers boom to life and everyone in the gym flinches at once. The volume drops instantly and someone calls out an apology through a microphone, to scattered laughs and applause. Forrest and I widen our eyes at each other, smiling.

"Welcome dancers, welcome guests!" the emcee continues. Forrest winks at me, *winks at me*, and looks toward the stage. I half listen to the speaker introducing the event and the first few crews, replaying that wink in my mind. Why did he wink?! Was it flirtatious? Does he like me back? Was it just a fun wink, like a *hey here we go the event is starting* wink? Did he even know he winked? Do people wink without knowing it?

"Oh my god," Jayden whispers excitedly, grabbing my arm, yanking me back into the present.

"Aaaaaand representing Seattle . . ." the emcee shouts at the same time, "206 Maverix!"

The crew's name incorporates the area code for Seattle, showing their pride in their hometown. They take the stage and we all cheer as they throw their hands up, urging the crowd louder, and Alexander is right there in the middle, posing, clapping, smiling from ear to ear. 206 Maverix are third in the tournament, up against a crew from Tacoma, and they bound back to our station by the wall to watch the competition begin.

Third. That's an odd number, a safe number, and I relax a little. *Everything is going to be fine*, I tell myself.

Everything is going to be fine.

Everything is going to be fine.

♥

As the crews battle, my thoughts fade below the boom of the bass, and I'm swept up in the breakers' flow. Jayden narrates the dancing from beside me, pointing out different moves, and I start to see how the dancers put them together into unique combinations all their own. They drop to the floor, legs spinning around their heads as they balance on their hands, then back up, feet moving in patterns I can't follow, bodies twirling and twisting like tornadoes to the scratch of the DJ's track.

When it's time for Alexander's crew to take the stage, Jayden heads toward the front of the crowd, and Anna takes his place next to me, checking her phone. Forrest is at my other side, where he's been the whole time, talking to Stef and Makayla.

"This is so cool," I say over the music, and Forrest half tilts his head to me, grinning, still watching Alexander.

"Right?" he says. "Wait 'til you see him. It's going to blow your mind."

I watch the stage as the crews take their positions, waiting for the music as the DJ transitions from the previous track. I'm glad Jayden has been going to breakdancing club, and it seems like he and Alexander are really good friends. I just don't know what that means for our group. Will Jayden leave us for Forrest's friends, or will our friend groups merge? I don't want to lose Jayden, don't want us to change, but the other option means hanging out with Forrest all the time. And if I tell him I like him, and he doesn't feel the same . . . I squeeze my eyes shut.

A hand touches the small of my back, and my eyes fly open. "You OK?" Forrest murmurs in my ear. His breath makes the skin on my neck prickle.

I shake my head, not daring to look at him. "I'm fine!" His hand is still on my back, right above the waistband of my jeans, and his touch zaps my whole body to life.

"OK," he says, and pulls his hand away, leaving me buzzing. I stare at the stage and try to focus on what the emcee is saying, on the beat of the music behind his words, on anything but the way my heart is pounding, the way I'm drawn to Forrest like he's a magnet and I'm helpless metal.

"Look at Jayden," Anna murmurs in my other ear. I do, and see him standing right in front, eyes fixed on Alexander, rocking back and forth from toe to heel. "They need to just get together already."

Wait.

What?

I squint at her. "What are you talking about?"

She frowns. "Jayden and Alexander and their massive crushes on each other? Did you not know?"

I turn back to the stage. Jayden's hands are clasped in front of him, his face tipped upward as if toward the sun, gaze fixed on Alexander, who's moved out in front of his crew, into position for his battle. Alexander looks down at Jayden, and even though he was already smiling, now he's grinning, the expression taking over his whole face as he gives Jayden the tiniest wave.

Anna pokes me gently. "Wait, did you seriously not know? Makayla and I were talking about it at lunch the other day while you were with Forrest, and we just assumed you knew too."

I'm silent, staring at the stage, but I'm not seeing the competition anymore. All the moments from the last few months flash in front of my eyes: their group project together, Jayden's new familiarity with Forrest's group of friends, his sudden interest in breakdancing—

"Halloween," I say. "His costume. Alexander helped him make it."

"Are we talking about Jayden and Alexander?" Makayla appears on Anna's other side. "They started FaceTiming recently. He goes into his room and they talk for *hours* and when he comes out he's all glow-y but he *still* hasn't told me."

Anna grabs my arm. "Oh my god, they're starting!"

Forrest cups his hands around his mouth and whoops. "Here we go!"

Alexander struts toward the center of the stage, the half-circle of his crew behind him, up against a tall Black girl from the other crew. I watch Jayden watch him, and feel a pit open up underneath me. I'm standing in the gymnasium, but I'm falling, falling, falling. How could I not have noticed? Now that I see it, it's obvious, just like Anna said. Jayden is the living embodiment of the heart eyes emoji, following Alexander's every move.

I'm a horrible friend. All I think about is myself. When Makayla came out, I spiraled, and now Jayden has this crush and I didn't know, I had no fucking idea, because I've been caught up in my own head, in my stupid feelings, in these stupid thoughts. I'm a horrible friend and they're all going to leave me and I deserve it, I deserve it—

The crowd cheers and I dig my nails into my arm, as hard as I can.

THAT'S NOT REAL. IT'S NOT HAPPENING.

THAT'S NOT REAL. IT'S NOT HAPPENING.

THAT'S NOT REAL. IT'S NOT HAPPENING.

I breathe out, the pinch of my nails anchoring me, and watch Alexander. His movements are more fluid than other dancers', and as he glides from a handstand to the floor and back, he incorporates his arms and hands in graceful framing gestures.

"He vogues too," Forrest says. "It's part of his style. It's so fucking cool."

I've seen voguing videos come across my feed, and now I can pick it out in the way Alexander moves, combining breaking and voguing into something entirely new. The crowd shrieks and gasps as he death-drops and spins his legs to pull himself onto his hands, feet twirling in the air. As I watch his dancing, the thoughts quiet, and I relax my hand around my upper arm.

I'm OK.

They battle back and forth until finally the DJ calls it in a dramatic wail, drawing out the syllables of the winning crew's name: "Twoooooooo ohhhhhhh SIX! MAVERIX!"

We all scream, drawing laughs and claps from the crowd nearby as the crews leave the stage. They're swarmed by people high-fiving and hugging them, and we rush toward the clump, fighting our way toward Alexander, who's fielding admiration from several dancers in other crews. When he sees us, he abandons his fans and zooms over, his face glowing.

"We won!" he shrieks. Behind him, the other dancers laugh, looking on with fond expressions like he's not just their competitor but also their kid, someone they admire and feel pride in at the same time.

"That was *amazing*!" Jayden says, and they hug tightly. Alexander hugs me next, surprising me, and after a second I hug back, relaxing into his embrace. His cologne is spicy, and he's wearing a lot of it. He moves to Forrest then, and the rest of us in turn, our little huddle a circle of warmth in the loud gymnasium. It feels good, but it's not going to last. I know Anna is thinking about me right now, how I'm such a bad friend that I had no idea about Jayden, how she's done with me and our friendship. She'll tell Makayla, and then Jayden, and they'll see it too. The moment is a candle I'm holding, my very presence enough to douse the flame. *That isn't real. It's not*—it isn't right now, but it will be. I can feel it, sweeping toward me like a tidal wave—*STOP IT*—this is going to end, and they're all going to hate me.

"I'm going to the bathroom," I say, backing away, and it doesn't seem like anyone notices. I turn and slip through the crowd, out of the gym doors, into the lobby of the community center. I scan the walls and find a sign pointing me in the direction I need: the restrooms, six all-gender single stalls lining a side hallway, and I push open a vacant one, locking the door behind me.

The linoleum floor is cool under me when I sit, and I press my hands to the hard surface like it can anchor me. I close my eyes, breathing deeply, and repeat the words to myself, the ones I've said so many times I can see them, like wheels wearing a groove in my brain.

It should work, but it doesn't. I try over and over, set after set, until I'm breathing fast, tears streaming down my cheeks, hands clutching clumps of hair at my temples. The fear is intense, swirling into devastation, a maelstrom that's pulling me under. I can't feel this, I can't handle it, it's too much.

"That's not real. It's not happening." I rock back and forth, the words coming out of my mouth now instead of staying in my mind. "That's not real. It's not happening. That's not real. It's not happening." Someone is probably right outside and they can hear me, they can hear me losing it, they're calling the police right now and I'll go to a mental hospital and never come back and all my friends will forget about me and Forrest won't care and I'll just be that crazy person they knew—

My phone rings and I start. It falls out of my hoodie pocket and hits the floor, still ringing.

Forrest is calling. Forrest is calling me.

I answer.

"Where are you?" he asks.

"Um." I scramble to my feet and unlock the door. I can't say where I am, that's too weird. "I'm. Um. I'm outside! Just needed a break. From the, um, crowd?" I head out of the bathroom hallway, toward the exit, away from the gym. I push through the door and step outside, the air hitting my face with a chill that snaps me back into my body like a rubber band.

"Oh, OK! I'll come join you," he says, and hangs up. I'm at the side of the building, and I circle around to the front, phone still in my hand. The line of cars dropping people off is gone, and there's a small crowd milling around out here too, a few folks smoking cigarettes out by the street. I stand next to a huge planter holding a shrunken rhododendron. When Forrest emerges, I raise a hand hesitantly to wave, and he walks over.

"You were gone for a *minute*," he says.

"I was?"

"Yeah, like two whole battles," he says. "I got worried."

Has he noticed? Has he realized that I'm actually crazy? "Sorry."

"It's all good." He sits on the broad rim of the planter. "You staying the whole day?"

I nod. "Do you think 206 is going to win?"

"That would be fucking dope," he says, picking at his cuticles. "They haven't been around that long. Alexander has only been competing with them for a year-ish? He used to do mostly solo competitions, or sometimes he'd be in a random crew for a second, but it never really stuck. The first one was a bunch of bros, and Alexander . . ." He chuckles. "That's not really his vibe."

I sit next to him. Forrest's presence, the sound of his voice, pulls my focus, the thoughts fading away in the warm glow of being near him. Our legs are inches apart. "Were they homophobic?"

He shook his head. "Nah, they were always pretty chill and respectful according to him, but . . . it was just a lot of super-masc energy and he didn't really feel at home. He likes hanging with femmes, so this crew is a good fit."

"What about you?" I nudge him. "You're not femme."

He looks at me sidelong, smiling. "No, but I'm like . . . soft masc." He flutters his nails, freshly painted black. "What about you? Do you like femmes, or mascs, or . . ."

His eyes are on mine, greener in this light, and I bite my lip, looking down at my shoes. "I don't know! I like both, and everything else. I think the person matters more to me than the gender or the expression."

"That's cool," he says. "I'm kinda the same."

"Cool." I press my feet into the pavement, very aware of my hand resting on my thigh, right next to where his hand rests on his.

"So . . ." He trails off. A bird twitters in a nearby tree, but otherwise, everything is quiet. All I can feel is how close he is to me. The thoughts, the fear, the maelstrom inside me, it's all gone. Just . . . gone. "The other day . . . it was really fun hanging out. And . . . I was wondering something."

Everything slows down, like we've entered a parallel universe where time passes differently. I shift my body, turning slightly, and my knee presses into his. The warmth flows from his body into mine at that spot, and I look up, into his eyes. Our faces are inches apart now. How did we get this close?

"Sid! Forrest!"

We both jump, whirling around to see Makayla waving at us from the doorway. "The next round is starting! 206 is competing first!"

"Oh shit!" Forrest hustles toward the community center, and I follow, heart pounding. We weave through the crowd inside the gym, back to our spot, just as the emcee calls the 206 Maverix up to the stage. I want to ask Forrest what he was about to say—I *need* to, almost, and the need is itching under my skin. I press my lips together tightly, because if I speak, I won't have control over what I say. The words will come spilling out, and it will be humiliating, and Forrest will think I'm just some weirdo who's in love with him. But I'm not in love with him. I just feel at home around him. When we're talking, all my anxiety movies stop, the theater in my brain goes dark, and I'm in the present, anchored wherever he is. And he smells good. And has nice eyes. And lips. And I want to lean in and—

"Can I tell you later?" he asks, right in my ear, and I jerk, startled. "I'm sorry, I'm sorry." He curls a hand around my arm and squeezes it once before letting go.

"It's all good! Yeah, totally," I say, smiling at him in what I hope is a normal way to smile.

"OK, sick," he says, and looks at the stage as the music kicks in. "Oh my god, Alexander is up first!"

I watch Alexander twirl and pose, trying to focus on the music, the moves, the crews cheering their dancers on, but all I can feel is the imprint of Forrest's hand, still warm around my bicep. Later, he'll tell me whatever he has to tell me *this will end* and everything is going to be fine *it will end*—

EVERYTHING IS GOING TO BE FINE.

EVERYTHING IS GOING to be fine.

Everything is going to be fine.

FORREST DOESN'T HAVE TIME TO TELL ME LATER THAT DAY. The Maverix lose the second round, and Alexander is crushed, crying in Forrest's arms. I keep looking at Forrest, hoping he'll say something, give me a look, but he's focused on Alexander. We stick it out 'til the end of the competition, because Alexander says that's the right thing to do, but we all head home before the dance party: Forrest in Stef's dad's car, Alexander with someone in his crew who lives near him, me and my friends in the twins' van.

I can't sleep that night. I lie in bed for what feels like hours, replaying every moment of the competition, looking for clues of what to expect when Forrest and I talk. Does he like me back? Or is he tired of me? Is he hoping everyone will pick him when we revote, and he's worried about how I'll react if they do? Maybe that's what he was going to say at the community center before Makayla interrupted us.

What if he dies and you never know? He's not going to die. *But he could, he could have a heart attack or get shot tomorrow while walking to school, someone out to get trans people and they see him*—THAT'S NOT REAL, IT'S NOT—*blood everywhere, his body on the ground outside the school as I walk up, a crowd gathered around and I push through to see him lying there, broken and gone*—IT'S NOT HAPPENING, THAT'S NOT REAL—*fall to my knees crying, his face cold and still, I never got to tell him how I felt*—

"Stop," I groan out loud, turning over and pushing my face into the pillow. "Stop. Stop." I chant the word over and over until it loses all meaning but I keep going because if I don't, the thoughts will start and I can't do this.

I can't do this anymore.

♥

The next morning, I sit at the table, backpack at my feet, waiting for Dad to pick me up for our hike. I'm exhausted, but I'm ready to get out of the city for the day, into the forest, where my thoughts will finally leave me alone.

I hope.

I fiddle with my phone, swiping back and forth between apps and my texts, absentmindedly rereading my thread with Forrest. Seeing it makes me calmer, almost as if Forrest is in the room with me.

It's five minutes past the time Dad is supposed to be here, and I flip to our conversation, even though there's no new messages, just his last text to me: *Great, pick you up Sunday at 10*.

He'll text me. Any minute now. He's just running late.

I reread my texts with Forrest again, smiling at the memes we sent back and forth the other day.

It's fifteen minutes past, and Dad hasn't texted. *He's done with you.* No. I'm not doing this today. I squeeze my left arm, nails digging into my skin. The house is quiet, Mom relaxing in her room, Shar in the garage.

Thirty minutes past. I sit staring at the phone, at my texts with Dad, and finally tap out a message: *Where are you?*

"Sweetie?" I look up to find Mom in the kitchen, frowning at me. "What are you still doing here? Wasn't your dad supposed to pick you up, like . . ." She checks the clock on the stove. "Forty minutes ago?"

I nod.

"What happened? Is he running late?"

I shrug. "I don't know."

"He hasn't contacted you?" Her frown deepens, her voice rising slightly. She's getting angry, and I don't want her to, I don't want them to fight—

"It's fine!" I say, getting up and grabbing my pack. "He probably just overslept. Or forgot. I'm going to . . ." I trail off, gesturing at the back of the house, and rush past her.

Earl Grey darts out as I come into my room, and I shut the door. Brekky is dozing in the middle of my bed. Dad probably did oversleep. That's it. That's all it is, and he'll text me later, and he'll apologize, for real this time, and we'll be OK, everything will be OK.

My phone pings, and I almost drop it as I pull it out of my pocket.

Hey kiddo, I'm really sorry. Something happened. I can't get there today. I'll make it up to you later.

Something happened. I stare at the phone. What does that mean? Is he OK? I'm on a city street, suddenly, watching Dad pull out from his apartment and a car careens around the corner, out of nowhere, smashing into the back of Dad's Corvette and it goes flying into a telephone pole, his head whipping onto the wheel and then back and he slumps to the side, blood streaming down his face, and he's in a hospital, texting me now, telling me something happened, but he's got a concussion, a really bad one, so bad that in two hours he'll collapse and I'll never see him again—

Something mushrooms inside me, dark and spidery: *He's going to die. He's going to die, and I'll never see him again. He's going to die, and I haven't even told him I love him.*

I grab my phone and call him. The phone rings once, twice, three times, and goes to voicemail. "Wazzzuuuuup! You've reached Kyle—" I hang up and call again. Voicemail. I hang up and call again. Voicemail.

He's going to die, chants a voice in my head. *He's going to die. He's going to die. He's going to—*

The phone rings. It's Dad. I pick it up.

"Are you OK?" I ask.

"Hey!" His voice is jovial, a little louder than normal. "Sid. I'm fine. It's all good. Something came up last minute."

I blow out a breath. He's OK. He's alive. It worked. The sets I do—I called him three times, and he called me back.

He was all right, because I checked on him. "I thought . . . from what you said . . . I was worried."

"You were worried about me? Aw, kiddo, it's all good. I just, uh . . ." He trails off. I can hear voices in the background now, muffled, like he's in a room somewhere with a bunch of people.

"Where are you?" I ask.

There's a long pause, so long I almost wonder if the call dropped, but I can still hear the other voices wherever he is.

"I'm at a meeting," he says finally, and his voice is flat now. "Listen, kiddo, I need to be honest with you. I drank last night."

I grip my phone tighter, my whole body stiffening.

"I drank last night, and when I went to start the car this morning, well . . . the Breathalyzer got me. And I realized I fucked up. I called my sponsor, and he brought me to a meeting. I'm sorry, Sidney." His voice cracks. "I can't pick you up today, because I need to be at a meeting."

"Oh." My voice is tiny, a pebble dropping into a lake.

"I know this is me letting you down for the millionth time, and I'm sorry about that. You're the best thing to ever happen to me. The reason I'm still here. I love you, kiddo, and I'm going to keep working the program, and I'm going to make it up to you."

I feel like I can't breathe, but I need to say it back, need to say it so I know that I did. "I love you too, Dad."

"How about we hike again in a couple weeks? Once I've been back on track for a while."

"Yeah, totally."

"Great. Be good, kiddo."

We say goodbye and hang up. I sit there, phone in hand. Brekky appears at my side, headbutting me, and I pet him, but I can barely feel his fur.

Dad was supposed to pick me up, he knew he was going to, and he still drank. He relapsed.

I curl up on my bed and stare at the wall, replaying the call. Brekky nestles against my back purring, the sound eventually shifting to quiet breathing as he sleeps.

You're the best thing to ever happen to me. The reason I'm still here.

What does that mean? Did Dad think about . . . I don't even want to think the word. Thinking it feels like invoking it, like it **will** happen if I acknowledge that it *could*. I've even wondered before if he might, and—*no. Stop.*

Stop.

Stop.

I imagine Brekky batting the thoughts away, like they're toy mice, skittering across the floor and out of my head.

I thought the set of three worked this time, but I was worried about the wrong thing. If I'd thought of Dad relapsing, I would have checked on him earlier, and maybe if he'd heard my voice, he wouldn't have gotten drunk.

My chest hurts, and I press my hand just below my collarbone, like I can hold myself together. I need to talk to someone. I can't tell Mom, because if she knows Dad relapsed, she'll probably freak out. If I tell Shar, she'll tell

Mom. If I tell my friends, I'll just be even more of a burden than I already am.

I pick my phone up, and open my thread with Forrest, and calm settles over me. Talking to him will make me feel better. It always does.

Hey, I say.

He replies within a minute. *Hey yourself.*

I smile weakly at the phone. *How's your Sunday?*

It's good, pretty chill. Yours?

Not great.

What's going on?

My dad relapsed.

Oh, shit. Wow, Sidney. I'm so, so sorry.

Tears sting my eyes, sliding down my cheeks, and I hug the phone to my chest. It buzzes again, and I look at the screen.

What do you need?

I don't know, I say. *Distraction? I just don't get it. Like, if he wants to stay sober, just STAY SOBER. Just don't drink.*

I hear you, Forrest says. *It doesn't make any sense.*

Can you send me some memes? I ask. *I liked that cat video the other day.*

You got it, he says. *Incoming.*

Our thread fills with videos, and I watch them one after another, laughing at some, cooing out loud over others. *These are perfect*, I say.

Good, Forrest says. *I can do this all day. Just let me know if it gets annoying and I'll stop lol.*

I grin, kicking my feet a little. *Sounds good.*

♥

In the morning, I'm dragging. Dad is on my mind, wherever he is right now; he could be in a meeting, or maybe he's drinking again. I miss my train and catch the later one, which gets me to school just as the first bell rings. I fight through the crowd in the halls, sliding around clumps of students flooding every direction to their classes, and get to Ms. Lundahl's room just as the second bell buzzes.

She's talking about the essay, and I know I need to pay attention, but it takes everything I have to keep my eyelids half open. The room is blurry around me, and her voice fades to a background hum. Every so often, my head jerks forward and wakes me up. I straighten my posture every time, eyes fixed on her, hoping no one saw me, only to slide down, down, down again into a sleepy daze.

"Sidney!" Forrest calls out when the bell rings for second period. I stop at the door and wait for him; Stef and Alexander are already in the hall, heading for their next classes.

We fall into step, and he looks over at me. "How are you holding up?"

Something warms inside me. He cares about how I'm doing. "I don't know. I keep thinking about him, and . . ." I swallow, eyes filling with tears.

"Hey, hey." He puts a hand on my upper arm, and it steadies me and lights me up at the same time. How many feelings can one person have in their body at once? If there's a limit, I must be approaching it. "It's going to be OK. It's not your fault."

"Thanks." I sniffle, wiping my eyes, and meet his: calm, and kind, more brown than green today. "I was wondering. Do you want to hang out after school today? You were going to tell me something at the competition."

"Oh, right!" He blushes, the red spreading over his cheeks to the tips of his ears. "Um, sure. Yes. That sounds great."

"OK, cool."

We stand there for a moment, his hand still on my arm. The bell rings, and we both jump and say a hurried goodbye, splitting in opposite directions for second period.

I think I know, now, what he's going to tell me.

I think.

I hope.

CHAPTER 18

BY THE END OF LAST CLASS, MY STOMACH IS IN KNOTS. IF I didn't know better, I'd think I had food poisoning. I race to the bathroom to offload an anxiety poop, then make my way to my locker. Down the hall, Forrest is cackling about something, probably goofing off with Stef or Alexander.

RUN, my brain says. I push the thought away, shut my locker, and head down the hall.

"Sidney!" Stef waves as I approach.

"Aren't you about to miss your bus?" Forrest says to her, and flashes me a smile. "Hey." The sound of his voice makes me grin automatically.

Stef sucks her teeth. "Trying to get rid of me?"

"Yes," Forrest says. "Yes, I am."

She eyes us both, first him, then me. "What are you up to tonight, Sidney?"

"Um. Hanging out with Forrest." My voice comes out way higher than I intend.

"Oh!" She looks between us again. Forrest must not have told her. Why didn't he tell her? "Have fuuuuu-uuuunnn," she singsongs, backing away slowly.

"Shut *up*!" Forrest yells.

"Never!" she hollers in reply, and turns on the toe of her platform boots, racing away down the hall.

"I don't know how she runs in those things," Forrest says, shutting his locker.

"My feet hurt just looking at them," I say.

"She says they're the most comfortable shoes she owns," he says as we fall into step beside each other.

I laugh. "She's such a goth."

"How was the rest of your day?" he asks.

"It was . . . a day," I say as we push out of the doors and into the chilly November air. Watery sunlight breaks through the clouds, warming my face just a little.

"That's real," he says.

"What about you?" I ask, glancing at him. "You know about my tragic family life. What's going on in yours?"

"Ugh," he says, making a face. "Don't even get me started."

"I'm sorry," I say. "Do you want to talk about it?"

"I don't want to bring you down even more," he says. We turn the corner onto the main street and head toward the train station. It's louder here, the street busy with cars and businesses.

"You won't," I say. "Seriously, I need to think about someone else's problems for once."

"Fair enough," he says with a laugh. We pass a tree and he reaches up, plucking one of the few bright red leaves still hanging on to its almost-empty branches. "They've just been fighting a lot. My dad makes way more money than my mom, but he's trying to nickel and dime her for everything. She wants to split custody, but he thinks we should stay with him. And I don't want to. Like, I love my dad, don't get me wrong, but if we're gonna stay with one of them, I'd rather be with Mom."

"I know what you mean," I say quietly.

"Yeah?" He glances over, twirling the leaf in his fingers.

"My parents fought over me too, but it wasn't really much of a fight. My mom won custody and Dad has visitation rights." I scuff my feet through the leaves piled on the sidewalk.

"I'm hoping my mom wins custody of us too," Forrest says.

"They ask you," I say. "During the court proceedings. You get a chance to say what you want."

"Really?" He looks over at me. "Did you . . . ?"

I nod. "They had a therapist interview me. They usually wait 'til you're twelve, I think, and I was eleven, but it was almost my birthday so I guess that was close enough."

"So you didn't have to say it in front of your parents?"

"No." I grimace. "God, that would have been so awkward."

"For real."

We enter the station, tapping our fare cards on the card reader, and ride the escalator down to the platform. As we near the bottom, lights flash in the tunnel, and the train emerges just as we step off. The seats are full, so we stand, clinging to the overhead railings as the train zooms away to the next station. I can see us in the dark glass of the window, reflected back like a parallel universe.

The night before the therapist was supposed to interview me, Dad took me out to the arcade and won me a stuffed animal. Afterward, in the car, he cried, asking me to pick him, saying he loved me, that it wasn't fair, that he was trying to get sober and having me around would help. But even then, I knew it was bullshit. I'd seen him try over and over, and I just wanted it to end.

In the therapist's office, staring at her soft blue carpet, after I'd answered her questions about life at home, about my relationship with my parents, I'd said it. "I want to stay with Mom." She nodded, and noted something on her pad.

"So the new season of my show just dropped," Forrest says, bringing me back to the present. "I binged the entire thing this weekend. Do you want to hear about it?"

I nod and he's off, catching me up on everything that's happened in the past few episodes, and the sound of his voice anchors me in the present again.

♥

At my house, I feed the cats while Forrest uses the bathroom. I think of the last time he was here, holding his hand as I pulled the cactus needle out of his finger. The look in his eyes. I think he likes me back, and I think that's what he wants to talk about. The thought floods me with jittering energy.

"Are you hungry?" I ask when he comes back into the kitchen. "We have snacks."

"I'm good," he says, leaning on the counter across from me. He looks so effortlessly cool and confident, the way the hoodie falls open across his chest, the way his jeans hug his hips, the sliver of his boxer's waistband visible above the belt. My cheeks get hot and I look away quickly. I'm thinking about his underwear and he's standing. *Right. There.*

"So, um," I say. "You wanted to talk to me about something?"

"Yeah."

The kitchen is silent, and after a moment I chance a look at him. He's staring at the floor, chipping away at the polish on his thumbnail. His scalp is bright red through his curls.

"I . . ." he says, and goes quiet again. Brekky wanders into the kitchen, his lunch finished, and winds around my legs. I pick him up, just to do *something* but he squirms and I let him go.

"So." Forrest is still chipping at his polish. "I know we started meeting because of the alliance. But it's been really fun, getting to know you. I think you're really cool, and smart, and funny."

I hug myself, to keep from jumping up and down.

"Hanging out with you last week was really great. And at the competition. I really like being around you, and I just wanted to tell you . . ."

From the other room, the cats' feet patter as they chase each other, but my eyes are fixed on Forrest. He looks up finally, his face the most serious I've ever seen it, hands clasped in front of his chest.

"I like you, Sidney."

My whole body goes still. The house fades away, and all I see is him.

"You like me, like . . . as a person? Or . . . ?" My voice is squeaky, like I sucked up a bunch of helium.

"Well, yeah, but also, I have a crush on you," he says, and the Jenga tower in my mind scatters everywhere.

"I like you too," I say, and his eyes widen.

"For real? Like—like I like you?"

"Yes. Um. Like a crush." My brain-to-mouth connection is fried by his words. "I have a crush. On you. And I like you as a person. But also as a crush. Oh my god." I cover my face with my hands.

"Sidney." I hear footsteps, and gentle fingers wrap around my wrists, pulling them down. Forrest is inches away, staring into my eyes. "You don't have to hide."

I stare at him, heart pounding. His hands are still holding mine, and I curl my fingers so we're squeezing each other's. He peers down at our grasp and rubs his thumb over the back of my hand. Sparks jolt through my skin.

"Thanks," I say, because it's the only word that comes to mind. He's gazing at me, his eyes a vast meadow, a place where I can finally rest. I look at his mouth, his lips a soft pink, slightly parted.

He speaks. "Can I kiss y—"

"Yes," I say, nodding vigorously.

He smiles and leans forward, and I watch as his eyes close, dark lashes brushing his cheek, and then his lips are on mine and my eyes close and all I do is feel.

His lip balm tastes like vanilla, our mouths fitting together like they've been waiting to do so, all soft pressure and warmth. He presses me back against the counter and my whole body wakes up, those sparks zooming all through me now. I don't even care that the edge of the counter is digging into my spine, or that Brekky is meowing at us from the floor.

I've kissed people before. In seventh grade, at a friend's birthday party, giggling our way through spin the bottle. At the homecoming dance last year with a girl I had a crush on. For a few months, we'd go to her house and make out—sometimes more than make out—until the day she came to school hand in hand with a girl the grade ahead of us.

I've kissed people before, and it was awkward, or fun, or even hot. But this is something different. Forrest likes me back. He's kissing me because he really wants to.

I hope my breath smells OK. Oh my god, what if it doesn't?

He pulls back, cheeks red, and I can feel mine are too. I stare at him, blinking. I need to say something, but my thoughts are fuzzy, from the kiss or the sudden anxiety that my breath is actually terrible.

"Sidney?" He tilts his head. "What is it, did my breath stink?"

"No, no!" I shake my head. "Does mine?"

"Not at all," he says.

"Cool."

"Cool."

We look at each other, and a giggle bubbles up inside me. He starts to smile, and then we're both laughing, still looking at each other.

"I like you," I say.

"I like you too," he says, and I pull him back in.

♥

We make out for what feels like hours, but when we come up for air, it's been only ten minutes. At some point, we moved to the couch, and I'm sitting on top of him, his hands gripping my waist.

"I can't believe I'm kissing you," Forrest says, his eyes sparkling.

I touch my lips and grin at him like a circus clown. "Freshman year me is in shock right now."

He laughs. "I know what you mean."

I shift to the cushion beside him, one leg curled against his thigh, the other still thrown over his lap. "What was that about? You were so aggressively anti–Queer Alliance then, and now . . ."

"I was jealous," he says, rubbing the back of his head. "You guys seemed so confident, and I was in the closet, and I just felt like Queer Alliance wasn't for me, would never be for me. I thought I was never going to get to transition, that I didn't deserve to, and even if I did, that it would be too hard. My parents fought all the time, even more than they do now because they were still trying to make it work, and everything sucked. I knew you thought I was an asshole, so I thought fuck it, I'll just be an asshole."

I grimace, my head shrinking back into my neck. "I really didn't mean for you to hear me that one time."

"But you did think that," he says.

Slowly, I nod.

He shrugs. "When I finally admitted to myself that I was trans, that I was a boy and it wasn't going away and that I had to transition or . . ." He trails off, but I know what he's going to say, and I put a hand on his arm. He covers it with his. "I got over myself."

"I'm glad you did," I say quietly.

"And also. I'm sorry I was an asshole."

"I mean, I kind of was too."

"Only in response to me."

"Oh my god, let me apologize." I shove him lightly, and he grins.

"OK." He leans over, and slides his hand across my cheek and around the back of my neck and pulls me toward him. A wave of energy whooshes through me, down my spine and up to the top of my head, and I climb on top of him again, kissing him back.

A moment later, my phone rings in my pocket, startling us apart. Shar's photo is on the screen, her smiling on the sand at the edge of the ocean, from a trip we all took this summer.

"Hey!" I answer in as normal a voice as I can manage, resettling my glasses on my nose. I hold my finger up to my lips, and Forrest mimes zipping his shut.

"Hey kiddo, just letting you know I'm coming home early today."

"Are you OK?" Worry spikes in my chest. Maybe Shar's been in trouble this whole time we've been making out—

"Yeah, yeah, I'm good! We just finished early before the roofers come tomorrow. I was thinking I could grab some burritos for us."

I exhale. "That sounds good."

"Great." Someone honks and she curses. "Sorry. Hey, I'm going to sign off, but I'll probably be home in about thirty minutes, maybe shorter depending on how food pickup goes."

"OK, see you then!" We hang up and I scoot off Forrest's lap, onto my feet. "My stepmom is going to be home soon."

"I should probably go anyway," he says, standing. "Homework."

"Oh god, don't remind me." I press my fingers to my forehead.

"How's your essay going?" He walks to the door, pushing his feet back into his sneakers as he pulls on his jacket and shoulders his backpack.

"Nowhere," I say, and he laughs. Brekky headbutts his leg, and he bends down, scratching the cat behind the ears. He straightens and we stand there for a moment. I look down, scuffing my foot on the floor.

"So . . ." he says. "I'll text you?"

I nod. I want to reply, but everything that pops into my head sounds too casual, or too intense, or too . . . *something.* "Sounds good," I say brightly. He turns and opens the door, slipping out quickly before Brekky can follow him, and then it's just me and the cats, standing in the living room. I reach out and lock the door, then head back to my bedroom, fighting the urge to go to the window and watch Forrest walk away. That would be weird. Probably. Maybe it's weirder if I don't? It's too late, though; he's probably already out of sight.

I flop across my bed, my feet hanging off one side, my head hanging off the other. I stare down at the floor, reaching out to trace the pattern of the wood grain with my fingers. The house feels too quiet now that he's gone. In the kitchen, the refrigerator hums, and a few minutes later, the heater comes to life for another cycle. Brekky chirps, and then his weight lands beside me with a soft thump. He walks across my back and settles against my other side to lick his leg.

Forrest likes me. Forrest kissed me. I kissed him back. Should I have kissed him before he left? We didn't even hug. Oh my god, did I completely mess everything up? I squeeze my eyes shut. He probably thinks I'm a weirdo now, a weirdo who doesn't know how to date.

Are we dating now? We didn't talk about anything; we just made out. Do I hold his hand when I see him tomorrow?

Tomorrow is the Trans Awareness Week panel. And next week, on Friday, is the reelection.

"Fuck!" I yell, and roll over, away from Brekky, into a sitting position. He meows a complaint and resettles himself against my pillows.

I take my glasses off and bury my face in my hands. What happens to Forrest and me if I win the revote? What happens if *Forrest* wins? And what happens to our friends? If Jayden likes Alexander, and I like Forrest, and we all date, that means our friend groups will merge. Someone will inevitably break up and it will all be ruined.

"I'm sorry, Sidney," Jayden says through sobs, telling us he can't be around Alexander anymore. "Forrest needs to ditch them or I'm out."

Forrest's face pulls into a frown. "They're my friends, I can't do that."

"Please," I beg him. "Jayden's going to leave our group."

"So the answer is me getting rid of all my friends?" He shakes his head. "No. Maybe we should just break up, if that's what you want me to do."

"No, no—"

He's walking away and I collapse on the ground. My chest is hurting, tears rolling down my face.

"Sidney!"

I startle, pulling my face out of my hands.

"Sid?"

It's Shar. She's home. I jump up, looking around wildly, then swing open my closet door, looking at my face in the mirror hanging there. I don't look too upset, but my heart is still racing like what just happened really happened.

Am I . . . hallucinating? Is that what this is? What if it's not anxiety at all? What if it's something much, much worse?

"Sid!" Shar's voice is closer.

"Hey!" I call out.

She knocks. "You OK?"

"Yeah, sorry, just taking a nap," I say, staring at the door from across the room.

"OK. Food's on the table. I'm going to lie down for a bit too."

"Sounds good."

Her footsteps recede down the hall and into her bedroom. I wait a moment, then dart into the bathroom before she can see me. Inside, I splash water on my face. I don't know what's happening, but it's getting worse.

Something is wrong with me.

IN THE MORNING, I PACK MY LUNCH IN THE KITCHEN WHILE Mom finishes up in the bathroom. When she comes in, her face is pink, like she just finished washing it. She must be running late again.

"Sidney!" Her arms close around me from behind, hugging me for a moment. "You were in your room all night last night. Did you sleep OK?" She puts her thermos under the spout of the coffee machine, waiting as her espresso pod pours into it.

"Yeah," I say, but it's a lie. I woke up over and over, out of nightmare after nightmare, and I still feel half in that horrible dreamworld, anxious and a little sick.

"Good." She caps the thermos. "Let's check in about homework soon. I know it's been a minute and it seems like you're doing good this year, but I just want to make sure everything's still on track."

"OK," I say.

"Great." She squeezes my arm and kisses my cheek, and then she's gone and I'm alone.

My essay draft is due in three days, on Friday, and I still have just two pages languishing in my laptop. I need to avoid this talk until then, because I can't let Mom know I've fallen behind. She thinks I'm doing well in school, and she thinks that because I've been lying to her. I've been so focused on Queer Alliance and Forrest that I let homework slip away.

Forrest. I'm going to see him for the panel in the library today. My chest flutters at the thought, half with butterflies, half with dread. What do I do when I see him? I want to kiss him, but maybe it's safer to ignore him. I can't ignore him, though, I can't hurt him like that. Oh god, I have no idea how to act around him. I feel shaky and nauseous, and for a moment I think about staying home, pretending I'm sick, but I brush the impulse aside. I'm supposed to help him moderate the panel today, and I can't leave him and the alliance in the lurch.

What if this was his plan, all along? To pretend to be friendly, to distract me so much that I'd forget about the revote—telling me he likes me would be the perfect way to do that—

STOP.

STOP.

STOP.

I press my hands to my face. I can't believe I even had that thought. Forrest wouldn't do something that awful.

Are you sure? whispers a voice in my head.

"That's not real," I say into the quiet of the empty house. "It's not happening. That's not real. It's not happening. That's not real. It's not happening."

I glance at the clock. If I don't leave now, I'll be late.

I push the bubbling thoughts and images down and head to the train station, arriving on the platform with a few minutes to spare. I zone out, staring down onto the tracks. They're made of concrete, a cylinder scooped down into the ground below the edge of the platform, two metal railings running side by side down its length and disappearing into the tunnel at either end. I shuffle my feet forward, lining them up at the edge of the yellow strip that marks the no-standing zone. It would be so easy to jump in front of the train when it arrives.

I frown. Why did I think that? I don't want to do . . . that.

Do I?

A breeze picks up, and I peer down the tunnel to see the approaching train. I could jump, right now.

"No," I say, and step back, then look around. Nobody heard that, right? Me talking to myself in public?

No one's noticed me, and the train pulls up, its doors opening right in front of me. I move into it in a daze, finding an open seat and sliding over to sit by the window.

Why did I think that? I don't want to jump in front of a train, I don't want to die, I don't want to . . .

Do I?

Why would I think that, if I didn't secretly want to? When you're suicidal, you think about dying. You think about the ways it could happen, the ways you could do it. Like jumping in front of a train. It's weird, how easy it would be. I never really thought about that.

If I haven't thought about it before, maybe I'm not suicidal. But people don't just have thoughts like that for no reason. Imagine if someone asked me what I was thinking in that moment. "Oh, nothing, just picturing killing myself!" That's not normal. Fear flickers inside me, like kindling catching a spark.

I close my eyes. I'll imagine it again, see how it feels, me on the edge of the platform as the train thunders out of the tunnel like a bullet from a gun, stepping forward, off the edge—

My eyes snap open and I pull in my shoulders, tensing my body, the image still playing like a hologram in my mind as I stare out the window into the concrete darkness. I don't want it, I don't want it, I don't want it, I don't want it, I don't want it—if I don't want it, I can't be suicidal. If I was, then I'd want it.

But maybe that's how it gets you?

I replay the movie and check again, scanning my chest, my shoulders, my stomach for any trace of desire, and the more I look, the less sure I am of what it even feels like to want something, but it doesn't matter because I need to keep going, I can't stop, I have to figure it out somehow, before it's too late.

♥

At school, I skip my locker and dawdle in the bathroom until first bell rings. When I walk into class, Forrest is already seated. His face lights up the second he sees me, and I can't help smiling back, even as my stomach lurches. In my seat, I can feel him looking at me, and I pretend that whatever Ms. Lundahl is saying is the most fascinating thing I've ever heard.

My phone vibrates in my pocket. When I slip it out, it's a text from him. *Can't wait to run the event with you later*, he says, and my heart sinks. I want to respond, I want to tell him the same thing, I want to co-moderate the panel and kiss him afterward in front of everyone, but every time I imagine it, that romantic movie's catastrophic sequel rolls through my mind right behind it. Our breakup, breaking everything in its path, including me.

Forrest wouldn't even want to date me anyway if he knew what the inside of my head was like. I don't know what's happening to me, but it's not good. *I'm* not good—for anyone, and especially not Forrest. He likes me, and I like him, and I can't even text him back. Jayden has a crush on Alexander, and instead of being excited for him like Makayla and Anna, I'm worried about how it's going to affect me.

Maybe I don't have anxiety at all. Under my desk, I open a search browser on my phone and type in "sociopath symptoms."

My phone buzzes again. It's Dad this time, the first time he's texted since this weekend. Why is everyone texting me *right now*? I slide the phone into my pocket without looking at the message. At the front of the room, Ms. Lundahl is droning on about something I should probably care about, but all I can feel is the fluttering in my chest, the churning of my stomach.

I have to stop getting anxious, or I'm going to break down in class in front of everyone, and everyone will know what a freak I am.

Stop, I tell myself.

Stop.

Stop.

It doesn't work.

♥

I take my time at my locker once the lunch bell rings, longer than I need to. I never got to finish my Google search in class and it's been itching under my skin ever since, the need to know, the need to figure this out. If I'm a sociopath, my friends deserve to hear it, so they can get away from me. I click on link after link and scan the articles: "6 Traits of a Sociopath," "Here's Why Spotting a Sociopath Is Harder Than You Think," "Antisocial Personality Disorder Signs and Symptoms," and on and on.

"Sidney!"

I close the browser as fast as I can and look up. Anna is coming toward me down the hall, a big smile on her face as she waves at me. I shut my locker and fall into step beside her.

"How was your morning?" she asks, linking her arm through mine.

I shrug. "It was fine."

She squeezes my bicep. "You OK? You seem down."

"I'm just tired."

"I feel that."

The hallway in front of the library is busy, lockers opening and slamming shut all around us in rhythmic cacophony, clumps of people talking and laughing as they push through the crowded corridor to the cafeteria. Anna leads me around a group and then we're passing through the library's double doors, into an eddy of quiet outside the wild current.

"Hey y'all!" Mx. Prager calls out cheerfully, waving from their desk, and I smile weakly as we hustle past them toward the back of the library. Nyx and Stef are already there setting up for the panel, one at each end of a table as they slowly slide it out of the way.

"Hi," Nyx says breathlessly as we approach. The two of them push the table lengthwise against the bookcases, and Anna and I take the cue to grab another one and do the same. Together, the four of us move all the tables aside to leave a large area in the center.

"Where's Forrest?" I ask as casually as possible.

Stef fixes me with a pointed stare. The corner of her mouth twitches. I wonder if he told her. "He's making up a quiz during lunch," she says, pushing the first few chairs into a row.

"Cool," I say, nodding.

I can feel her eyes on me as we set up the rest of the rows, but I ignore her. We leave a square of carpet at the front for a stage area, with three chairs facing the rows, angled slightly toward each other.

We're just finishing up as Jayden and Makayla join us, and the others trickle in as we eat lunch. Most of the Queer Alliance is here, and they fill the first few rows, eating and chatting. More people join, some of them friends with our members, others I don't recognize.

I hear him before I see him.

"Are! You! Readyyyyy?!" Forrest bellows over the chatter. We all turn, and he's there at the back of the rows, posed like he's the Hulk ready to smash.

"Forrest," Mx. Prager calls out, and he grimaces.

"Sorry!" He whisper-calls over his shoulder, and everyone laughs. He shrugs, smiling, and scans the room until he spots me. He looks different, and it takes me a minute to pinpoint why: He's wearing jeans instead of sweatpants, and sneakers instead of slides. His hood is pushed off his head for once, his curls spilling out in full view. It's so cute, the way he clearly tried to spruce up for this.

When his gaze falls on me, it's like a spotlight, and I can't help but smile. I press my lips together, feeling the ghost of our kiss. He motions for me to come to him, and with everyone watching, all I can do is stand and weave through the spaces between chairs until I reach him.

"Hey," he says. His eyes are sparkling.

"Hi," I say. I sound stiff, and his smile falters for a second, but he pulls his backpack around, digging out a couple sheets of paper.

"I printed out the questions for us," he says, handing me one of the pages.

"Great," I say.

He steps closer, and I freeze, my eyes widening. He stops, frowning, and starts to say something, but then someone comes up beside us and we both turn.

“Sidney, Forrest, I’d like to introduce you to our guest,” Mr. Harrison says. “This is Dean Foster, executive director of the Trans Youth Center here in town.” He gestures to the man standing behind him.

Dean is clean-cut and slim, a few inches shorter than Mr. Harrison, with strawberry-blond hair in a tight fade. He’s wearing a dark green sweater and black jeans, with new-looking sneakers. I always pictured executive directors in collared shirts and suit pants, like Mom in her blazers and slacks, but Dean looks more like a fun older cousin.

“Hi there,” Dean says, shaking each of our hands with a smile. “It’s an honor to meet you both. I’m ready whenever you are.”

“Sweet,” Forrest says. “Shall we?” He sweeps an arm toward the front, and then we’re all walking there together, taking our seats as Mr. Harrison calls the room to attention.

“Welcome, everyone,” Mr. Harrison says. “As the advisor for Queer Alliance, I’m going to take a moment to introduce our speaker, and then our co-presidents will chat with him. There will be time for Q&A at the end, so hold your fire and we’ll try to get to everyone.” He glances over at us, smiling. “It gives me great pleasure to introduce Dean Foster, the executive director for the Trans Youth Center here in Seattle, and a former student of mine.” Dean does a half bow from his seat, as if he’s onstage. “Dean was once a dorky teenager walking these very halls—”

“And now I’m a dorky adult,” Dean interjects.

Mr. Harrison laughs. “We didn’t have Queer Alliance then, but Dean was a trailblazer in his own right. I’ll leave it to him to talk more about that, but suffice to say he made quite an impression as Romeo in the school play. Sidney and Forrest, take it away." He gestures to us before retreating to a chair in the front row.

Everyone is looking at us now. I feel hot and cold with fear, stomach turning over. Am I going to faint? I might faint here, in front of everyone, and I'll ruin the panel and everyone will be mad at me because they worked so hard on it, and—

"Dean, thanks for coming today," Forrest says. His voice cracks on the first word, but miraculously no one laughs, and Dean acts like it didn't happen.

"Glad to be here," he says. "It's quite a throwback for me."

"For sure," Forrest says. "So, you were in theater, and now you're the executive director of the Trans Youth Center. I went there to get on hormones last year, it was super chill. How did you end up in that role?"

"I'm glad you had a good experience with us," Dean says. "In my time here, I played Romeo in the school play, and that actually led me to come out as trans. I think I was one of the first students to be openly trans at Jefferson High."

The crowd murmurs. "That's really cool," Forrest says. "I mean, it must have been hard too."

"It was a lot of things." Dean smiles, his eyes flicking to Mr. Harrison and then back. "My experience at Jefferson was part of what led me to create the Trans Youth Center after I graduated from the social work program at the University of Washington. I still do theater on the side—I'm involved in an all-drag production of *Hamlet* right now—but the Trans Youth Center is my life's work."

I peer down at the page in my hands. I should say something, but Forrest has already asked the first two questions, and the conversation is flowing. I'll just interrupt it if I speak up.

"Sidney," Forrest says, nudging me with his elbow.

I look up, and everyone is staring at me, waiting for me to speak. Dean is watching me too, eyebrows raised, as if he doesn't understand why I'm here.

"Are you going to help me co-moderate at all, or are you just going to sit there?" Forrest asks through a clenched jaw. The crowd murmurs in agreement.

"I'm sorry," I whisper, and he scoffs.

"Whatever," he says. "You clearly aren't fit to be president. Good thing I've been campaigning behind your back this whole time."

My mouth opens, tears stinging my eyes, and I turn to Mr. Harrison for help, but he's just standing there, glaring at me, arms crossed.

Everyone laughs, and I twitch, breathing shallowly. Forrest and Dean are talking, Forrest's elbows firmly by his sides. I sneak a glance at the audience; everyone is watching them, smiling and nodding along, including Mr. Harrison. No one is looking at me.

That wasn't real. It was an anxiety movie.

But it felt real. My heart is still pounding, tears welling behind my eyes. I don't deserve to be here. Forrest is ten times more prepared. I never should have been president in the first place. When it's time for the revote, everyone will pick Forrest, and ask me to leave.

Oh my god. I'm going to cry, here in front of everyone.

I squeeze my right arm, the one between me and Forrest, and dig my nails into my skin, pinching one, two, three times.

That's not real. It's not happening.

That's not real. It's not happening.

That's not real. It's not happening.

Dean and Forrest are smiling and nodding, and I nod along with them.

"So," Forrest says, "I think we just have a few more questions and then we'll open it up." He looks over at me, at the paper in my hands, crumpled inward on the left side where I'm clutching it. "Sidney, you wanna ask the next one?"

"Sure!" I say, scanning the text. I have no idea where we are in our list, so I pick the second to last one, just to be safe. "Dean, what was your favorite part of going to Jefferson, and what was the most challenging?"

"What a great question," Dean says, clapping his hands together. As he starts to talk, I take a deep breath, quietly, slowly, then exhale, and glance across the crowd to the clock above Mx. Prager's desk.

Fifteen minutes. Then we'll be done. I just have to hold on until then.

TEN MINUTES LEFT.

Forrest calls on someone. I can feel him looking at me afterward, but all I can hear is the buzzing in my ears.

The paper crumples in my hands.

Everyone is clapping and smiling and there's something ringing in my ears, ringing in the room, the bell is ringing.

Forrest is standing. I can stand. I stand, grab my backpack, Forrest and Dean, all smiles, turning away to greet Mr. Harrison, I'm turning away and Anna's in front of me and then she's not and I'm at the front of the library and I'm in the hall in a bathroom, single stall, door locked.

I was going to fix everything fix myself so my thoughts couldn't ruin my life but it's all happening again and there's nothing I can do to stop it and I'm going to kill myself and I don't want to my face is hot and wet and my head is pounding and my nose is so clogged I can't breathe through it. I gulp air through my mouth in shuddering gasps, scooting across the floor to the toilet paper roll in its holder. Tearing off a strip, I blow my nose until it's clear. The devastation is a forest fire, completely out of control.

It's ten minutes into sixth period. I don't want to walk in looking like this. But if I skip, the school will call Mom.

I leave the bathroom.

WHEN SIXTH PERIOD ENDS, I TAKE MY TIME HEADING TO MY locker, hoping the halls will be clear and Forrest will be gone by the time I get there. I stop in front of the library and pretend to look at the exhibit while students stream around me, arm in arm with their friends. Everyone seems so happy and normal.

Finally, it starts to get quiet, and I make my way to the junior hall.

And there he is.

Leaning against my locker, waiting for me.

Walking to him is like trying to run in a dream, when you feel like you're going fast but your limbs move like they're pulling through thick molasses. As I approach, he straightens upright, clasping his hands one over the other in front of him.

"Are you all right?" he asks, his eyes soft and worried.

"I'm fine," I say quietly, stopping a few feet away.

He frowns. "You didn't seem that way during the panel."

I look down.

"Sidney." He steps forward, his hand coming into my line of vision and folding gently around mine. "What happened? We were supposed to co-moderate, but it was like you were on another planet."

"I have a lot going on, OK?" I yank my hand away, and he pulls his up as if to protect himself.

"So talk to me about it." He crosses his arms.

"I can't!" My voice cracks.

He steps back, his frown deepening. "I don't understand. I thought you liked me."

"I do! I do." I'm crying now. "I just . . . can't do this."

His face goes completely flat and still. "What do you mean?"

"I'm not . . ." I swallow. "I'm not . . . good."

"What are you talking about?"

I look away, clutching one hand in the other. The hallway around us is emptying, and a few people glance at us curiously as they hurry out. I could just run away right now, run away, out of the building, down the street, and before the movie can play, I shake my head, squeeze my eyes shut. "Stop."

"Stop what?" His voice is raw with confusion. I open my eyes. He's staring at me, head tilted, eyebrows furrowed. If I didn't look crazy to him before, I definitely do now. I just talked to myself in front of him.

"I'm sorry," I say. "I can't talk about this. I have to go." I turn, hurrying down the hall, but he follows me.

"Sid, what's going on? We *kissed* yesterday, and now you're acting like . . ." He trails off. I speed up, but he keeps pace with me. "Sid, talk to me. I like you. I want to date you and shit."

"Forrest, please." I push the door open with as much force as I can, taking the steps down to the sidewalk. "Just leave me alone."

He stops, and the distance between us lengthens, pulling at me like a rubber band as I barrel toward the parking lot and the street beyond it.

"Is that really what you want?" he calls out.

I don't respond. I just keep walking.

I'M SO AFRAID. THE STREET IS FILLED WITH CARS. IT WOULD be so easy to step out in front of one of them. I hug the opposite side of the sidewalk, trail a hand along the wall of the grocery store that sits next to the street, its painted concrete exterior cold and wet. It's raining. I have to stay as far away from the street as possible, or I might lose control and step off. A big truck would take me out for sure. Or I could pick an SUV, that might do it—*Idontwanttodie*—I have to get home somehow, but if I go into the train station, I might jump in front of the train. The grocery store is gone and my hand hits branches, a hedge of small bushes in front of a boxy condo. It hurts. A truck hitting me would hurt. But just for a second, before I hit the ground—*stop*—head smacking the pavement—*stopidontwannadie*—the train station's mouth opens up and I walk into it, scan my fare card on autopilot, take the escalator down, down, down into its belly. I can't stop. Am I actually under my own control or is this other thing, this something wrong, taking over? The train station is crowded. If I jumped everyone would see, they'd scream, someone would rush to the train, beating on its side, but it would be too late, I'd—*STOP STOP STOP! THIS ISN'T REAL, IT'S NOT HAPPENING, THIS ISN'T REAL, IT'S NOT HAPPENING, THIS ISN'T REAL, IT'S NOT HAPPENING*—back against the metal side of the escalator as the train roars into the station, eyes shut as it comes to a stop, step inside where it's safe, I'm safe, grab the metal pole but that's too close to the doors and if I'm too close to the doors I might slip out when they open again and run to the front and jump on the tracks as the train pulls away and walk to the back of the car, the last row, an open seat, and someone sits beside me, thank god, I can't push past this person to get out, but what if I do?

What if I do?

What if I do?

What if I do?

What if I do?

AT HOME, I GO STRAIGHT TO MY ROOM. THERE ARE SO many ways for me to hurt myself in the house. Knives in the kitchen. Medication in the bathroom cabinet. How did I never think about this before? How is it so easy to die by suicide? I always thought it was this big deal, this extreme thing, but now that I've had the thought I can't unthink it. Did I feel this way before and just didn't know? I don't want to die, so why am I thinking about all the ways I could? I don't want to die, but what if I lose control and accidentally kill myself?

I get under the blankets and wrap myself up tight, phone clutched in my hand. I want to call someone, anyone, but I don't want them to worry, or think that I've lost it completely. And who am I supposed to call? Not Dad, that's for sure, and I don't want to freak out Mom or Shar. I already drove Forrest away. Jayden's probably so excited about his new crush, and my problems will totally kill the vibe. Makayla is Jayden's twin, so if I call them, then he'll know too. And Anna—

Anna.

I open our text thread. The last thing she sent me was a meme, and looking at it, I smile. Anna's such a good friend. *Hey*, I type.

The ellipses pop up instantly. *Hiiiieeee*

I'm—

I delete and try again.

Something is—

No, not that.

Can you come over?

Of course, she says.

I lie there, staring at the thread. I need her. I don't want to die. I check her location, and watch her tiny dot move around her house and then out of it. It moves faster than normal, so I know she must have called a car. I keep my eyes fixed to her as she snakes through Capitol Hill, down its east side; past Judkins Park, where we went to a protest rally a few years ago; across Rainier Avenue and up the back of Beacon Hill, and then the dot pauses on the street outside my house. I push back the covers and set my feet on the floor. She knocks, and it takes everything in me to get up and walk out of my bedroom, but I do.

When I open the door, she steps inside and wraps me in a hug. My head nestles into her neck, and I squeeze back, feeling the comforting softness of her in my arms.

"You give the best hugs," I mumble.

"I know," she says, and squeezes me tighter for a moment before releasing me. Her face is serious. "I'm going to make you some tea, and we're going to go in your room, and you're going to tell me what's going on, because I know you and I know something's up."

I nod. She heads to the kitchen and fills our electric kettle, then selects two mugs while I stand there and watch her. Brekky meows from the floor, Earl Grey echoing him from the cat tree.

"I should feed them," I say, and cross to the cabinet where we keep their wet food. Brekky headbutts my hand as I open it, and tries to climb inside, on top of the pallet of cans. I pull him out. "Get out of there, you ridiculous little boy."

"Herbal or caffeinated?" Anna says.

"Definitely herbal," I say. I do not need to add a caffeine buzz to whatever the fuck is going on inside my brain right now.

"Chamomile? Peppermint? Rooibos?"

"Chamomile is good." I crack open the cat food and scoop the portions into clean bowls, then carry them to the feeding station, the cats trailing me the whole way. They chow down, and I follow Anna back to my room. She hands me my mug, and we sit down the bed.

"So," she asks. "What's up?"

And I tell her everything.

♥

When I'm finished, she's quiet for a little bit, turning the mug around in her hands. Maybe this was too much. Maybe I overwhelmed her.

"Wow," she says finally. "That's a lot."

I look down. "Sorry."

"Oh my god, NO." She reaches out and squeezes my knee. "Not 'a lot' as in you're too much. 'A lot' as in . . . wow, you've been dealing with a lot."

"Oh."

"I'm not surprised you have a crush on Forrest," she says.

"You aren't?" I can't even hide the incredulity in my voice.

"No." She waves a hand. "And also, I don't think you're crazy. But that definitely doesn't sound like anxiety."

"Yeah." I raise the mug to my nose, breathing in the sweet, musty smell of the chamomile tea. It's familiar and calming. "I just . . . don't know what's going on with me. I'm . . ." My voice gets watery and thick, my throat closing up. "I'm scared."

"Sidney." She scoots closer to me.

"I'm sorry I've been a bad friend." I'm crying now, through my words.

"What are you talking about?" she says. "In what way have you *ever* been a bad friend?"

"I'm self-centered, and I make everything about me, and all I can think about is my own problems, and—"

"OK, those are all basically the same thing, so that's one thing, and it's not even true," she says. "Nothing you just said about what it's like inside your head sounds remotely like that. Honestly, it sounds like torture."

I cry harder, because she's right, and she puts her arms around me, hugging me tightly. We rock back and forth, in a comfortable embrace, until my tears slow. The door swings open a little bit as Brekky pushes through, and a moment later, Earl Grey pokes her head in too. Brekky jumps up on the bed, curling up against Anna, and Earl Grey prowls over to my bookcase, jumping on top of it to look out my window.

"So . . . I think you should tell your moms," Anna says finally, pulling back from our hug.

"Urrrgh." I shut my eyes. "They're going to freak out."

"They're supposed to freak out," she says, twisting side to side to stretch out her back. "They love you. And they don't want you to . . ."

"I don't want to either."

"I'll help you," Anna says. "I brought my homework. We can study until they get home and tell them together."

I press my face to my knees, squishing my glasses against the bridge of my nose. "I'm so behind on the essay. I'm going to fail Lundahl's class for sure."

"Maybe." Anna shrugs. "Maybe not."

"How are you so chill?"

"I mean, I'm not, at all. But also, therapy and medication." She bends her wrist gayly, wiggling her fingers at me.

"Maybe *I* need therapy and medication," I mutter.

She snorts. "Maybe you do."

♥

As usual, Shar gets home first. Her truck pulls up, and the cats scatter, dashing to greet her. Our walls are thin, and I can hear everything: the passenger door slamming shut, her key turning in the lock, her work boots on the floor as she heads to the kitchen. She sets something down on the counter, probably her backpack with her lunch and water bottle and whatever else a carpenter needs to bring to work.

"It's gonna be OK," Anna says, her quiet voice bringing me back to my room. I was so focused on listening to Shar's arrival that it almost swallowed me up. Anna touches my knee from where she's sprawled out beside me, doing a reading for history class.

"Sid?" Shar calls from the kitchen, and a moment later she's tromping toward my door. A knock sounds.

"Hey," I call back. "Anna's here studying with me."

"Oh, great!" She peeks her head in, smiling at both of us. "I'm gonna take a nap, then probably get started on dinner once your mom gets home. Anna, you're welcome to stay."

Anna glances at me, then grins at Shar. "Thanks!"

Shar withdraws, and I look down at Anna. "Please stay."

"Shar's cooking. Of course I'm staying," she says. "When do you want to tell them?"

"Before dinner," I say. "I just want to get it over with."

She nods, and turns her eyes back to her laptop. I watch her for a while, then zone out, staring out the window. Images play in that weird liminal space behind my eyeballs, and my room fades out until I'm alone in the dark theater of my brain, watching the past few days over and over and over. Forrest probably hates me now. Who could like someone who literally walks away while you're telling them you want to date them?

A little while later, the sound of the front door opening jerks me back to reality again. I look at Anna, and she gives me the thumbs-up. I take a deep breath, and slide off the bed. Here we go.

We nearly run into Mom as we step out of my door.

"Hi sweetie," she says, and catches sight of Anna behind me. "You two hanging out?"

"Yes. Um. Actually. Anna came over to help me with something. Can I talk to you and Shar?" I shove my hands into my pockets, gripping the fabric at the bottom.

She frowns slightly. "Of course."

We follow her down the hall and into the room she shares with Shar. Its walls are painted an eggshell white, like the living room and kitchen, with gauzy curtains and framed photos of our family above the bed, a queen-size that takes up half the room. A small brown leather armchair sits in the corner opposite the door, Earl Grey asleep on top of the fleece blanket piled on its seat.

Shar is lying down on her side of the bed and cracks an eye when we come in. "What's up?"

"Sid and Anna want to talk to us about something," Mom says, closing the door. She crosses to the chair and slides Earl Grey to one side so she can sit; the cat lets out a croaky meow of protest, then resettles in her new spot. Shar straightens up, yawning, and motions us to the bed.

I perch on its other side, Anna standing next to me.

"What's going on?" Mom asks. I can already tell she's worried, and I hate that I'm about to make that even worse.

"I'm, um." I clasp my hands together, rubbing one thumb over the other. I didn't think about how to say this, but it's too late now. "I've been having these . . . thoughts. For a long time, actually. But they started getting worse last year. And this year. I thought it was anxiety, but . . . it's something else. I get these, like . . ." I spread my hands out, as if I can show Mom and Shar in the shape of the air between my fingers. "Visions. I don't know. They feel so real. Of you guys getting hurt, or Dad, or . . . people turning on me. And I hear these voices all the time. Telling me to do stuff. Like run away, or that my friends hate me, or . . ." I swallow. Tears sting my eyes, and I take off my glasses, pressing the heels of my hands against my eyeballs. Anna grips my shoulder. "Today they've been telling me to kill myself."

The room is silent. Even Earl Grey stops purring for a moment, only to start again.

"I was standing in the train station this morning and this thought just popped into my head," I say, rushing onward. "That I could just jump in front of it. Why would I think that? I don't want to die. But I couldn't even walk down the street today without thinking about jumping in front of a car. I'm afraid I'm going to do it, and I don't want to, I don't want to, I don't want to die!" My voice breaks on the last word, stretching it out into a wail and then I'm sobbing, bent forward on the bed. Mom's arms close around me a moment later, someone else's hand on my head, Shar and Mom both murmuring to me as I cry. Anna's holding my arm with both hands now, squeezing my bicep.

"Sweetie," Mom says. "Honey. We're going to figure this out, OK?"

I nod, the top of my head rubbing against her chest, and slowly sit up. Mom pats my face with one of Shar's cloth hankies, as Shar gives me a small smile and leaves the room, coming back a moment later with a glass of water for me. I sip and then take the hanky from Mom, blowing my nose.

"I'm sorry I didn't tell you," I say. "I didn't want to upset you or anything. I haven't been able to focus on school because it's just been getting worse and worse, and I have a huge essay due on Friday that I've barely started."

"Your well-being is way more important than school," Mom says in a low, fierce voice.

"But last year . . ."

"Is this why you were struggling then?"

I nod.

"Sidney. I'm so sorry." Mom cups my face with her hands. "I thought I asked you what was going on."

"You did, but . . . you were so mad." My voice drops to a whisper. "I thought you'd just get more upset if I made excuses."

"Oh, no. No, no, no. My baby." Mom scoots closer and wraps her arms around me. "I'm sorry for anything I did that made you feel that way."

I start crying again, and I can tell by the way she's breathing that she's crying too, and that just makes me cry harder.

"Anna," Mom says after a while. "Thank you for helping Sidney. I'm guessing that's why you came over today."

"Yeah," Anna says. "Sidney's my best friend."

"You're a good kid," Shar says. "I'm going to make us all some dinner, and then we can talk about what to do next."

"Thank you, sweetheart," Mom says.

"I got you." I hear Shar's footsteps grow faint as she moves out of the room.

I let out a deep, shuddering sigh into Mom's shoulder. I told people the truth, and the world didn't end. I told people what my brain is doing, and they didn't lock me away or tell me I'm crazy. They still love me. They're going to help me.

Mom squeezes me closer, her arms warm and comforting, and for the first time in a long time, I feel safe.

CHAPTER 24

MOM CALLS ME OUT OF SCHOOL FOR THE REST OF THE WEEK and takes an emergency leave at work. My whole body fills with relief when she tells me. I won't have to face Forrest or the rest of my friends just yet. Even though I know it will be all right if I tell Jayden and Makayla what's been going on, I'm still not completely sure. Part of me is still scared, still whispering to me about how it could all go wrong. I try not to listen, I try to block the voice out, but it doesn't really work.

She emails her therapist and gets a list of recommendations for people who work with teens and take our health insurance. I don't leave the house the entire weekend; I'm afraid if I go out the thoughts will come back and I'll lose control this time. To keep my brain as quiet as I can, I watch hours and hours of shows and movies. On Monday, Mom calls me out of class again, then emails my teachers and asks them for extensions on all my missing work. It feels good to be babied.

On Tuesday, Mom drives me to my appointment with the first therapist on the list.

"Remember," she says once we're parked. "If you don't like her, we have more options."

I nod. We get out of the car and make our way inside. It's a newer office building in one of the neighborhoods in North Seattle, nestled on a side street, next to a community garden. The elevator takes us up to the seventh floor, and we step off into a waiting room lined with windows, a hallway stretching away from it on either side. I can see doors spaced along it, and a few people wait in chairs for their appointments.

We've been sitting for only a few moments when a woman appears. "Sidney?" she says. Mom squeezes my arm, and I stand, moving toward the therapist.

"Hi there," she says with a warm smile, her eyes crinkling. "I'm Tracy."

"Hi," I say, following her. She's a few inches shorter than me, her hair cut like Shar's but brunette. She's dressed in classic Seattle wear: dark jeans and a black fleece jacket open over a crew-neck shirt.

"My pronouns are she/her," she says.

"They/them," I answer.

"Great." She pushes open a door farther down the hallway and we walk into her office. It's a small room, but cozy, a dark green two-seater couch against one wall, with a bright yellow accent rug and a round wooden coffee table.

"Tea?" she asks, turning on the electric kettle on her desk, which sits against the wall opposite the couch. She sits in the office chair and spins to face me.

"Sure." I sit down on the edge of the couch. "I didn't know therapists made their clients tea."

She chuckles. "It's not required, but I like to. I have some fidgets there too, if you want one." She points out the bowl on the coffee table, and I lean forward, rifling through it until I pick up a squishy rubber cat. It reminds me of Brekky.

"Chamomile or peppermint?" she asks, and I pick chamomile. A moment later, a steaming mug sits in front of me, and Tracy is peering at me over her own cup.

"So. Tell me what's on your mind. Your mom gave me the rundown, but I'd love to hear it in your words."

"Yeah." I nod. It feels easier, somehow, to open my mouth this time and say the words. "So. I've been having these . . . thoughts."

I tell Tracy the whole story, the way I told it to Anna. She asks me questions here and there, about what the voices sound like, where they come from, if I see the images in my head or in the world around me, how I react when I have the thoughts. She asks about what's happening in my life, if there's anything stressing me out or weighing on me, so I tell her about Dad, and about Forrest, and the Queer Alliance, and my homework.

When I'm done, she takes a sip of her tea. "Have you ever heard of obsessive-compulsive disorder?" she asks.

"OCD?" I frown. "Yeah . . . that's when you're like, a clean freak, right? Like, you can't stand germs and have to wash your hands a lot."

"Not exactly," she says. "There is what's called contamination OCD, where the primary fear is of being, well . . . contaminated somehow, often by germs. For people with that subset of OCD, they have a lot of thoughts or mental images about this fear, this obsession, and they engage in actions—rituals, or compulsions—to try and manage those thoughts."

"I don't have that," I say.

"Yeah, it doesn't sound like you do. But there are other OCD obsessions too. Anything you can think of can be an obsession. So someone might be obsessed with the idea that harm could come to someone they love. They're having a lot of thoughts about it, a lot of fear and maybe mental images of how that harm could happen, or inner voices telling them it will, and their compulsions might revolve around trying to prevent that harm or ensure that it hasn't happened. The compulsions can be external, like having to call that person to make sure they're OK, or they might be internal, like reviewing your last interactions with that person or the route they might take to work or the activities they do every day, to figure out whether they're all right or how they might potentially come to harm." She turns the mug in her hands, watching me.

"That's . . . me," I say slowly. "It happens a lot."

Tracy nods. "Rejection or abandonment could be another obsession. Or suicide."

When she says that word, it's like my whole body lights up from my toes to the top of my head. "You mean . . . I don't actually want to kill myself?"

"You've told me you don't want to."

"I don't." I shake my head. "But why would I have those thoughts?"

"That's what happens with OCD," she says. "That's why it's so tricky. It convinces us that our thoughts are our reality—or that they could be. That there's meaning behind these thoughts. They're called intrusive thoughts."

"I know that phrase," I say. "Like—*I let the intrusive thoughts win!*"

Tracy smiles. "Totally. But the meme isn't accurate to what intrusive thoughts actually are. They're not the random, benign impulses we get. Intrusive thoughts are opposite our values, opposite what we actually want and think and feel and believe. And everyone has them."

"Really?"

"Yep." She nods.

"Everyone has them," I repeat. "Everyone has random thoughts about jumping in front of a train. Or their dad getting killed in a freak car accident. Or all their friends turning on them."

"I know." She leans forward in her chair. "But it's true. The difference is, most people say 'oh, that was a weird thought,' and move on. With OCD, we give that thought meaning. We think it says something about us. And it's usually to do with something deeply important to us, which is why it's so distressing."

"Oh." I'm kind of hearing what she's saying, but I'm still stuck on that part where everyone has thoughts like mine. Except not everyone freaks out over them. "Why does MY brain have to do this? Like, what went wrong?"

"Nothing is wrong with you," she says. "No one really knows for sure what causes OCD. Like a lot of things, it's probably a combination of nature and nurture."

"Do *you* have OCD?" I ask.

"I do!" She raises her mug. "Cheers to both of us."

I snort and lean forward, grabbing my mug. It's still warm, and the taste of the tea is calming. "Cool, so how do I make it stop?"

"That's a great question," Tracy says. "We don't. Trying to stop the thoughts can be a compulsion, and engaging in compulsions makes the obsessions worse, even if it initially helps. Instead, we work on accepting the thoughts, accepting the uncertainty of what could happen, and . . . we just let them be and move on."

"I have to accept . . . that Shar might get killed?" I raise my eyebrows. "I have to accept that my brain plays me little horror movies about all the ways I could commit suicide?"

"Yup." Tracy nods. "It's easier said than done, I know, and there are other tools that come into play besides mindfulness and acceptance. The gold standard of OCD treatment is exposure and response prevention, where we help you experience your fears without doing compulsions. That helps teach your brain to process your intrusive thoughts as just thoughts."

"What about the voices, though? And the images . . . they just feel so real." I swallow, staring down at the mug. "Are you sure I'm not crazy?"

"There's nothing wrong with having a mental health condition," Tracy says. "And certainty isn't the point. But I can tell you what you've told me: The voices are inside you, not something you hear externally. The images are in your mind, not something you're seeing outside yourself. The thoughts and images you're experiencing are very upsetting to you and not aligned with your values or what you actually know or want or believe. That's OCD. If you were hearing and seeing things externally, or if you wanted to die, that would be a different conversation and a different diagnosis."

I nod. "OK."

"We're almost at time," she says gently. "But I want you to know this doesn't have to be your experience forever. Successful treatment is very possible. And medication is something we can try too."

I nod again, and set my mug back on the coffee table. "Thanks," I say. Something inside me settles, like a cat finding the perfect place to curl up. I have a diagnosis now. And it's something she can treat.

I don't have to feel this way forever.

♥

The first thing I do when I get home is text Anna. *So . . . apparently I have OCD.*

She doesn't respond right away, and I set my phone down, crossing to my window. The backyard is in full fall mode, our small square of grass littered with red and golden leaves from the maple tree that shades it. As I watch, a squirrel hops across the lawn to the base of the trunk and starts digging. Probably burying food before winter, so it has something to sustain it when the months get darker and acorns get harder to find. Do squirrels really eat acorns? I pull out my phone to look it up, but a text from Anna is waiting.

OMG THAT MAKES SO MUCH SENSE, she says.

It does?

She sends me five links in rapid succession, and I watch the videos one by one. *I saved these when I was trying to figure out my brain a few years ago*, she says. *I don't have OCD but . . . I was kinda just looking everything up at that time hoping something would jump out.*

The videos are relatable. Too relatable. One is from a creator I've seen on my feed before, a therapist who also has OCD. I'd never watched one of her videos, always scrolling away in search of something funny, or something about books, or queer history, something I was interested in. Mental health wasn't one of those things. Besides Anna telling me I had anxiety, I mostly tried to avoid thinking about my mental state at all. But the therapist is talking about suicidal OCD, and, hey. That's me.

Now I know.

"I don't want to die," I say quietly into the room. I know it to be true, the same way I know I love our cats, and Shar, and my mom, and my friends.

And Dad.

I do love Dad. I just don't know what my other feelings about him are.

Are you going to tell Jayden and Makayla? Anna asks.

I stare at her text. I want to. But not over the phone. *Yeah, I wanna do it in person, though.*

We could all hang out after school this week, she says. *I know you're taking the week off. But you could meet us at whoever's house. Or we could come over there.*

After a long moment, I reply. *That sounds really nice.*

♥

When they knock the next afternoon, though, I almost don't let them in. The movies play immediately, filling my head with all the ways this could go wrong, and I stand immobile in front of the door, one hand on the knob.

They knock again, and I take a deep breath, opening the door.

"Sidney!" I stagger back a few steps as Jayden crashes into me, his arms wrapping firmly around my shoulders.

"Hi?" I lift one hand, patting his back. He squeezes tightly and then lets go, stepping back, eyes bright.

"I missed you," he says solemnly.

"Really?" I say, before I can stop myself. God, I sound insecure.

"Yes, really, you dork," he says, sliding past me. Makayla follows him with another hug at the ready, and I relax into their arms, hugging them back.

"It's nice to see you," they murmur into my ear, and this time I keep the insecure thoughts inside and just hug them tighter. Anna smiles at me over their shoulder, a plastic grocery bag in her hands.

"What's that?" I say once we're all inside.

"Hair dye!" she says, holding the bag up. "I thought we could dip dye my ends while you fill these two in."

"Anna's been very mysterious," Makayla says from the floor, where she's petting a purring Brekky. "She said you were going through it, but that we shouldn't worry, so I've been doing my best. But I want to know what's going on. If you want to tell us." She looks up at me.

"I do," I say, and I mean it. I want them to know. And it's not really fair to expect Anna to be the only one who does.

"Good," Jayden says. "I'm hungry. Can we order pizza?"

We all chorus a yes and Anna pulls out her phone to place the order. With that done, we head back to the bathroom, Jayden dragging one of the kitchen chairs after us.

Somehow we all squeeze in together, with me perched on the toilet, Jayden across from me on the bathtub's edge, and Anna seated on the chair, head tipped back so her hair hangs into the sink. Makayla's been appointed the hair dyeing wizard for the day, so they stand next to Anna, setting the box dye on the sink and pulling Anna's protective cape out of her backpack.

"You're such a pro, Anna," I say as Makayla encloses her in the black fabric.

"Well, when you dye your hair as often as I do, it makes sense to invest," she says. Her hair is its natural dark blond right now, the dye from her last at-home job—a bright teal—all faded out. Makayla rips open the box and pulls out the dye, the gloves, and the applicator. As they get to work brushing color onto the ends of Anna's hair, I take a deep breath. Jayden reaches out and sets a hand on my knee, and the warmth anchors me. These are my friends. They care about me. I let the warmth fill my body, and for the fourth time in the past few days, I explain everything that has been going on.

They listen, murmuring at the right places, Jayden squeezing my knee now and then. I see Makayla's eyebrows fly up when I describe catching feelings for Forrest, but she doesn't say anything, just keeps working on Anna's hair. I don't look at Jayden; if he really does have a crush on Alexander, I don't even know what to expect from his reaction.

"So yeah," I say finally. "I have OCD, I guess. And I fucked everything up with Forrest and everyone is going to vote for him this Friday, which is fine, because I can never go back to Queer Alliance anyway."

They're all quiet for a moment, the silence broken only by the soft sound of the applicator turning the bottom three inches of Anna's hair a bright magenta. Makayla finishes the last strands and washes the applicator under the faucet, the dye swirling around the white porcelain bowl and down the drain.

"I'm so sorry," Jayden says finally, squeezing my leg.

"Thanks," I mumble. Maybe this was too much. Maybe it's too heavy, too weird, too—

"Sidney, we love you so much," Makayla says, sitting beside Jayden. "I'd give you a hug or something, but . . ." They hold up their gloved hands, covered in dye, and I smile a little.

"I know it's a lot," I say.

"Nope," Makayla says immediately, at the same time as Jayden.

"Jinx!" he crows, pointing at her, then shrinks back as she pretends to grab him with her dye-covered hands.

"Anyway," she says, grinning at me. "I just want to be there for you, you know? I think I can safely say we all do."

Jayden and Anna murmur their agreement, and I nod, tears filling my eyes. Jayden leans over and hugs me, and I hug him back.

"For what it's worth, I don't think you fucked things up with Forrest," he says. "My inside sources tell me he's been talking about you all week. He's super worried about you. And confused. And upset. But mostly worried."

"Your inside source wouldn't happen to be named Alexander, would he?" Anna says dryly.

I pull away and sit up in time to see Jayden blush. "Yeah, about that . . ."

"You have a crush on Alexander!" Makayla shrieks.

"How did you know?!" Jayden shrieks back.

"Dude." Anna rolls her eyes. "You are *not* subtle. The sudden interest in breakdancing? The heart eyes whenever he walks by?"

"The *nightly FaceTimes*?" Makayla arches her eyebrows.

"Uggghhhhhhhhhhh." Jayden drags his hands down his face. "OK. Yes. I have a giant crush on him. And . . ." He freezes, a sneaky smile curling his lips. "*He likes me too!*"

Makayla and Anna scream so loud that I flinch and start laughing, and then we're all laughing.

"Why didn't you *say* anything?" I poke his arm.

"Well . . ." He shifts, making a face. "You hated his bestie. Or I thought you did. And then it seemed like y'all were maybe cool, but I don't know, things were so peaceful and I didn't want to mess it all up."

"I'm really sorry," I say quietly. It makes me sad to know my problems with Forrest kept Jayden from pursuing someone he liked. At the same time, it's nice that he cared enough about how I felt to not pursue it. And then I feel selfish for thinking that. The emotions swirl inside me, and I follow them down—

"Hey." Jayden shakes my arm. "It all worked out. And now we can double-date."

"I don't know," I say. "Like, that would be so cool, but . . . I acted all weird the last time Forrest and I talked. I told him I couldn't be with him like that, and I was so awkward—"

"So talk to him and explain," Jayden says. "I really think it will work out. And even if you don't end up dating, maybe you can salvage the friendship."

"I don't know." I stare at the floor.

"I don't think you have to leave Queer Alliance forever," Anna says gently. "And I don't think everyone is going to automatically reelect Forrest. You've done a really good job, and everyone likes you. People in the club have been asking us about you all week. Maybe you could come back for the meeting on Friday?"

I chew on my bottom lip, thinking. Maybe Anna is right, but maybe she's biased because she's my friend. I don't know if I can take one more thing going wrong. Although, at this point, QA is probably better off if I'm not in charge.

"I'll think about it," I say.

Jayden nudges my foot with his. "If you do decide to go, you won't be doing it alone. We've got you."

WHEN FRIDAY MORNING COMES, I WAKE UP EARLY AND LIE there staring at the ceiling. I've been thinking about everything my friends said since yesterday, and I'm no closer to a decision. Part of me wants to talk to Forrest so badly. I play out all the scenarios where it ends exactly the way I hope, but I can also see all the ones where it ends in catastrophe.

In the darkness, Brekky resettles himself on my feet, and I keep still so I won't disturb him. I haven't missed a Queer Alliance meeting since I started going, and now I've missed one last week and potentially another. The idea of staying home today feels weird. Especially because yesterday was Trans Day of Remembrance, the end of Trans Awareness Week. I should have been at school, leading the event the way I'm supposed to as co-president.

My alarm beeps, and I blow out a heavy sigh.

"I can do this," I say into the room, and sit up. "I just have to go to school. That's all I'm doing."

Brekky protests as I move my feet out from under him. I flip on my lamp and squint in the sudden light. At my closet, I throw on black sweats and a T-shirt, with a hoodie over it. In the bathroom, I brush my hair and teeth, and clean my glasses. There's still a faint pink hue from Anna's hair dye around the mouth of the drain.

"Sidney!" Mom says when I walk into the kitchen. "You're up."

"I want to go to school today," I say.

"Are you sure?" she asks.

I nod.

"Then let me drive you," she says.

"OK," I say.

♥

I text my friends in the car to let them know I'm on my way. The sky is just starting to lighten as Mom and I take the freeway over Lake Union toward the school, and it seems like it's going to be a clear day, just a few clouds dotting the pink horizon as it blends into a blue sky above us. I twist in my seat to look back, and I can see her: the mountain, watching me go.

After almost a week at home, the school is loud and bright. I keep my head down, heading straight for my locker. When I reach it, all my friends are standing there, and they hug me in turn.

"I'm really glad you're here," Makayla says.

"You can totally do this," Jayden says.

"I'll meet you outside your fourth period and walk you to Queer Alliance," Anna adds. The ends of her hair are a perfect bright magenta, clashing gloriously with her orange sweater.

"I wish you could come to my first period too," I say, leaning my head into her shoulder.

"Forrest is in that class with you, right?" Makayla asks.

"And his friends." I blow out a breath.

When the bell rings, they all walk me there, and Ms. Lundahl smiles at me when I step into the classroom. She was the first teacher to email my mom back and grant an extension. "Just have them turn in the rough draft by Thanksgiving break," she'd said.

I head straight to my seat, keeping my eyes on my desk, scrolling on my phone. I hear Forrest when he comes in, chattering away to Stef and Alexander, and a second later they all go silent. They've seen me, and I feel them looking at me; I can even see them in my periphery, stopped just inside the doorway, but I don't move. As more students push in behind them, they finally head for their desks.

As class starts, I peek at Forrest out of the corner of my eye, and slowly turn my head to look at him. He's staring at his desk, hands fidgeting in his lap. I've never seen him this subdued before, and my heart aches. This is my fault. I need to talk to him, to explain somehow, and if he still likes me like Jayden thinks he does, maybe there's a chance for us.

♥

As the clock moves closer to lunchtime, my stomach feels worse, and the voices get louder. I guess they're not really voices, because they're inside me, but they're still impossible to ignore: telling me to run, that this is a mistake, it's going to end terribly, here are all the ways it could end and destroy my whole life—

That's not real. It's not happening, I tell myself.

That's not real. It's not happening.

That's not real. It's not happening.

It's hard to just let the thoughts be there without reacting to them. Tracy made it sound so easy.

♥

"If you weren't here, I'd be hiding in the bathroom right now," I mutter to Anna as she walks me to the Queer Alliance meeting. She laughs, pulling me in with the arm she's linked through mine, and squeezes my bicep with her other hand.

"You could totally do it on your own," she says. "But I'm happy to help."

We round the corner, into the short hall that leads to Mr. Harrison's classroom, and manage to stay linked as we squish together through the doorway. Makayla is scooting chairs into place, and Jayden is standing with the back of a chair in his hands, talking to Alexander, both of them blushing furiously.

"They're so cuuuuute," I say in Anna's ear, and she nods vigorously.

"Hey," a voice says behind us, and we both turn. Forrest stands there, hands in his pocket, hoodie up. His eyes search my face, and he looks like he wants to ask me a question but doesn't know where to start.

"Hi," I say.

Before we can say anything else, more people appear behind him and we split apart, me and my friends on one side of the circle of chairs, Forrest and his friends across from us. It's like the beginning of the year, only instead of annoying each other, we're pining for each other.

At least, I am.

"Welcome, welcome, welcome," Mr. Harrison says, appearing from his doorway. His eyes land on me. "Sidney, we are so glad you're back."

"We missed you," Riley says, and I smile at them. They blow me a kiss with freshly bejeweled nails.

"So, I know we were going to have a reelection at the start of the new quarter," Mr. Harrison says. "Now that both our presidents are here, we can proceed—"

"Mr. Harrison?" Nyx says quietly, and then again, louder. Mr. Harrison stops and holds out a hand for them to continue. They shrink a little, glancing around the room, but Mercury grabs their hand and they straighten up in their chair. "While Sidney was gone, the rest of us have been talking."

I clasp my hands, squeezing until my knuckles turn white. I can guess what I'm about to hear, and I want to accept it with grace, not wild sobbing.

"I know that having two presidents is out of the norm for Queer Alliance," they continue. "Well, I don't know, because this is my first year, but some of the rest of you know, and, um, anyway, it's been a different approach. At first, things were a little . . ." They look from me to Forrest. "Tense. But since then, both Forrest and Sidney have been really great leaders in different ways. So we've all talked in the past week or so outside of Queer Alliance, and we decided we don't need to do a reelection. We want to keep them both."

My mouth drops open. Nyx is smiling at me, and at Forrest, and the rest of the club is nodding in agreement.

I'm not losing the presidency.

And neither is Forrest.

At the beginning of the year, I thought the world had ended when we tied. I was so attached to being the president, the *only* president. And now I don't want to be. I can't imagine being president without Forrest, and it's strange to think about how much he annoyed me before. I know him now: his sense of humor, his family life, his fears, his ideas. He's not out to ruin the Queer Alliance. He never was.

Anna squeezes my arm. I hadn't noticed we were still linked, but the realization warms my heart. She's right here, like she always has been, along with Jayden and Makayla.

In that moment, a golden bubble expands inside me, out of me, around all my friends and this room and all the people in it. I picture Shar on her job site hammering away, and Mom at her desk, and Dad in an AA meeting, and Brekky and Earl Grey curled together on the couch, and Forrest kissing me in the kitchen.

I want to kiss him again. I want to hold his hand, and make him laugh, and talk about everything and nothing, and watch that show he introduced me to, and—

My eyes are stinging, and I blink back the tears. I'm going to do it. I'm going to talk to him. I'm not going to let the fear of what might happen keep me from what I want right now.

"I accept," I say, and across the circle, Forrest smiles at me, slowly, hesitantly.

"I do too," he says.

♥

In sixth period, I pull out my phone under my desk and open my text thread with Forrest.

Can we talk after school? I type and send it before I can think twice.

He doesn't respond during class. When the bell rings, I head to my locker and take my time, gathering the crumpled papers and candy wrappers from the bottom and throwing them in the trash, tidying up the magnets and pictures I've stuck on the inside, slowly putting the things I need into my backpack. Every few seconds, I glance down the hall, but he doesn't come to his locker.

By the time the hall is mostly cleared out, I've run out of ways to stall. I shut the locker and close the combination lock, spinning it a few times, then pull out my phone to check my texts one more time.

Nothing.

I blow out a heavy sigh. My eyes are stinging. This is what happens when I put myself out there. I should have known better. Forrest doesn't want me. He hates me now, and he's right to, because I'm—

"Sidney!"

My head jerks up and there he is, walking toward me.

"Hey!" I croak out, my voice breathy. Oh god, don't cry in front of him. I was already awkward once, I can't make it awkward again.

He stops a few feet away, hands curled around the straps of his backpack. "It was good to see you in Queer Alliance today."

"Yeah. I. Um. I wanted to come back."

"Are you OK?" he asks. "You've been out all week, and you seemed really upset on Tuesday . . ." He trails off, biting his lip. Everything he isn't saying about what happened last week looms over us in that word. *Tuesday.* The day I freaked out.

No. I didn't freak out. Tracy said there's nothing wrong with having a mental illness.

"I have OCD," I blurt. "I see all these things in my head—well, I don't SEE them, exactly, they're not hallucinations, they're just, like, mental images, about bad things happening to me, to other people, people I love, or my relationships, and they were getting really bad, and I do these things, these rituals to stop them, like saying phrases, but it wasn't working anymore, and I really like you, and I was scared that it would all end badly, like *really* badly, with you hating me and all my friendships falling apart and I couldn't risk that, and that's why I was so weird last week, and I'm really, really sorry. I really like you. And I want to date you too."

He stares at me, eyes wide. The hallway is utterly quiet, and somewhere in the school a door slams. I clasp my hands together tightly as I watch his face.

"You have OCD," he says.

I nod.

"My cousin has that," he says.

"They do?"

"Yeah. She has the stuff about germs—"

"Contamination OCD," I say, remembering what Tracy said.

"But you have a different kind?" he asks.

"Yeah. I just started seeing a therapist for it."

"Wow."

The silence stretches, and I get that itching sensation in my chest, in my head, and I need to ask him—

"Are we OK?" I say. "I'm really sorry. Like, so sorry."

"I don't know," he says, and it's like an arrow to my heart. "I mean. When we kissed, I was stoked. I've had a crush on you for ages."

"You have?" I don't know what he means by that. How long is ages? This year, or even longer? Have I been missing more than I thought, this whole time?

"But you told me to leave you alone last week, Sidney. You walked away from me. You seemed really upset, and I didn't call or text you because I didn't want to upset you more or ignore what you asked for, but I was *worried*." His voice cracks again, but this time tears follow it, streaking down his face. He wipes them away with a sleeve. "I was afraid you were gonna, like . . . and then you were out of school, but your friends were here, and Alexander told me that Jayden told him you were having a hard time but you were OK, and I was so relieved, but it also . . . really . . . hurt." He pushes the last words out, like they're hard to say, and every one hits me in the stomach. I hurt Forrest. I thought I was avoiding hurting him by walking away, and instead I did even more damage, maybe, than I would have otherwise.

"So I don't know." He shrugs. "I think I need some time."

"OK," I say in a tiny voice.

"I just need some time," he repeats. "I'm gonna go."

And this time he's the one to turn and walk away, and I just watch him leave.

I GO HOME, AND I DO MY BEST TO IGNORE THE BARRAGE OF images swirling in my head: Forrest ignoring me in the halls, Forrest telling all my friends how terrible I am and all of them abandoning me to join his group, everyone in Queer Alliance voting that I leave the club. Maybe that counts as a compulsion, pushing the thoughts away, but I don't know what else to do.

For a while, I try to do homework, and I get a few more paragraphs of my rough draft written, but then somehow my phone ends up in my hand and I start scrolling and suddenly it's been two hours and I'm on my bed, Brekky curled beside me, and I can hear Mom and Shar talking in their room. They came home and I didn't even notice.

A tap sounds on my door. "Hey Sidney," Mom calls from the other side.

"Come in," I say dully, and she enters, crossing to my bed and sitting down beside me.

"How was school today?" she asks, squeezing my foot.

I shrug. I don't know how to put it all into words.

"How are you feeling?"

"OK. Ish."

"Ish?" she asks.

The tears fill my eyes again—it's like they're right at the surface, waiting for a moment to come out—and she clicks her tongue in sympathy. "You wanna talk to me, sweetie?"

"I don't know," I mumble, sniffling. "My brain is just being . . ." I wave my hand at my head. "What if it never gets better? What if it pushes everyone around me away?"

"I know what you mean," she says, and I don't know what I was expecting her to say, but it wasn't that. "You know . . . I never told you this, but after the divorce . . . I was really anxious and depressed. I was on medication for a while."

"You were?" When Mom and Dad first separated, I could tell they were both upset; Dad, because he would rage and snark about Mom whenever I was with him, and Mom, because she was quiet and sad, like a light bulb with a dimmer switch turned down to almost nothing. She was worried about me all the time too; she hardly let me go over to friends' houses, and whenever I got back from hanging out with Dad she would watch me as if I was a porcelain doll that might break at any moment. When she won full custody of me, she'd cried. I'd known she was sad, and I tried to be as good as possible, so she wouldn't have to worry about more than she already was. As time went on, I stopped noticing her sadness as much, and then she started pursuing her new career, and I didn't think that much about how she was doing.

But maybe it wasn't just starting a new career, and then meeting Shar, that helped her.

"It was anti-anxiety medication," she says, as if she can hear the question in my mind. "It took the edge off, made it so my brain didn't spiral so much." She twirls a finger, and I nod. I know that feeling. "I don't know too much about OCD, but I do remember my dad was pretty anxious too. When we went on trips, he used to go back into the house over and over to check that the stove was off. One time it took an hour before we were finally able to leave. We were really annoyed as kids, but now . . ." She trails off. "Tracy gave me some websites to look through, so I can learn more about what might be going on, but whatever you want to share, I want to hear."

I nod.

"And I wanted to check in about your dad too," she says. "He told me that he relapsed, but that he got right back on the wagon. He said he told you as well. How are you feeling about that?"

Huh. Dad told Mom what he told me. I didn't realize they talked like that, but I guess it makes sense. They're both still my parents, even if I live with Mom. And if he was honest with her about that too . . . maybe he really is trying.

"I don't know," I say finally. "I kind of . . . don't trust him."

"I hear you," she says.

"Like, he's tried to get sober so many times, and it's never stuck, and I don't get it. If he really wanted to stop, why would he relapse? Why am I not—" My voice cracks, and then I'm crying again. "Why am I not a good enough reason?"

"Oh, honey," Mom says quietly. "Addiction is really challenging, and his struggle to stay sober has nothing to do with you or me. It's about what's happening inside him, the demons he has to fight. Substances are really powerful coping mechanisms for that, and he has to build new ones, and that takes time. And relapses are part of that."

She scoots closer to me, wrapping my hand in hers, and I squeeze back. Her brown eyes are soft and kind as she gazes at me. "I believe he's trying, that he always has. But I realized a long time ago it's not my role to walk beside him in that. You get to choose your relationship with him too."

I nod. I don't fully get what she's saying, how addiction is about what's inside him. But my thoughts and my compulsions feel that way too, when they come—like something taking over my body, something I can't control no matter how much I try. Maybe, in time, Tracy can help me learn how to handle them. Maybe Dad will learn how to handle his addiction.

"He loves you," Mom says. "But whatever he does or doesn't do, it's not your fault or your responsibility."

"Thanks," I say. I want to believe her, but I'm not sure I do.

She pats my leg. "OK, you. I'm going to help Shar finish cooking dinner."

I give her a thumbs-up, and she leaves, pulling the door closed with a quiet click behind her. I pick up my phone again, staring at the wallpaper I chose months ago: a photo of a waterfall, from a hike I did with Mom and Shar near the end of summer.

Even though I'm still angry at him, I miss Dad. Is he at a meeting right now? Is he lying in bed, thinking of me? Is he even sober? He texted me a few days ago, and I still haven't read it.

I take a deep breath, and open our thread.

Hey, kiddo, he wrote, and the words make me tear up. I can hear them in his voice, warm and reassuring. *I just wanted to let you know I'm thinking of you. I understand if you need some time, so no rush, but whenever you are ready to hang out, I'm here.*

I squeeze my eyes shut, tears leaking out and trailing down my cheeks. I sniff, wiping them away, and curl up on my side, staring at his message. For a moment on the mountain with him at our last hike, so many things felt possible, like we could have an actual relationship, one where I could tell him things and he would listen and care. But what if he relapses again, and I just keep getting hurt?

I don't know if I'm ready, I say. *I'll let you know.*

His reply is instant, as if he's been staring at his phone since he texted me, waiting for my reply. *OK, sweetie. I'll be here.*

The tears well up again, and this time I let myself cry.

♥

When I get home from studying with Jayden the next day, Shar is in the kitchen eating a peanut butter and jelly sandwich.

"Kiddo!" she says through a mouthful of bread.

"Hey," I say, dropping my backpack on the floor by the door and kicking off my shoes.

“We haven’t been out in the shop for a while,” she says. “I’ve been saving the bookcase to finish with you.”

The bookcase. I haven’t thought about it in weeks, but I could really use some power tools right now. Hammering, drilling, and sawing sound like exactly what my body wants to do. And it’ll keep the mental movies quiet for the next couple of hours.

A few minutes later, we’re out in the shop, getting suited up in protective gear. The bookcase is right where we left it, but the stain has set in, and instead of the blond, raw wood, it’s a deep, rich shade of dark brown.

“I have to confess I did do the initial wood gluing of the pieces,” Shar says as she rummages around in her tool organizer. “However . . .” She turns around, holding up the drill with a big grin. “You remember how to use this?”

“Uhhhhh . . .”

“I’ll take that as a no.” She grins. “We’ll be putting in screws today, and then we’ll be just about done.”

She walks me through how to use the drill and has me practice on a piece of scrap lumber until she’s satisfied. Then she stands back, and it’s my turn.

I turn the drill on, feeling it whir to life in my hands. She’s predrilled shallow holes already, so all I have to do is fit the screw into place and drive it the rest of the way into the wood. Sawdust collects at each drill point in small piles as I move around the bookcase. It’s satisfying, seeing how it all fits together, how every step leads to the ending Shar planned for.

When I’m done, I turn off the drill and set it down. Shar high-fives me.

“This is looking really good,” she says, hands on hips, surveying our work. “Third time’s the charm.”

“What do you mean?” I push the goggles up on my head, massaging the bridge of my nose where they’ve already imprinted a groove.

“This is my third try making this bookcase,” she says, brushing the sawdust piles off the table. “The first attempt . . . well, I did *not* measure correctly, let’s just say that. The second time, I got it all built and there weren’t enough shelves. That one’s in our closet holding shoes now. So this is round three.”

I look at the bookcase. It’s beautiful, with five shelves, the wood smooth and perfectly stained. I never would have thought Shar had messed something like this up; building things is her whole job.

“Shit goes wrong sometimes,” she says, shrugging. “Shall we clean up and get this bad boy on its feet?”

I nod and join her in sweeping the sawdust into a small pile. She dumps it in the garbage while I tuck the drill back into its drawer. Then she releases the clamps on the bookcase, takes one end, and I take the other. We slide it off the table and set it upright. When we step back, it stays standing, a little taller than me. Shar laughs, clapping her hands together. “Nicole is going to *love* this.”

We each pick up the ends again and move toward the door, turning it on one long side to fit through the door frame, and walk it slowly toward the house. Shar reaches out one hand, the other gripping the top shelf with all her strength, and opens the back door. We move through, into the kitchen, and around the corner, careful not to step on any cat tails as we go.

Where the old bookcase used to stand is an open space. For the past few months, the books it used to hold have been piled on top of the other bookshelf and stacked on the floor nearby. We set the new bookcase down and slide it backward. It fits perfectly.

"Yes!" Shar pumps her fist, and I can't help smiling.

There it is. A whole thing, and we built it. Well, Shar did a lot of it. But I helped.

Shar bends to start replacing the books, and I follow her lead. Brekky keeps trying to climb into the open shelves, and each time we remove him, he meows in complaint, making us laugh.

"What's going on out here?" Mom asks behind us.

Shar spins around like she got caught doing something she wasn't supposed to. "I wanted to get it all done before you came out here," she said. "But—ta-da!" She steps aside, gesturing at the bookcase, and Mom squeals, clapping her hands.

"You finished it!" she says, throwing her arms around Shar.

"Told you I would," Shar says, and they kiss.

I smile, shoving more books onto the shelves. Mom grabs a stack to help, and one book at a time, we put the bookcase back together.

♥

On Monday morning, I stand in the bathroom, staring at myself in the mirror. My hair is brushed and so are my teeth;

I'm fully dressed and my backpack waits by the door; all I need to do is walk out.

"You can do this," I tell my reflection. I don't look like I believe me, but I turn away and head for the living room.

Outside, it's chilly, the sky still dark as I walk to the train. The car is crowded when I get on, like usual, and this time I have to stand, holding onto a pole as the train zooms through the tunnel. I'm spaced out, music loud in my headphones, and it's not until I get to my stop that I realize I haven't had a single suicidal thought. Well. An OCD thought, I guess. Since I'm not really suicidal. It's just an intrusive thought. One that everyone has, apparently.

I stare at the people riding down the escalator next to mine as it rises. There's a tired-looking businesswoman on her phone, a young guy texting someone, an old man bent over his cane who smiles at me when I look at him. Do all of them really have intrusive thoughts too? I need to ask Tracy about that tomorrow, because it doesn't seem possible.

I push through a door at the back of the school and into the echoing tornado of the hallway, snaking through the chaos to my locker. I stuff my coat inside it, put my lunch box on the top shelf, and shut the door, swinging my backpack onto my shoulder.

When I turn, I see Forrest.

He's at his locker, doing the same thing I was just doing, minus the lunch box, because he eats in the cafeteria. I want to say hi, but he asked for time. Maybe the time isn't up yet.

He looks up and it's too late to walk away, because he sees me too. He lifts a hand and waves. I wave back, and he motions me toward him.

I walk along the bank of lockers until I'm standing right in front of him. "Hey," I say.

"Hi." He shuts his locker and shoulders his backpack.

"How are you?" I ask.

"I'm good." His eyes are a mellow brown in the light. "I thought about you a lot this weekend."

"I thought about you too," I say. "And I'm really sorry. Again."

"I know," he says. "I just wish you would have talked to me."

I nod.

"I hope . . ." He swallows. "In the future . . . you'll tell me if it gets bad again."

I go completely still as he rubs a hand over the back of his head. If he wants me to tell him, does that mean—

"Do you want to go out with me?" he asks.

"Yes!" I shriek, and he bursts out laughing. His face lights up, and seeing him happy makes my heart expand until it feels like I'm going to explode, because I'm happy too.

"So you're my boyfriend?" I reach out and poke his shoulder.

He pokes me back. "Yeah. And you're my . . . date . . . person? What should I call you? Co-president?"

I snort. "Oh my god, no. I like partner."

He smiles. "You're my partner."

I poke his shoulder again, and he pokes me back, and then we're poking back and forth, giggling wildly. I can't believe this is happening. I'm dating Forrest. I'm. *Dating. Forrest.*

As quickly as my heart expanded, it contracts. We're dating. Which means we can break up. And when we break up—

His face, rigid with anger, screaming at me about something, I don't know what it is but I know I did something bad, and I am bad, and he's done with me—

"Sidney?"

I snap back to earth. Forrest is watching me, hands in his pockets.

"I . . . had a thought," I say. "Um. An intrusive one. It's an OCD thing."

"You looked like you spaced out for a second," he says.

"Yeah. It's like a movie that plays in my brain, except instead of something entertaining, it's a highlight reel of my worst fears." I give a double thumbs-up.

"That sounds terrible," he says. "Like anxiety on steroids."

"Yeah." The inside of my skull is itching, and I want to ask him to never leave me, never break up with me, *we're OK, right, you don't hate me, please tell me so the thoughts will stop and I'll be OK*. But I'm not supposed to do that, I don't think. I have to let the thought exist. All of this could end, and I just have to accept that. I have to live with all the possibilities of us, layered over each other, every branching pathway we could take, and find out where we go.

"Hey." He holds out a hand, and I take it. His palm is warm, his fingers curling through mine and pulling me closer, until we're a few inches apart. "I got you."

“Thanks,” I say softly. His hand in mine is solid. And right now, I know what I want to do. I’m going to open my mouth and ask him what I’ve been wanting to ask him since he called me his partner a few minutes ago.

“Can I kiss you?”

He nods. I let go of his hand and slip my arms around his waist, and he pulls me close, and then we’re kissing.

This is real.

It’s happening.

AUTHOR'S NOTE

I was diagnosed with OCD in 2019, right before I turned thirty. Many people are misdiagnosed, or undiagnosed, for years thanks to common misconceptions, lack of knowledge and awareness in public and clinical settings, and the stigma associated with intrusive thoughts and compulsions. Thanks to this combination, I had never considered the possibility until my therapist mentioned that some of what I was struggling with sounded similar to their clients with OCD. This began my journey of learning about the disorder and looking back on my childhood and teenage years through a new lens.

Like Sidney, for much of my life I thought OCD was about contamination, and that compulsions consisted of washing your hands repeatedly, or needing to flip light switches on and off a certain amount of times, or checking and rechecking the stove for hours. What I've learned is that it can consist of those things—and those are just some in a vast array of possibilities. However, contamination and externally visible compulsions are still the public's primary stereotype about OCD.

Another stereotype? "Being OCD"—that OCD is a trait, and it means you really like to organize and have everything a certain way, that you're a "neat freak." There are subsets of OCD that bear some similarities to this, such as "just right" OCD, but one cannot "be" OCD, it is not enjoyable, and it has nothing to do with organization and cleanliness.

Much of Sidney's experience with OCD is drawn from my own. I wrote this book for myself, for others with OCD, and for anyone who feels tortured by their own brain but doesn't know the cause. I wrote it for anyone who thought everybody's brains worked that way until one day they learned that wasn't the case. I wrote it because of the lack of popular media narratives that accurately show OCD and its complexity and breadth. I wrote it because everybody deserves to understand what is happening inside them and have tools to ease their suffering.

If you read this book and felt seen, I hope you take Sidney's realization at the end of their therapy session to heart: You don't have to feel this way forever.

Love,
Ray

RESOURCES

What is OCD? iocdf.org/about-ocd
What to look for in a therapist: iocdf.org/ocd-finding-help/how-to-find-the-right-therapist
Provider directory: iocdf.org/find-help

Learn more:

- *The Mindfulness Workbook for OCD: A Guide to Overcoming Obsessions and Compulsions Using Mindfulness and Cognitive Behavioral Therapy* by Jon Hershfield, MFT, and Tom Corboy, MFT; foreword by James Claiborn, PhD, ABPP
- *Getting Over OCD: A 10-Step Workbook for Taking Back Your Life* by Jonathan S. Abramowitz, PhD, ABPP
- *The OCD Stories:* a podcast hosted by Stuart Ralph, featuring interviews with providers in OCD treatment and recovery. Both entertaining and educating, it often touches on the personal experience of the interviewee as well as their professional knowledge and experience.

Some examples of OCD in popular media:

- *Work in Progress*: a Showtime series about a self-identified "fat, queer dyke" living with OCD and depression, who enters a transformative romantic relationship
- *Turtles All the Way Down* by John Green: a teen with OCD gets pulled into unraveling the mystery of a fugitive billionaire as her mental health worsens
- *The Rest of Us Just Live Here* by Patrick Ness: a teen with OCD struggles with everyday issues like graduating and working up the courage to ask out his crush in a town where the "chosen ones" who are usually the protagonists of a story are fighting evil in the background while everybody else just has to live their normal, non-heroic, non-magical lives
- "Serotonin" by girl in red: a song that expresses what it's like to live with OCD and describes intrusive thoughts and compulsions

ACKNOWLEDGMENTS

Thank you to my team, including my agent, Lauren Abramo, and my editors, Maggie Lehrman and Claire Stetzer, and everyone at Abrams who contributed to the making of this book. I feel so lucky to work with such talented, caring, and insightful people.

Thank you to the therapists who have accompanied me at different points in my mental health journey and created a safe and healing space for me to learn new skills, understand my brain, and make sense of my life experiences. Our work together is and was vital, profound, and felt far beyond our sessions.

Thank you to Stace Nagle, MA, LMFT, for contributing your thoughtful and invaluable professional expertise as my sensitivity reader for the representation of OCD and its treatment in this book.

Thank you to my friends, family, and partner, who encouraged me along the often difficult, yet rewarding, path of writing this book. Your love, support, and presence in my life is a gift I treasure deeply.

OTHER BOOKS BY RAY STOEVE